Praise for Ronna Wineberg's Previous Books

On Bittersweet Place:

"Wineberg's quintessential American story of belonging, family life, heritage, and pursuing the American dream will resonate with listeners." —*Library Journal* (audiobook review)

"...there are questions of identity, the evolution of cities in the 20th century, and the minute effects of sweeping historical change.... impressive." —Tobias Carroll, *The Forward*

"*On Bittersweet Place* is as much the coming-of-age story of the Midwest as a diverse and thriving urban center as it is Lena's." —*The Millions*

"...an impressive and moving coming of age story." —*Largehearted Boy*

Second Language:

"While chronicling the ends of relationships, Wineberg is actually planting the beginnings of new life for her characters....These stories possess full, beating hearts that capture our attention and our sympathy. We are immensely attached to the characters. We yearn for understanding in the same way they do.... Ronna Wineberg does a wonderful job of showing all her characters fully in the world they inhabit, writing almost in real time of the pain that walks hand in hand with beauty and joy." —*Other Voices*

"The following comments by Cynthia Ozick about writers and their work captures precisely the powerful stories in Wineberg's provocative book:

> ...the writer is an imaginer by trade, will suggest a course of connection, of entering the tremulous spirit of the helpless, the fearful, the apart. The writer will demonstrate the contagion of passion and compassion that is known in medicine as empathy and in art as insight (*Metaphor and Memory.* New York: Alfred A. Knopf, 1989, p. 266).

It is exactly what Ronna Wineberg does as a writer." —*Literature, Arts & Medicine*

Nine Facts That Can Change Your Life

Stories

RONNA WINEBERG

Serving House Books

Nine Facts That Can Change Your Life

ISBN: 978-0-9971010-0-3

Cover design by Mark McCoy

Author photo by Whitney Lawson

Serving House Books logo by Barry Lereng Wilmont

Published by Serving House Books, LLC
Copenhagen, Denmark and Florham Park, NJ

www.servinghousebooks.com

Member of the Independent Book Publishers Association

First Serving House Books Edition 2016

We don't see the world as it is.
We see the world as we are.

—Talmudic Saying

Also by Ronna Wineberg

Second Language
On Bittersweet Place

To Daniel, Genia, and Simone, always,
and to the memory of my parents

Acknowledgments

The following stories in this collection have been previously published, sometimes in slightly different form.

"Legacy" appeared in *Jewish Women's Literary Annual.*
"Happy to See You" appeared in *The Chrysalis Reader.*
"A Question of Place" appeared in *RE:AL: The Journal of Liberal Arts.*
"Taking Leave" appeared in *The Pikeville Review.*
"Terminal" appeared in *Ellipsis.*
"Matters of the Heart" appeared in *Pennsylvania English.*
"Foreign Lands" appeared in *Sou'wester.*
"Adjustment" appeared in *Oasis.*
"Open House" appeared in *Controlled Burn.*
"Bare Essentials" appeared in the *Michigan Quarterly Review.*
"A Celebration of the Life of the Reverend Canon Edward Henry Jamison" appeared in *The Laurel Review* and was a finalist in the *Moment Magazine*–Karma Foundation Short Fiction Contest.

Table of Contents

1.

Legacy

Over a year has passed since Morris Vogel last saw his grandson, Willy. Being with the child brings a powerful and unexpected pleasure, but also plays a subtle trick on Morris. It is a trick of perception—the sense that, when with Willy, Morris is really watching his son, Ted, forty years ago and, beyond that, looking at a replica of himself.

Today Morris sits at the piano with Willy and teaches him to play a simple melody from Pachelbel's *Canon*. Willy is almost five, musical and bright. Morris reads to him, books like *Doctor De Soto*, *Brave Irene*, and a children's story by Isaac Bashevis Singer that Morris brought the boy as a gift. Before bed, Willy climbs onto his grandfather's lap. Morris kisses his grandson's soft cheek and dark curly hair. Then Willy throws his arms around him. "See you tomorrow, Grandpa. I want to see you every day for my whole life."

Morris smiles when he thinks about this exchange later. His daughter-in-law, Emily, sets platters on the table for dinner—roasted chicken, salad topped with almonds, creamed potatoes, and broccoli in a thick brown sauce. The room is airy, with a high cathedral ceiling and large bay windows. The windows frame a view of the yard, and beyond that, the mountains that ring the western edge of Denver. Paintings hang on the only solid wall, portraits in muted shades of brown and green of people Morris doesn't recognize.

"Wine, Dad?" Ted asks, holding an opened bottle. "We should celebrate. We don't see each other that often."

"Wine," Morris repeats. "Just a bit." He pats his stomach. "With this ulcer, I've got to be careful."

Ted is a leaner, younger version of his father, with traces of gray in his dark-brown hair. He is an emergency room doctor, impatient, used to making swift decisions. Morris is proud of his son's accomplishments. Tall and athletic, Ted has Morris's deep-set brown eyes and thick brows, and the same intense expression. Morris is shorter and broad. When he and Ted stand face-to-face, Morris looks up to his son.

Emily brings the last platter and sits down. She is a petite woman, thin and bony, with green eyes, a slightly crooked nose, and a small, angular face. She isn't really pretty, but her presence is graceful. "What a relief," she says with a sigh. "For once we'll eat on time. Willy is finally settled in bed. We can have a calm dinner."

Ted stands as he pours the wine and then raises his glass. "To more visits," he says formally. "More time together, less time in between."

Morris's thin lips open into a smile and he nods. He would like to make his own toast, but it isn't his way. Tonight, especially, he regrets this and longs to feel comfortable here, to say something of lasting importance.

The three touch glasses. The brushing of crystal against crystal chimes.

Morris has always felt uneasy with Emily. She is not Jewish. Her father was born in Germany and came to the States as a boy. From the beginning, Morris opposed the marriage. He and Ted stopped speaking for two years then. It wasn't their first rift, but this one was deeper and more lasting. Ted was a difficult, willful child, and Morris supposes he was a difficult father, a harsh one—like his own father. He and Ted were both stubborn and opinionated, each sure the other was wrong. But does a parent really have a right to dictate a child's life? Morris wonders. They have reconciled, yet Morris stays away from here. He doesn't know how Ted and Emily will raise Willy, with any religion or not. Still, he secretly wishes he can someday forgive this marriage.

Emily passes the platters, first to Morris, who spoons small portions onto his plate. He hasn't much appetite, preoccupied as he is by thoughts of his grandson. He wants to share this feeling of his—of Willy becoming Ted becoming Morris. But he doesn't know what to say. Besides, he feels lightheaded, not from the wine, but from being here.

Ted asks about Morris's business, the furniture store he owns in Chicago, though Morris knows his son is not really interested. "Business is good," he says, "thank God."

"Do you ever think of retiring?" Emily asks.

"Absolutely not," Morris replies, more fiercely than he'd like. "I've done this most of my life. It's a reason to get up every day."

"You'll have to think about selling the store sometime, Dad. You're not seventy-five anymore."

"I don't have to be reminded." Ted likes to give him advice. "But would that cure the aches and pains?"

"You look well," Emily says. "Thinner. It suits you."

"I try. But it's not so easy, especially with a dinner like this."

Emily smiles. Morris knows she is pleased with the compliment. But, in fact, the food is too elaborate for him. He eats slowly while she talks about Willy and the plans she's made for his visit.

Morris hardly listens, thinking instead about the expanse of years that await his grandson. He yearns for this, the possibilities. Having just turned eighty-four, he finds himself where he did not plan to be—his first marriage of forty years to Ted's mother ended, his second marriage unsteady. Business is fine, his health adequate. But how long will that hold up? His fingers are still nimble enough for him to play the spinet piano at home. Melodies he learned as a boy; these bring him some solace. His second wife didn't join him on the trip here. She doesn't like to travel. Although this new marriage was a mistake, Morris can't tolerate the thought of another divorce and, worse, taking care of himself, facing the nights alone.

Emily goes into the kitchen to start the coffee, a special blend, she told him, that she bought for tonight. Morris loves good coffee, one of his few consistent pleasures. He and his son sit quietly, as if waiting for a rapprochement. The April evening enters lazily through the windows. Morris feels a hint of intimacy, the possibility.

"I have to meet with Willy's teacher tomorrow," Emily says, returning to the room. "Maybe your dad would like to come with me. It's about schools, Morris. We have to decide what to do with Willy next year, to send him to kindergarten or hold him back."

"Oh?" Morris says. "It's hard to believe Willy is old enough for school already. Time goes so quickly. Life eats it up."

Rain begins to fall outside, pattering softly against the windows.

"You know, Dad, a child has to be five years old in kindergarten. Willy's birthday falls on the deadline."

"Let's see. You skipped, Ted, didn't you? But it doesn't matter, really. There's always something to decide with children. The worry never ends. Even now."

"If you want to worry, there will always be something to worry about. It's not a difficult decision. I don't want Willy to lose a year," Ted says. "Why should he be held back?"

"He shouldn't be pushed," Emily replies firmly. "He may not be ready."

"Of course, you can't really know what's best," Morris says. "It's pointless to try. You'll see. The world will take Willy and do what it wants." He turns to Ted. "It happened to you, it happened to me. The most you can hope for is to help cushion the blows."

"Maybe," Ted says. "You're a pessimist, Dad. You've always been. Besides, you see yourself in Willy, like you saw yourself in me."

"That's no crime." Morris is surprised Ted has noticed this. "We have the same genes. But there's no way to know what will shape the man. For me, if my life had been different—"

"It would have been different," Ted interrupts. "I'm not going to try to shape Willy like you tried to shape me. And why dwell on the past and be a prisoner of it?"

"The past helps people understand." Morris strokes what hair is left on his head. "You learn from it. Surely, you of all people want to learn."

"It was a different world in Europe then. Emily is talking about a simple choice about a little boy."

"No. I disagree." Morris inches his plate away. For the first time tonight, he feels animated, determined to make his point. "I was like Willy exactly. A smart boy. With promise." He glances at the photograph on the mantel, at his grandson's brown eyes and dimpled smile. "The whole world was there for me, as I hope it is for Willy. But I had a teacher who shaped my life. And then life was beyond my control. To this day."

Morris sees that Ted is shaking his foot beneath the table. Even as a child, Ted was impatient. Emily, though, watches Morris, attentive. He hesitates for a moment to tell them his thoughts, for fear of offending her or polarizing the two of them, but he can't help himself. He wants them to know about his past, to know what shaped him.

"I was older than Willy," he says. "But still a boy. I can't remember the man's name." He pauses, straining to think. "I know the face. And the voice. All day long he shouted at us in the classroom. He addressed me by my last name. '*Zi Vogel*,' he would yell." Morris shakes a knobby finger at Ted, shouting, "'*Zi Vogel*. The answer. *Zi Vogel*. Speak up.' Just like that."

"Terrible," says Emily. Morris thinks she looks frail, as if his words will sweep her away.

"Oh, yes," he says. "Sometimes the man took a ruler and hit a hand or pinched an ear. We were children. I was terrified. If you answered incorrectly, he made notations on a card. We didn't know what happened to this. We were sure he showed the cards to the principal. That you could fail because of his notes. That whole year I was afraid. I had a constant pain inside, in my stomach."

"Maybe the beginnings of the ulcer," Ted says.

"Not at all. It was fear." Morris narrows his eyes. "My first thought of the day was how I hated that man. I pretended to be sick, but my parents were strict. Unless I had a fever, I was sent on my way."

"Did he do anything more?" Emily asks.

"Oh, yes. Our examination was after vacation, one test for the whole year. My sisters remember that summer as a happy one, the last stay with our grandfather in the house by the lake. There was all the time in the world to roam, swim, to read there, yet I was miserable. I couldn't study, but I couldn't enjoy myself either. And no one noticed. My parents were away; my grandfather was ill; my sisters were always busy. Besides, I tried to hide my problems. I worried it was my fault the teacher acted in this way. And it seemed unmanly to be afraid. So the time crawled by, and, secretly, I hoped the vacation would never end. In the evenings I sat outside, praying for an escape, divine intervention. If only I believed in God now. I hoped for an accident so the teacher would be killed. Or that something would happen to me or my family."

Emily begins to interrupt, but Morris waves to stop her. He wants to continue, needs to. How could she ever really understand?

"Of course," he says quietly, "there were no accidents. Life proceeded as it does, at its own pace and according to its own plan. I was soon back in Vienna, on the way to the examination. My mother made me wear a tie. It tugged against my neck. I arrived early and went to the bathroom many times, nervous. Then I tried to study my book.

"When it was my turn, I walked in, and suddenly the classroom seemed huge. There were just the two of us. I felt as if I would be swallowed. Even though the window was open, the air was heavy and smelled stale. The teacher sat behind his tall wooden desk. When I took my seat, close to his desk, I couldn't find a comfortable position. He tapped his fingers on his desktop, signaling we would begin. He smiled a kind of half smile. 'I trust, *Zi Vogel*, you had a nice vacation, eh?'

"I didn't answer.

"'There is no time to waste,' he said. 'We will start.'

"I noticed then his teeth were badly chipped. Every time he spoke, I could smell his breath, an onion scent. He began by asking a question, and he held his pencil to write my answers. '*Zi Vogel,'* he said, 'the capital, please, of Bolivia.'

"Each time I looked down, grinding my teeth, trying not to cry. I was in such a state, I couldn't think. I struggled to be calm and stared at the large wall clock behind him. The long minute hand was like an executioner's blade. It jerked from number to number. And the clock hummed so loudly. I remember how my heart beat, in almost the same rhythm. Like this."

Morris forms a fist and hits his knuckles against the table. "Bum, bum, bum," he says. The sound, a thud, breaks the stillness of the room. "So, you see."

Emily nods, and Ted watches his father.

"Even now, like the sound of my heart," he says.

"You were nervous," Ted says. "That's all. Nerves."

"Perhaps," answers Morris. Ted has always been impatient with emotions, too, Morris knows. "But perhaps it was something more fundamental." He pauses, easing his chair back from the table. Rain falls harder now; the room has grown dim and damp. "As the hour passed," he says, "I felt worse. In the middle of the exam, I realized I'd forgotten to wash my hands that morning and in the bathroom at school, too. Suddenly, I was repelled by their dirtiness. I checked to be sure my pants were zipped and prayed I wouldn't have to expel gas. I must have squirmed. He became impatient.

"'Negative, again, *Zi Vogel*,' he yelled. 'Your vacation went to waste, no?'

"I mumbled something, and he said, 'You have been ill?'

"I mumbled again.

"'Do you have anything to say for yourself? A defense perhaps, *Zi Vogel* ? Speak up, so I can hear you.'

"Again, I shook my head. He scribbled on a paper and waved me away.

"I ran outside to the schoolyard. I threw my tie on the ground and cried. My mother knew something was wrong as soon as I came home. She was ill again, consumption. In her bathrobe.

"'Morris,' she greeted me, as she always did, with her soft voice. But she looked pale and thin. A bag of bones. She asked me about the test, looked at my face and knew. I couldn't bear to disappoint her. So I accused her of interfering and ran to my room. I hated myself even more for snapping at her."

"If you had talked to someone," Emily says, "that would have helped. That's what parents are for."

"Oh, I used to confide in my oldest sister, but this time I couldn't bring myself to. She was a good student. I was certain she wouldn't understand." Morris shrugged. "So I suffered alone. The day we found out the results of the examination, my best friend gave me a paper with a skull and crossbones, and my name on it. 'The old man will fail us all,' he laughed. I was in no mood for joking.

"Of course, I failed. It was no surprise. Because of this I had to repeat a year in school. I was devastated. My mother became upset. But my father was furious. He was a religious man and strict. He questioned me, yelled, and though I tried to explain, he didn't wish to hear. He believed in accepting consequences like a man. He put me on a restricted schedule. I had to spend three hours after school in my room with my books. I was a prisoner. Every night I had to recite my school assignments aloud to my father.

"All that year, I felt in a fog, always angry but still feeling that perhaps my fate was deserved. Oh, I tried to adjust, make the best of it. I played our piano to pass the time. My mother gave me lessons, as if this would ease my sentence at home. The anger was always there, though. I studied hard to be sure to pass. Still, I held back a little out of spite. I don't know why. And I never could redeem myself in my father's eyes."

Morris pauses and sees that Emily regards him carefully, the way he wishes Ted would. There is a softness about her, for which he is grateful. Ted gazes out the window into the darkness.

"So, you see," Morris continues, trying to reach Ted. "There was nothing to be done. This set a pattern, a spiral of inferior luck. From then on school was difficult. I was a bright boy, too. But my hands were tied."

"It was a difficult circumstance," Ted says, turning to him. "People rise above that. You choose to remember."

"No. I can't help but remember. And it happened again, with other consequences. The next time I understood." Morris places his knife perpendicular to his plate. He has never told either of them this story. "Much later, when I was first in *Gymnasium*, my mathematics teacher gave our class the test questions and answers a few days before the examination. All you had to do was memorize them. It was a simple thing. I memorized everything. I felt I had to redeem myself on every test. At the examination, I answered everything correctly except for one small question. It was foolish. A whim. But I purposefully did not answer one point.

"The next week the results were announced. We sat in the auditorium and the names of those who passed were called out. In every class my name was announced, except for math. I couldn't believe that one small question made me fail. Math was my strongest subject."

"That's strange," Emily says, "if you had answered all but one question."

"Correct," Morris replies. "It was impossible for me to have failed. Later that day my mathematics professor took me aside and whispered, 'Vogel, you'll take math again. After the summer. So, what's a year? You'll pass without a hitch.'"

"Your parents should have done something," Emily insists.

"Oh, they knew, of course, but there was no question why I failed. And, by chance, a few years later it was confirmed in Paris, when I was on my way to the States. 1939. I had missed my train and sat on a bench, reading. But I was in no hurry. Finally, I was out of Austria. I still did not have my papers yet to come to America, and I had no work. My old math professor happened to be at the train station, too. His sister lived in Paris. I hadn't seen him for a few years. His hair had turned completely white. He approached me and I knew him immediately. Fate follows you, like memories, even if you try to escape.

"'Vogel.' He put his hand on my shoulder. I remember his words exactly. 'Vogel, you haven't changed a bit.' He stood close to me and smelled of tobacco and beer. 'I have a confession to make. An apology.'

"I tried to stop him, to interrupt. But he persisted. 'No, it's been on my mind for years,' he said. 'You remember the examination? The grade was politics, nothing to do with you. Oh, it's good to be out of Austria. They needed a Jew, Vogel, as simple as that. A Catholic was failing, so they needed to fail a Jew.' He patted my cheek. 'Here, in France, you won't find that anymore. You'll be safe.' He embraced me, wished me luck. His train arrived and he was gone."

For a moment, no one speaks. "Good God," Emily says finally. "Are you listening, Ted?"

"Yes," he whispers.

Morris continues, raising his voice. "At that moment I needed no one, only my wits."

"But you knew at the time," Emily says.

"It was no secret what the Viennese thought of Jews."

"Still, you should have done something. You were a boy, your parents…"

"Emily," Ted says sharply. "He's a Jew. It's that simple. There was nothing to be done."

"I'm lucky, I survived, but this was a blow of the greatest sort," Morris says, more loudly than he intended. "A psychological blow."

"Your mother—" Emily begins.

"There's nothing to discuss," Morris interrupts. "She didn't get out."

"No, I meant, just that, you were a boy that first time. Maybe she could have helped you then, talked to you. I know it was a difficult time in the world, in Vienna. But still, maybe she could have helped."

"Yes, perhaps. Perhaps not. But her legacy was the same as mine. I couldn't escape it. The same as yours, Ted."

No one speaks. Rain clatters against the window. Inside the room, stillness hovers above the three of them. Morris imagines the silence stretching from his boyhood to now. *They cannot possibly understand*, he thinks, *living here with their paintings and minor problems*. Then he notices he feels weary and flushed. His heart is pounding and he is embarrassed; he realizes he has been talking on and on, like a nervous schoolboy or regretful old man. Yet, even so, he feels a great, unexpected relief.

Emily gathers dishes from the table, and Ted regards his father quietly, as if Morris has passed on an unwanted burden.

Morris wishes Ted would embrace him. No; more truly, Morris would like to disappear, run upstairs and check on Willy. Make sure he is safe and that he will always be safe. An irrational urge, he decides, and impossible. And Morris understands his grandson won't face the dangers that he faced as a boy. The chord of Judaism is passed from the mother. But there will be other dangers for Willy, new ones.

Morris walks to the piano at the far end of the room. It's a baby grand, a rich mahogany, like the one he played as a child but grander than the piano in Vienna. He plays an easy Beethoven sonata from memory.

After a few minutes, Emily places her hand on his shoulder. Her touch is light and graceful, as if a small bird perches there. This is an affectionate gesture, Morris thinks, one she's never made before, and he is grateful. He suddenly regrets the distance between them and wishes he could give something in return. He brushes a hand against hers, then rests both of his hands on the piano. He would like to please her, and to reach Ted, but his fingers linger on the keys. He knows he cannot bend.

Melody

When I was ten years old, I smashed my best friend, Melody Andrews, against her locker in the hallway after school. I shoved her hard, harder than I had ever pushed anyone before, jammed her face into the sharp vents of the metal door. The locker door clanged loudly in the long, empty hall. "Don't say that about me again, ever," I warned her. "I hope you die. I'll make sure you do."

Melody had been joking the night before with the boy who lived next door. It was October. They were talking in his backyard, and I overheard.

"Libby's a fat pig," Charlie Cohen said. "She picks her nose. Her mother eats Jell-O and pigs' feet."

"Yeah," Melody said. "Nobody likes them."

I was stung to hear her voice. I was in my bedroom, the window open.

"She eats her boogers," Melody went on. "The whole family does the same thing."

"You can be in the club if you won't talk to her," Charlie said. "We're letting in two girls. Do you wanna?"

"Sure thing," Melody said.

That night I cried bitterly. Melody and I often played together. She was the person I liked the most, whom I most wanted to be like. Her family had fine and beautiful things. Her mother had a soft voice and long red nails. Her father was a lawyer, dressed in neat gray suits, and shook my hand. My mother was pudgy, wore orange calico aprons, and had curly black hair streaked with gray. My father stayed late at his business, selling shoes and counting boxes in the back of his store. He never did what he promised—he didn't come home on time or spend the afternoon with us when he said he would. He bought things we couldn't afford: leather books, lamps, and antiques. My mother said, "Harvey, are you dreaming? Who's going to talk to the bill collectors when they call? Are *you*? Is Libby? Your big-shot friend Mr. Weberman? I'm finished doing that."

I jammed Melody against the locker for a long time. I wanted to crush everything about her.

"Stop it, *stop it*, Libby." Melody tried to wiggle free. "You horrid ugly thing. Charlie Cohen was right. You're hurting me." I gave her one last shove, and she started to cry. Then I released her. Her nose was bleeding.

I ran to the school playground and hid behind a tree. I wanted to do more, to kick and strangle her. It was not just that she had been mean. Even then, I knew people could be mean. Melody had betrayed me. I had told her secrets and let her into our house. I had let her become my friend.

Then, for a moment, I felt scared, because I had allowed myself to hurt her, and I wasn't sorry at all. I wasn't one bit sorry, just the way I felt about my sister when I did what I knew I shouldn't—hit her or wrote on her dolls. I didn't feel badly even when my father discovered my behavior and said, "This is serious, Libby." I would have done everything to my sister again. I would have smashed Melody again. Suddenly I felt frightened I would do all those things again. Maybe I wouldn't be able to stop myself. Maybe I was the little girl with the curl. My mother liked to sing the words from the nursery rhyme. "There was a little girl, who had a little curl," she sang, "right in the middle of her forehead. And when she was good, she was very, very good. But when she was bad, she was horrid." I shuddered when she said that. My mother laughed and stroked my curly brown hair. "It's just a song, Libbila; don't worry so."

I sat behind the tree in the playground until there was a hint of darkness, and I was sure Melody had gone home. My mother had just begun to allow me to walk to school by myself. I knew I'd better start back.

I wiped my eyes with my blue cotton jacket and walked slowly up Devon Avenue. This was the route I always took. I knew the names of the store owners, the previous owners, and what the businesses had been before they changed hands. The dress shop once had been a bakery; the jeweler had replaced a butcher; the bath shop had been a grocery. My father had told me this. He told me lots of bits of information, like what a great man Mayor Richard J. Daley was, what highway improvements were being constructed near Lake Michigan, which aldermen were honest, which ones were crooked. The mayor had announced that the city was building new terminals at O'Hare International Airport, my father said, and it would become an important center for travel. My father told me Chicago was the most beautiful city in the world.

Most of the stores were closing for the day. I stared at the sidewalk and hoped no one would notice me. Then I wandered down a side street and walked past my favorite house. The house had four stories and was built of three shades of red brick. A mansion, the kind my father pointed out to us. I liked to imagine the house was a castle and that the people who lived there were kind and gracious, even though my mother said I was getting too old to pretend anymore. I was certain their children had tidy rooms with shelves filled with toys and that the floors were covered with thick pink carpeting that felt like a bed when you lay on it.

I gazed longingly at the house, and then hurried back to Devon Avenue, past the gas station where my father took our car every time it had problems. I ran by the bank where my mother went for money, and the Tiny Town market where we shopped. All these people—the clerks and shop owners—knew me as Harvey's and Charlotte's daughter, and told me I looked just like my parents. The grocery clerk swore I would grow up to be as pretty as my mother. The bank teller said I would be smart and dashing like my father.

When I arrived home, it was dinnertime. The screen door was closed, but the heavy wooden door stood half-open, so I peeked into our small kitchen. I smelled the pot roast and potatoes, saw the bright yellow walls, and my mother wrapped in her orange calico apron, her curly hair pinned behind her ears. She wore white terrycloth slippers. She was talking on the telephone, slicing tomatoes as she spoke.

"What a shame," she said. She paused to listen. "That's not like her," she said, "either one of them. There must be a misunderstanding."

I decided to pretend to be sick and slip past my mother. But she motioned to me and said, "Hold the wire a moment please, Edna." She covered the mouthpiece with her hand and whispered, "Come here, Libby. It's Mrs. Andrews. She's telling me you shoved Melody and made her nose bleed." My mother peered at me as if she could burrow inside my mind. "Did you do that, Libby Simon? I want the truth."

I shook my head no.

"That's what I thought." She sighed and went back to Mrs. Andrews. "Of course not. Libby wouldn't do such a thing." My mother listened, arranging slices of tomatoes around a plate of red Jell-O. "I don't know," she said. She wiped a hand on her apron. "I'll speak to you later this evening."

My mother looked me up and down. I stared at the pot of potatoes cooking on the stove. She told me she wanted to know exactly what had happened between Melody and me. We would discuss it later, though. Dinner was ready. Then she frowned and said my father would be out again on business tonight. Only the girls would eat. She told me to wash my hands and keep better track of time so I wouldn't come home so late.

My sister, Shelley, bounded into the kitchen when she was called. She always did what my mother asked. She was three years younger than me, and she liked to follow me around the house. The three of us sat at the round table covered with a yellow plastic tablecloth. We ate dinner, my mother serving us, my sister telling jokes she'd learned in school—what was red and white and black all over, no, no, she giggled, black and white and red all over, not the color red, but read like a book. Try to guess, Mommy. My mother laughed, but she couldn't guess. Of course, I knew the answer: a newspaper. Everyone my age knew. Those were old jokes, I told Shelley, stupid jokes that everyone wanted to forget. My mother said if people didn't have anything nice to say, they shouldn't speak at all.

After dinner, she told Shelley to change into pajamas. My mother spoke with Mrs. Andrews again. Then she sat with me at the kitchen table.

"I want the truth, Libby," she began. "I don't understand why Melody would lie. I don't know why you would."

I looked down at my math homework on the table. "I don't know what she's talking about," I mumbled.

I could tell my mother was watching me. I thought she might smile then and hold my hand—she did that sometimes—and say, "Libby, it's not so bad, whatever it is. The important thing is to be honest." This time, my mother didn't touch me. She told me to stop using a sharp tone of voice. Then she sent me to my room until I was ready to tell her what had happened.

That night, Shelley went to sleep in my parents' room. She went to bed earlier than I did. She and I shared a bedroom, but my mother said tonight I didn't need the company. She would move Shelley back to our bedroom later.

Our bedroom was small and crowded with books, dressers, and toys. When I lay on my bed I could gaze out the window at Charlie Cohen's big white brick house with its sprawling lawn.

Even if I tried to explain to my mother why I had pushed Melody, I would have to start with Melody and Charlie Cohen, and I knew this might hurt my mother and her pride. She always insisted I wash my hands and face and change into clean clothes before I went to Melody's house. She told me to act like a lady there. She didn't like Charlie's family one bit.

They weren't our kind, she told me, even though Mr. Cohen was a dentist and they lived in the biggest house on the block. My mother said Charlie ran around wild. He never read and could go anywhere alone, watch all the television he wanted, and curse. There was a color television in his bedroom, and he could watch the one in the kitchen while he ate dinner. Mrs. Cohen chewed gum, smoked cigarettes, and wore big gold hoop earrings and loud print dresses that clung to her large breasts. She was a careless housekeeper, my mother said. Mrs. Cohen never swept and left her white living room sofa bare, without plastic covering.

I glanced at a photograph of my family that hung on the wall in my bedroom. My mother's arm was draped around me, and she was smiling. She would never understand what I had done and why. She wanted me to be just like her.

She always went to cook for people who were old or sick and she liked to take me along. She gave them clothes, too, and invited people we hardly knew to eat with us at our house.

My father often told me proudly that she was the kind of person who had never met a stranger. Sometimes he complained, though, that she wasted her time, cooking and inviting—for nothing, he would grumble, for the *schleppers* who had to take charity. He muttered that she put more time into taking care of other people than taking care of us and working at the business. And for what, he said, reading those religious books; it's a bunch of nonsense.

My mother never took me with her on Sunday afternoons. She wanted to, she said, but she couldn't bring a child because she went to a special building to dress the dead. She sponged off the body and dressed it in a clean white smock and hat. This was a wonderful task, my mother told me, to say prayers and prepare a person for the world to come. This was the highest good deed, a *mitzvah*, because the person didn't know you were helping and couldn't return the favor. "You need to learn a thing or two about good deeds, Libby," she told me.

Now I kicked off my shoes and stared at the white bedroom walls. I couldn't tell her that I had hurt Melody on purpose. I couldn't admit to her that sometimes I saw our lives through Charlie Cohen's eyes, too. We were a bunch of chubby people who ate Jell-O and argued and lived in a small, dull house.

I wished I could tell my mother everything and that she would understand. I wanted her to wrap her arms around me and say: "Libby, we love you. What's done is done; don't make it such a secret." I wanted her to say: "No matter what happens, don't hurt anybody. It's not like you, Libbila."

But it was like me.

After a while, she called me downstairs. Just as I walked into the kitchen, Mrs. Andrews telephoned. My mother wound the phone cord tightly around her hand as she listened.

"Yes, yes," she finally said to Mrs. Andrews. "I understand."

When she finished the conversation, she marched over to me. I was sitting at the table. Her belly stuck out like a shelf from under the sash of her blue terrycloth robe. Her long earrings of old coins and her bangle and charm bracelets jangled.

She asked me again what had happened with Melody, and I didn't reply. My mother didn't say any of the things I'd imagined. Then I made a mistake. I looked right into her eyes. She stared at me as if she could see everything about me, what I loved and hated, every tiny piece of my thoughts. Then she began to change. She did this sometimes. Her face became flushed; she pressed her lips together and glared hard. "Your grandparents didn't come to the *Goldene Medina* for you to sit and lie to me," she yelled. "Your father and I don't work to the bone for you to carry on like a brat."

My mother grasped my shoulders and squeezed them. "Answer me, Libby," she shouted. "*Tikkun Olam.* That's what you do, try to repair the world. You don't add to the world's troubles." She began to shake me. Her nails dug into my skin.

I was afraid she might never stop. I bit my lip so as not to show her any emotion or give her the satisfaction of knowing she had reached my heart. My skin stung, and I thought: When you are like this, I will never love you, I will never love you again. "Don't touch me," I shouted.

"I'm telling you, Libby," my mother screamed and shook me. "We're not going to raise a savage. Go to your room and stay there until you tell me the truth."

I yanked away from her, ran to my bedroom, and slammed the door.

My father came home late. When he tiptoed into my room and kissed the top of my head, I pretended to be asleep. Later, I heard him arguing with my mother. Their bedroom was next to Shelley's and mine. Whenever I had trouble falling asleep, I overheard them.

Sometimes I heard them laughing and sighing. Sometimes I heard them yelling.

They usually argued about my father's business. His store was on the south side of Chicago. It was a regular United Nations, my father liked to say with pride. Black people shopped there, Poles, Greeks, Italians, Romanians, Russians, even people from Mexico. Customers mingled in the front of the store. There was carpeting in the front, and beautiful, shiny leather shoes and handbags sat on display. The back of the store was larger. Rows of tall, rough wooden shelves stood against the wall, filled with boxes of shoes and handbags, piles of towels and denim pants, bolts of fabric, transistor radios, wristwatches, and toasters. Calendars with photographs of smiling naked ladies were taped to the walls.

The naked-lady calendars belonged to Mr. Max Weberman. He was my father's business partner and had invested money in the store.

"We'll get nowhere, Harvey," my mother often yelled, "doing whatever that Weberman says." He asked my father to do things she said weren't honest, things I didn't understand.

But that night my parents were talking about me.

"She's not the center of the universe," my mother was saying. "She can't hurt people and lie."

"Calm down, Charlotte," my father murmured. "You'll wake her. Children do those things."

"Not our daughter, not to a girl like Melody. You know the family. Libby will get a reputation. And Mrs. Andrews is president of the parents' organization at the school."

"So the family has money. I wish I had money, too. All children lie; they hit."

"What's the matter with you, Harvey? Suddenly it's okay to lie, to hurt people? The next will be to steal, like your big-shot friend Weberman."

"Leave him out of this. Without him, we're back in your father's apartment, slapped in like sardines. There are no saints in this house."

I heard the rustling of their sheets.

"Harvey, Harvey," my mother cried. "When will you open your eyes? Libby is a demon to Shelley; she's sullen to me. She has you wrapped around her little finger; that's what I see."

At breakfast, I didn't talk to anyone. My mother set the table as she always did, as if we were guests. She put neatly folded white cloth napkins on the table with forks and spoons, and a dish beneath my chipped white china cereal bowl. She set a cup and saucer at my place, too, though I drank only milk. Then we sat together while she drank her coffee, and I gulped my milk.

Often when Shelley and I ate, my mother would clean the kitchen or wash dishes or wipe the cabinets. When she did this, she sang loudly and sometimes she whirled around the room, clutching a dishcloth or box of napkins. She had a musical voice and made up songs, like "Libby, my little Libby, how I love you," or "Harvey and Shelley, you're my dreams." I never recognized the melodies. It bothered me to hear her, and I asked why she sang. She said because she loved us and she was happy.

It seemed to me there were other ways my mother could show that she loved me. She could sit with me like Melody's mother did at their house, and be happy to hear whatever I wanted to say.

That morning my mother didn't sing. She told Shelley not to tease me. My father didn't describe the progress of the construction projects on Lake Shore Drive. At first, he put his arm around me and said, "Libby, don't keep your thoughts to yourself." After a while he told me sternly that I should stop fiddling with my cereal and sulking. I had upset my mother. He had heard about what happened to Melody. "There will be a punishment," he said, "because you refuse to tell the truth."

At school, Melody and I glared at each other. During recess, Charlie Cohen said he had heard about the lowlife, awful thing I'd done. "I'll let everyone know," he laughed.

Some kids paid no attention to him. A few said I had showed my true colors. Others congratulated me. They were impressed by my courage and said it was time someone had finally stood up to Melody.

In the evening, my father sat with me on the sofa in the living room. My punishment was for both the problem and the lying, he said. For five weeks, I would go directly to my room after school. I couldn't talk on the telephone or play with friends or my sister.

My mother ordered me to write a letter of apology. I finally told my father the whole thing was an accident. Melody was as much to blame as me.

"Accidents like this should never happen," my mother said. She stood next to me like a guard while I sat at the kitchen table and printed on a sheet of her best beige stationery with the pink flowers on top:

> Dear Melody,
>
> I am very sorry about the misunderstanding, and anything I did to hurt you. I did not mean to hurt you and I apologize if I did.
>
> Sincerely,
> Libby Simon

My mother said I needed to write a stronger, more sincere apology;

there wasn't a misunderstanding. I started to erase the words, but my father said, "No. The letter is fine as it is."

Mrs. Andrews told my mother it would be best if Melody and I didn't play together again.

For five weeks, I went to my bedroom after school. Shelley played in the basement. I did my homework and then read comic books or made up my own songs or fiddled with dolls. Sometimes alone in the room, I peeled off my clothes and stood naked in front of the mirror that hung above the dresser. I stared at my eyes that were too closely set together and at my nose, which angled instead of curving gracefully. Then I peered at my flat chest, my pudgy belly, and all the places that were private. I slid my hands over my body and felt impatient for everything to change. I wanted to run away and never be sorry for anything again. I longed to be beautiful and kind like Melody's mother. I longed to color my hair and wear bold dresses like Mrs. Cohen, live in a castle, do whatever I pleased, and be in love with a man like my father. I would make up my own songs, about important subjects, like Devon Avenue and people like Charlie Cohen. Songs about what was in my heart. I would sing these for people.

One night, my father sat with me in the living room. "Libby, don't fret," he said. "Problems like this work themselves out. You fall off a horse, you dust yourself off, get right back on. It will be like you never fell."

I wished my mother would say this to me. Even if she did, I wouldn't believe her words either. I was afraid Charlie Cohen would taunt me forever. I was certain everyone knew a terrible secret about me and would never forget.

At the end of the next school year, Charlie reorganized his club. He invited old and new members to join the club, and he even asked me.

One day a group of us stood in the school playground, joking about how little kids behave. "Remember the time Libby slapped Melody so hard her nose bled?" Charlie said. People laughed, although

Melody didn't. Then a few kids answered yes, they remembered; that's just the kind of stupid thing fifth graders would do.

I felt myself blushing, dug my hands in my pockets, and looked at the ground. I was sorry now I'd pushed her, but I knew I could push her again. I could push everyone in the club.

I often dreamt about Melody. In the dream, we always stood on a mountaintop. There was a beautiful view of the sky and land below. I would push her, and she would shove me hard, right off the edge, and laugh, "So long, fat pig!" I fell in slow motion. People gathered around Melody and laughed as they watched me fall.

My parents were there, too, and Shelley. My mother wore her pink silk dress with the thick black sash. She looked beautiful. Shelley wore a fancy dress, and my father wore his best suit and the blue tie we'd given him for his birthday.

When I tried to gesture to them to help me, my mother pointed wildly at me, but my father just glanced at her. I could tell they were discussing what to do, and I could hear their voices as I fell, my mother saying, "Harvey, do something," and my father's reply, "Calm down, Charlotte; let's think this through."

In my dream, I called out and told them to hurry, but they stopped looking at me. My mother put on her white gloves, waved, and walked away. Shelley followed her. I could tell that my mother was going to the special building where she dressed the dead. My father hesitated, but my mother grasped his hand. I fell faster and faster until I couldn't see them anymore, and then I became afraid. I was terrified I would fall until I crashed against the ground. I heard their voices. "*Tikkun Olam*," my mother said brightly. "Come, Harvey. Let's repair the world."

Happy to See You

I stand in the front hallway of the house, my baby, Jennifer, straddling my right hip, the other hand holding the vacuum cleaner. The stereo is turned up high. I sing to Mozart, pretending my voice is a violin or a piano. I would like to dance, too, and sail through the room with the baby.

When I turn on the vacuum, it doesn't start. I kick the machine. There is a slow hiss of air and the smell of burning rubber.

Jennifer cries, so I switch off the vacuum and sway, trying to calm her. When she cries like this, I cannot think clearly.

The doorbell rings just as Jennifer quiets down. I'm not expecting anyone. Then I hear Anna's voice.

"Rebecca. Are you home?" She knocks on the door.

I yell, "Coming," but first hurriedly unplug the vacuum and push it into a closet, turn off the stereo, gather the books and newspapers scattered across the floor and hide them beneath the blue-striped couch. Jennifer bounces on my hip as if she's an appendage.

I unlock the deadbolt, open the door. Anna smiles. She looks beautiful in a stylish gray silk suit. Her wavy, honey-colored hair falls gracefully to her shoulders.

We hug and walk to the living room. I sit on the couch and rest Jennifer on my lap so she's gazing at the floor. Tiny pieces of lint spot the blue carpeting. I look away from the rug.

"I need to talk." Anna lays her leather briefcase on the coffee table and sits on the armchair next to the couch. "But first, let me see the baby."

I glance at the framed photograph of Anna and me on the piano across the room. We stand on the courthouse steps, lawyers dressed in sensible dark suits, poised to conquer the world. We wanted to help the poor then, to transform their lives.

I look back at Anna, who is smiling at the baby. "Hello, helloooo, little girl." Anna puckers her lips and blows kisses. "Yes, yes, yes."

Jennifer grins.

I stroke the fine brown hair on Jennifer's head. It's been months since Anna and I last saw one another; we drop in and out of each other's lives. "You look great," I tell her.

"But I've gained four pounds. I just can't lose the weight." She stands, resting her hands on her long, straight hips. Her body is flat and narrow, like a boy's. "Can you tell?"

I shake my head no.

She sits again and leans toward me. "It must be nice to be home with a baby and have so much extra time. I've been swamped at work. Tell me what it's like with the kids, what you do all day."

My husband, Brian, asks the same question. Sometimes I draw him a clock, parceling out hours as if they're pieces of a pie. I tell Anna that I feed the kids, play with them or sometimes yell at them in exasperation. All day. She says, "Be serious," so I describe the other things: the house, the laundry, the meals. I explain that with the baby and Sammy, the maintenance is incredible; Sammy is just three, still too young to help. It's easier on days like today when he plays at a friend's house. I try to explain how tired I often am.

Anna smooths the creases in her silk skirt. "But it must be sweet with the children," she says, "to help them discover the world."

I think about yesterday. I was walking with the children when we saw a neighbor's dog bound into the street. "Dog," I said, pointing him out to Jennifer. "That is a dog." She laughed. Sammy ran ahead on the sidewalk. A car sped up the street. There should have been time; you'd think the dog could have dashed away or the car would have stopped. But it didn't. We heard the screeching of wheels, the yowling and whimpering. The dog's leg popped open and so did his head. Blood was everywhere. Sammy ran to me sobbing. I tried to comfort him. It was a long walk home.

I want Anna to understand my world, for us to think in tandem as we used to, when we had no patience for husbands or children. Before I can explain, she begins talking about her work.

"There's no question the money at the firm is good," she says. "The clients treat me better than ours did. I don't know how we managed all those years visiting the jail every day. But I have to tell you. Yesterday I got a letter from Cody Morgan."

I shiver and move Jennifer toward my knees.

"He thanked me for helping him get sent to prison." Anna drapes her suit jacket across the back of her chair. "He wrote that he feels 'truly rehabilitated.' I couldn't believe it." She laughs, then looks at me. "I thought you were over that."

"I am," I answer, but clench my teeth.

"You take these things too seriously, Rebecca."

"Maybe. Still, he was the last straw."

"It was circumstance. He was crazy."

I nod and eye my watch to distract myself, gazing at the red second hand that moves slowly in its track. Then I glance at Anna.

"Look, I'm sorry I mentioned him." She puts her hand on my shoulder. "I'm hardly thinking; I'm famished. I had to talk to a client and missed lunch. Do you mind if I get something to eat?"

"I'll make lunch for you. I'd love to."

"No, you stay here; you have the baby. I'll find something for us both."

Jennifer kicks her feet against my legs as if she'd like to fly away, and I realize she hasn't napped yet. Afternoons when she sleeps, when there's no one else around, are the most peaceful moments of my day, the only time I can think or read or practice piano. I have to follow a rigorous schedule to find any free time. If I visit with Anna, Jennifer may fuss later, and I'll have to pick up Sammy from his friend's house. Still, I haven't seen friends in a while. Sometimes I long for them.

This scheduling reminds me of my former life in court. There wasn't a peaceful moment—lawyers to talk to, cases to argue, clients demanding something more be done. When Anna and I were in trial, everything else stopped. All that mattered was persuading a jury.

I hear Anna open the refrigerator. I check my watch again. I won't have a spare second today.

The last time I was with Cody Morgan, we were in the jail, in the small utility room where lawyers meet with clients when conference rooms are full, a room smelling of soaps and oils and ammonia. I was talking to Cody about his case when he suddenly stood up. He was six feet tall and broad, with red tattoos curling up his arms. He walked behind me and reached for a mop. Then he shoved me against the wall.

I should have screamed right away, I should have fought, but he wedged the wooden handle tightly against my neck. I could barely breathe. I saw a bottle of ammonia on a shelf from the corner of my eye. I slid my arm to grab it and I hit the bottle against the wall. My eyes watered from the smell. When Cody looked down, I thrust the jagged bottle into his face.

He grunted roughly and dropped the mop. He pressed his hands against his face and cursed me, his words like long, low moans. Then I lost control. I bellowed like a steer before slaughter. I heard the echoes of my yells until the deputies came and calmed me down. They twisted Cody's arms behind his back and led him away.

The next day, Anna took over the case. I met Brian a few weeks later.

Anna brings napkins and a plate of cheese-and-tomato sandwiches cut into perfect quarters without crusts. "I'll be back in a minute," she says, "then I'll tell you my troubles, and you can tell me yours." She goes to the kitchen to get two glasses of water.

I breathe deeply and gently hold onto Jennifer. I don't want to think about Cody Morgan. The house is quiet, and it's pleasant to sit and be tended to. I tell myself to relax. This is a comfortable room, the furniture nicer than what Anna and I shared when we were roommates. Anna lives alone now in a high-rise building, her third apartment in the last year. She thrives on change.

I don't like to move and am happy with the house and my things around me, like the massive rolltop desk across the room. It's a rich, dark walnut, with fine curved carvings on its legs. I like to arrange items on the desktop, piles of papers and bills, the minutiae of life. I can hide things in the tiny compartments. The beauty of it is that nothing stares me in the face. I can close the desk, but I know exactly where everything is.

Anna has a big desk in her office, too, but not as grand as this. Her office is grand, though, on the fifteenth floor of a tall building downtown, with large, gracious windows facing west.

My desk is my office. On a shelf on the right, I put clippings from magazines, travel ads like "Dreams for Sale—See South America's Jewels," or "Go Anywhere Your Heart Desires." I collect articles about music conservatories, summers in Aspen or Tanglewood. And on a shelf on the far left, I keep my list of what I want to do with Brian someday or what I'll do without him and the children if I have time again: Visit New Zealand and Peru; watch movies all day; become a concert pianist; set up a law practice with Anna or on my own.

Nights, when the baby is crying or Sammy has awakened, even after everyone has gone back to sleep, I stay awake and think: What if Brian died, or if I was crippled, or something happened to the children? To the world? Sometimes an idea will come to me then, and I add it to my list. I slip from bed and tiptoe to the desk. Even in the dark, I know just where to find my paper and pen.

I keep letters from old clients in a special drawer on the far right side of the desk. There's still one from Cody Morgan, though I never can bear to look at it. I save it to remind myself I've really had a past.

When Brian and I met, we liked each other right away. I finally felt ready to settle down. He wasn't like other men I'd known. He loved to play guitar, listen to music and read, like me. He wanted a family. I decided it was time for one, too. These days he's busy, selling computer equipment, working late. In the evenings, he watches television or works on the bed he's building for Jennifer. Or he plays guitar while I play piano. On Fridays, he comes home early, and we tell the children stories together. At those moments, I imagine we have all we need within the walls of our house.

He's never asked why I decided to become a lawyer or why I quit. I would tell him my lawyer father groomed me to become one. I gave up my music. I never believed I would get anywhere playing piano. Anna and I scorned our mothers' choices, houses full of children, husbands rarely around. Anna believed you could be happy only through social action. I did then, too.

Anna returns carrying two glasses of ice water on a silver tray. She's found our best crystal on a high kitchen shelf.

As we begin to eat, I ask her about her latest romance.

She stares at her nails; they're neatly filed and polished a pale pink. "Robert left me," she murmurs.

"He did?" I say with disbelief.

Her eyes fill with tears. "He'd moved in. We were getting along so well. Then he didn't come home."

"Oh, no."

"Four nights. Like my father. No explanation. No apology." She hides her face in her hands.

"You're lucky you didn't waste more time on him."

"When I realized he'd left for good, I drank a few shots of vodka." Anna looks at me. "Then I dumped the bottle down the drain. My God, I thought, am I turning into my father, too?"

"Of course not. You were upset." I want to hug her, but my arms are filled with Jennifer. "There will be someone else. Wait. You'll see. Someone just for you."

"There are hardly any decent men left. You were lucky with Brian. The men I meet are gay, or in love with a fantasy, or are still finding themselves. How long is it going to take them to find out who they are?"

Anna and I used to talk like this for hours. We both had lots of love affairs. These days I don't think about love affairs.

Jennifer waves her arms and grabs the sandwich in my hand. I try to occupy her with a plastic rattle I find on the couch, but she throws the toy on the floor.

"Can I hold her, Rebecca?" Anna reaches for the baby.

It's a relief to give up Jennifer. Anna carries the baby tentatively, away from her body, and Jennifer smiles, flapping her arms and legs as if swimming in air.

My hands feel light now, strangers to me. I think of how they were in court, grasping hands with clients, holding manila file folders, taking notes. My hands had a life of their own then, doing whatever they wanted.

I remember shaking Cody Morgan's hand, the feel of his rough, callused palm and short, fat fingers, the fingers that wrote the letter hidden in my desk, the fingers that shoved me against the wall. I remember words in his letter, like *beautiful* and *bitch*.

Jennifer begins to cry, and Anna walks toward me. "She wants something, Rebecca. You better take her. I think she's sick."

Thick, clear saliva spills from Jennifer's mouth. When I hold her, she spits up on my arm. I wipe her face with my shirt.

"Damn." Anna dabs a napkin on the damp streak that zigzags on the front of her blouse. "I've got a deposition at three."

"It'll dry by then." I rest Jennifer on my lap, and she wiggles vigorously. There's another sound and then a sour smell. Anna arches an eyebrow. I can tell she thinks it's just gas, but I feel thick liquid leaking onto my jeans. Jennifer needs her diaper changed.

In the nursery upstairs, I lay Jennifer on the changing table. Her face is flushed. She wails. I stroke her arm, coaxing her to be calm.

Anna follows and steps over board books and miniature metal

cars. She gravitates to a mirror in the corner and studies her reflection. "I need to fall in love again," she says. "I need that exhilaration."

I nod, thinking how hard she can be on a man. Then I wash Jennifer's bottom. She quiets down and stares at me with her round blue eyes.

"I've decided," Anna says. She lifts a tortoiseshell comb from her purse. "I want to have a baby."

I avoid her eyes.

"I knew I shouldn't have done it," she says impatiently, almost to herself. "I was only twenty-five. Anyway, that kind of thing can be fixed, reversed. They untie your tubes."

"I didn't know it was so simple."

She nods, as if it's settled and done. "These days they can undo anything." She fingers the stain on her blouse. "I won't wait forever. Plenty of women have babies on their own."

I sigh in agreement and fasten a fresh diaper on Jennifer. My jeans are wet; I try to clean the mess with a baby wipe. Jennifer reaches for my nose and laughs, her voice like tiny chiming bells.

As Anna combs her hair, she tells me that tomorrow she's going to California, then next week to New York and Washington. The firm pays and she'll stay a few extra days to ski in Tahoe and have a good time. "I might be lucky," she says. "Find a good man on the slopes."

I glance around the room. For a moment, I imagine Anna going off in the world, her hands light and free, while I stay behind with my children and the toys on the floor. For that instant, I long to go, too, to wear fine silk suits, have time to read or think, do what I want. When I tell Anna, she laughs.

"I'd rather not be working," she says. Then, more quietly, "Sometimes I feel like I'm just killing time. Waiting for something to happen in my life."

"We're all waiting, one way or another."

"When I don't need the money, I'll quit the law, move to

California, study flamenco dancing. There's a whole world out there. Who knows?" She laughs. "Still, there are interesting cases. And I love a good fight."

I have never liked to fight. I rub my nose against Jennifer's cheek. Her skin is soft and smooth; I know its contours like my own. She begins to talk in the way babies do, making sounds like trills on a finely tuned harp.

"Let me tell you about my newest case," Anna says. But she loses me. I imagine I could rest my face against Jennifer's forever, listen to her high, clear voice or watch her tiny fingers stretch open like petals of a flower, everything there only in miniature. What I love about Jennifer is how we are together. Interrupting, I try to explain this to Anna. "There's something soothing about motherhood. Something I can't really explain that—"

The alarm on Anna's stopwatch beeps. She searches in her purse. The keys jingle and hit the floor. She grabs them. "I've got to run. Tell me next time. You've got to get out more, Rebecca. You're becoming a hermit. No one sees you."

"It's wonderful to see you now."

She smooths a strand of hair from my face, and we hug again. Then she hurries downstairs. I follow behind with Jennifer, but Anna is out the door and gone.

I linger by the door. The space where her car sat blends into the empty street; it's as if she'd never stopped here at all.

This was what I wanted to tell Anna: how much I miss old friends and feel alone sometimes, as if I'm the only person in the world except for the children, their little lives pulling at me, their damp fingers pressing against my legs and hands. Whenever the baby and Sammy nap, I clean or sit at the piano. I don't read the newspaper anymore. I just don't want to know. I stick close to home. It's hard to bring the children places and hard to leave them.

At the piano, I practice scales. When my fingers are tired, I stop. The house is so quiet. Always, I go to check on the children. Watching their small sleeping faces is a kind of prayer.

Now that Anna is gone, I don't feel like vacuuming. I lift Jennifer high above my head and carry her upstairs. She laughs.

I sit to nurse her. In a few hours, I'll pick up Sammy, and Brian will return from work. I wonder which stories we'll tell the children tonight. Without thinking, I begin to sing in a way I never can with people around, composing words to whatever melody jumps into my head. Today it's "Edelweiss": "You're so sweet, you're my love, I'm so happy to see you." Jennifer's eyes open and close. I nurse her longer, cup her in my arms, then place her in the crib. She slips her thumb into her mouth and sleeps.

In the living room, dust coats the top of my desk. I rub off the fine gray wisps and open the drawer on the far right where I keep Cody Morgan's letter. I brush my hand across the letter. Then I close the drawer. I almost never lock up the desk, but now I do. I can open it any time I want.

A Question of Place

My husband and I had just returned from a vacation in the mountains when Melissa fell on the pencil. We had left the children with friends for five days, rented a small cabin in a state park, and had a wonderful time. We made love and talked, took long walks and admired the views, like any ordinary tourists.

I was in a dreamy state of mind and believed that John and I, and our three children, weren't ordinary. Not like the people we had seen on vacation, armed with their cameras, campers, and hopes. I told him that almost everyone seemed to be moving through life perplexed, pulled along by circumstance. I felt as if we were superior, set apart, like I'd felt twenty years ago when John and I met. As if, together, we led a charmed life. We had believed we could do anything then and nothing would touch us.

Usually John and I don't go away without the children, but we had wanted a kind of second honeymoon. And John needed a break. He had been working long hours and weekends. I was nervous about leaving. He said I was always nervous; he told me anxiety was in my genes. I had prepared every detail, the clothing and favorite toys—Melissa's pink blanket, Billy's baseball and bat, Laura's brown-and-yellow spotted bear. I left typed instructions and phone numbers.

When we arrived back in Denver after our trip, John said he wanted to stop at home to drop off our suitcases and check the mail and phone messages before we collected the children. As we walked into the house, he kissed me, and I felt an extraordinary calm. Though I missed the children, I didn't want to let go of the moment, the two of us alone.

On the answering machine were messages from a Chinese doctor who was scheduled to arrive and begin work in John's laboratory the next day. There were four messages in Chinese, all of them agitated. Just a few words of English were sprinkled in. John replayed the messages three times. I could see him shedding the ease of our week, see tension spread across his face and neck.

"The guy's English is no good," John muttered. "Maybe he's lost at the airport. I hate to go before getting the kids, but I have to find that doctor." John looked at me, and we went upstairs. "If you need me, Ellie, try my cell phone or the airport." He changed from his shorts and sneakers, tossed them on the bedroom floor. "Maybe the lab or…Chang Fu's house. Damn. God knows how long it will take to find the guy. They told me he knew English." Then he brushed his lips against my cheek and grabbed the keys.

"Are you sure you need to go?" I said. "Can't somebody else handle this?" I held his hand. "We were going to spend the rest of the day with the children."

"It can't be helped. It's my responsibility." He bounded down the stairs, and I followed. He hurried out the front door, then glanced back at me. "Sweetheart, can you lock up? And, hey, tell the kids I'm sorry."

The children climbed on me and kissed me. We told each other about the week. When we arrived home, though, they began to fuss. Where's Daddy? Why did you go away in the first place? they demanded. Maybe you don't love us. It seemed they understood I had been happy while I was away, and they couldn't bear that.

I tried to settle them. "Daddy needs to take care of something for work. It's very important," I said. I gave them souvenirs we brought from the trip. I told them how much we loved them.

I hadn't expected to retrieve the children without John, though I didn't mind, not really. It was one of those bargains you make with yourself. Things hadn't started out like this, but John worked long, odd hours now, setting up and checking his experiments. He's a doctor, a hematologist. He wants to unravel the mysteries of life.

We used to discuss every detail of the house and the children. John drew charts, plotted graphs of chores and childcare. We posted lists of duties on the refrigerator and strived to balance everything between us, as if we were partners in a great, growing enterprise.

Life had become so busy, though; really, it had run away with itself. The children were growing, John's work had become demanding, there was my small translation business, the house and yard, the dog and four hamsters—all the accoutrements of life we'd collected, almost inadvertently. I had wanted to be a linguist and had learned five languages. I used to translate lectures and poems; a teacher once told me that was my gift. Now I designed greeting cards in three languages and translated documents for an immigration lawyer. I earned enough for odds and ends. With my business, I could control the hours I worked and be more flexible than John could be. If we have children, I had decided, why should someone else raise them?

I was thinking about this as I sat at the kitchen table next to Billy and sipped a cup of sweet blackberry tea. I noticed John's cell phone on the table next to Billy's crayons. John must have forgotten it. He had become preoccupied lately. He and I had really been children ourselves when we met, I realized; our ideas and hopes were still so unformed then.

Melissa and Laura chased each other around the house. Billy grasped a red crayon and labeled a drawing of his friend's room where he had just stayed.

The girls began to yell, playfully, I thought. Billy raced to check on them. I looked at the paper he was working on: *bed. yelow lamp with 1 missing bulbe*. Then I heard a thud and a shriek.

"It was *my* pencil," Laura shouted upstairs. "She gave it to me. Melissa's an ugly Indian-giver." Only screams from Melissa.

I set my cup on the table and ran. Melissa was lying on the floor in the master bedroom, clutching her stomach, her blond curls limp. I saw the pencil—the new pink one we had just bought for her with the red stars and yellow hearts. It used to have a shiny, sharp point. Now the pencil was jutting out from the middle of Melissa's belly.

"She fell. She fell. I didn't push," Laura cried.

I knelt and carefully pulled the pencil from deep in Melissa's stomach. She was screaming, and I felt myself begin to panic. There wasn't a point on the pencil anymore, just jagged wood and blood. Blood on Melissa's belly. Her shirt. My hands.

Billy was yelling. "It's all Laura's fault. She grabbed it. She's a big grabber."

And Laura: "Am not."

I told Billy to hurry and bring me a wet washcloth and told Laura to find Melissa's shoes. I crooned softly to Melissa, "It's okay, sweet one, you'll be fine."

Then I lifted Melissa's hands away from her stomach and pressed the wet cloth Billy had brought on her skin. I told myself: You apply pressure to stop bleeding. You stay calm, and you apply pressure.

"Is she going to die?" Laura whimpered.

Billy nudged her with his elbow. "That is the all-time stupidest question."

"Quiet," I told them. I removed the washcloth and parted the skin around Melissa's wound.

If John were home, we would be taking care of the children together, I thought. I could have worried all I wanted, certain everything would be fine.

"It's just a little cut," I said. Melissa cried, and I stroked her face. But it wasn't just a little cut. I shivered as I checked it closely. The wound was a long slit, larger, deeper, and bleeding more than any I'd ever seen. There were layers of skin or muscle, white and pink; I didn't know what. The pencil had sliced her skin, like a knife slashing open a pouch.

"Is she going to die?" Laura asked again.

"No, sweetheart. Of course not." And I thought: *People don't die in this house. Don't you know that? Daddy can fix things. I draw rainbows and cartoons.*

I held Melissa in my arms, her head bent back, her legs and arms limp, and all that blood. I felt as if I wasn't holding a person anymore, just a body or rag doll. Something not quite alive, except for her screams.

"No one is going to die," I said firmly. For an instant I thought to call 911, but instead grabbed the car keys that sat on the dresser. Then like a policeman, I ordered everyone downstairs and outside. Billy held open the door. I carried Melissa and laid her gently in the front seat, tucking the washcloth in her shorts to absorb the blood. Laura and Billy sat in back. Laura clutched her spotted bear to her chest. Melissa cried.

I tried to calm everyone. "Let's whisper," I told them. "Let's watch outside the window and try to be the first to spot the moon."

It was dusk. The hazy silhouette of mountains rose in the distance against the western sky. Cars seemed to drive at a lazy pace, as if unwinding from the heat of the day. I started to speed, zigzagging from lane to lane, relieved when I came to an open stretch of road where I could jam my foot on the accelerator and really move.

Melissa began to whimper softly. Laura sang to her. "Pencils are sharp. Pencils are mean. Pencils are not for writing on skin."

"That doesn't even rhyme." Billy rolled his eyes.

"That's very nice, Laura." I looked at them in the rearview mirror. "Billy, Laura is doing a good job. You're seven, but she's only five. She's not as old as you are."

"Melissa is only three," Laura said.

"Yes." I lifted one hand off the steering wheel to stroke Melissa's arm and then I had a frightening thought. I realized I didn't know the location of the hospital. We'd never gone to the emergency room before. I had been to the children's hospital once, years ago. Now I couldn't remember which street it was on. The other hospitals were on the opposite side of town. Why hadn't I checked the address? I might never find the hospital or only when it was too late. Too late for what? My cell phone was in my purse, but it was dead. I'd meant to charge it. We were driving in a dark, unfamiliar part of town. Except for a few drunks and teenagers hanging out on the sidewalks, no one else was around. I locked the doors.

"Damn it," I muttered and gripped the steering wheel. "I've got to find that place."

Melissa touched her belly and cried loudly. Laura hugged her stuffed animal.

Billy asked, "What place?"

I could almost hear my mother, even John saying, "You should have found the address at home, Eleanora." I veered onto another street and sped through a yellow light. Then I raced around a corner. I was debating whether I could safely stop to call the hospital at a gas station when I saw it—a gleaming oasis, the clean white brick building with bright neon lights and arrows: EMERGENCY.

The corridor to the emergency area was light and empty. No one sat behind the white laminate desk. The floors were polished, countertops spotless. We could have been in the entryway of a modern office building. A nurse walked in. She wore a yellow blouse and black skirt and a nametag, but no uniform, as if she might be on her way to a movie.

She examined Melissa's stomach quickly. "Keep pressure on it," she said. "I'll have someone with you immediately." Then she directed me to another woman who requested information crisply: names, date of birth, insurance details. I carried Melissa. She was crying. Laura clung to my shorts. Billy patted Melissa's arm, trying to comfort her.

I asked to use the phone on the woman's desk. I called John at the lab, Chang Fu's, at home. There was no answer. I called the airport but there was no answer either. The woman was impatient and told us to go to a waiting area.

The room was crowded with other patients. We sat down. Melissa's bleeding had slowed, but the washcloth, her underwear, and her shorts were stained with blood. Billy and Laura walked around the room. Melissa clutched my shoulders. She wouldn't let me go.

As we waited, I held Melissa on my lap and thought about John. I wanted to talk to him. He and I met when we were nineteen. I had no intention of marrying then. It was a misstep, I've sometimes thought. I was young and idealistic. I wanted to save the world, to do extraordinary things—to do them on my own—to speak eight languages, become an ambassador and travel, help educate people. I wanted to change the way people lived. I had no intention of having children or duplicating my parents' lives.

But I couldn't help myself with John, couldn't help loving him. He had ideas about the world, seemed to understand it and feel just as I did. "I don't want an everyday kind of life," he told me when we met. He didn't have to say it. I could see that.

He took me away from everything I knew, and I went eagerly. We lived in Africa and Asia. He worked in clinics. I taught English, learned Hindi and Japanese. We climbed mountains and lived in huts. John wanted to have children, and he convinced me. We would create our own empire apart from the world. Yet even with children, I was sure we would never settle down.

There was nothing wrong with my parents' lives. My mother cooked, played bridge, and took care of the house, my father, my two brothers, and me. My father did accounting work six days a week. But I couldn't find anything right with their lives, either.

I wrapped my arms around Melissa as if she were a baby and rocked her on my lap. She liked that and quieted. A fat young woman paced in the waiting area, holding an infant over her shoulder as if the child were a cat. A boy in a wheelchair sat next to a man who must be his father, I thought. The boy's hands were like claws. Billy and Laura edged toward me. I kissed them and told them not to stare.

I used to wonder why my mother wasted her life on children, why she didn't do something more with herself, try to make a difference in the world. She always said patience was the key, not to try to solve the problems of the world all at once.

I used to imagine in Africa that if anything happened to John I couldn't exist. I would just die. But holding Melissa in my arms now, I understood that wasn't quite right anymore. I could go on without him. Melissa had taken some of John's place. I would die a hundred times for her, a million. I would give up everything. She seemed part of me in another way—as if she were my eyes, my limbs, my heart.

In the examining room, the doctor, who was a young resident with thick dark hair and gold wire-rimmed glasses, checked Melissa's stomach. She sat on my lap. His nametag read Dr. Lawson. I explained what had happened and told him that my husband was a doctor, as if to ensure that Dr. Lawson would do everything possible for Melissa, so nothing could go wrong.

Dr. Lawson said he didn't know my husband, but he needed to clean the wound and make certain there was no internal bleeding or damage. "The wound is deep," he said. "That pencil was like a weapon. We'll give Myra something for pain."

"Melissa," I said.

He nodded, then spoke to the nurse and told me they needed to get started. "She's lost blood," he said. "A piece of pencil might have broken off inside her. We'll try to get it out." He shook his head. "But these things happen. No matter how careful you are, no one leads a charmed life."

I told Billy and Laura to go to the waiting area, but they didn't want to leave me. They sat in the room with us and looked at picture books they found on the counter. When I laid Melissa on the examining table, she cried and kicked. I knew she was scared, and I tried to calm her.

"Hold her still," the doctor said. "If she wiggles too much, we'll have to tie her down."

Dr. Lawson and the nurse wore white plastic gloves. They gave Melissa a shot for pain, washed the wound, and then poked into it with a long needle, searching for pieces of the pencil. Melissa flailed her arms and screamed wildly.

"She's a tiger," Dr. Lawson said.

I tried to hold Melissa down on the table. Her eyes were half-closed, her mouth open. I could see her tonsils. She was wailing with all the energy she had. I suddenly felt as if I were pressing against a great weight, almost too much for me. The room felt stifling. Its sharp medicinal odor stung my throat. Sweat dripped down my face. Moisture bubbled on the foreheads of the doctor and nurse. Melissa's face was drenched with sweat.

"Here's a big one." The doctor held the pencil point. "Don't want to sew up that junk."

From the corner of my eye, I saw Billy and Laura huddle together on the floor and put their hands over their ears. As I grasped Melissa's shoulders, I turned to them and told them to leave the room until the doctor finished.

"We don't want to be alone," Laura grumbled. "Just make Melissa be quiet. Make her normal."

"Where's Daddy?" Billy whined. "Why does he have to be at work?"

"I want him," Laura said.

"Hush," I said. I wished I had insisted they go to the waiting room before. Now I couldn't let go of Melissa.

She cried and kicked, and as I pressed my hands against her I thought about John again. He should be here with us. He needed to be here to help soothe the children, comfort Melissa. He always said he'd provide for us and protect us. That was the bargain; we'd each do our part. He told me when we married, when we had children, and again this last weekend.

They sewed Melissa's belly with seventeen stitches. Seventeen slow, precise black stitches. She screamed the entire time.

Afterward, Dr. Lawson said to me, "You were lucky. If the pencil had gone straight into her stomach, instead of at an angle, it would have been worse." He gave me instructions for how to care for the wound, and he brought orange Popsicles for the children. "You guys were real troopers," he told them. "And that Myra has quite a pair of lungs."

Melissa sat on my lap, like a tired little animal. She rested her hands on her stomach and spoke in her quiet, musical voice—it sounded hoarse now. "Am I fixed, Mommy? Did that man fix me?"

"Yes," I said and hugged her. "Yes. As good as new."

Before we left the hospital, I telephoned John again at the lab, Chang Fu's, the airport, and home. Still no answer. I wanted to tell John what had happened. I didn't know how I could forgive him for not being with us. It was his place. He was my husband and partner. The father of our children. It wasn't a question of responsibility or working or intention. It was a question of place. Of where he belonged.

It had always been John's place to be with us, I thought as I drove the children home, though he was with us less and less. I was alone with the children too much. His work had taken on a life of its own. Pulling him away. Not just tonight. Every night, it seemed. He'd let this happen. And I'd allowed it. Nothing balanced between us anymore. This was what our marriage had become. I suddenly realized I had been giving everything, and I was lonely. But I'd never let myself notice before.

I could imagine my mother saying how lucky we were, to count our blessings. I would tell her what happened, and she would probably say, "Thank God, Eleanora; it could have been an eye or mouth. It doesn't matter if John was there or not. Melissa could have died." She would tell me she'd pray for us.

Melissa didn't talk or cry on the way home, but Laura whimpered. In the hospital she had asked me for a prize, for something special, for all the waiting. I told her then she should always remember that she was a very special and helpful little girl.

In the car, she cried again. Billy didn't tease her. He said, "Hey, c'mon. Don't feel bad."

Laura whimpered anyway. "I waited all that time, in that ugly hospital, all that time while Melissa cried. I was so patient. Just like you told me. Did you see how good I was, Mommy? And what do I get? What do I get that's special? Not one thing. Nothing at all."

The house was just as we left it, the kitchen and living room lights still shining, the blue china teacup on the table, the pencil resting on the bloodstained bedroom rug. I told the children they couldn't wait up for Daddy. We would explain to him what had happened in the morning.

Melissa fell asleep at once. Billy and Laura stayed up longer. "I was scared," Laura whispered. "I tried hard to wait."

"I know. You were so good and patient." I sat with her, then Billy, until they were asleep. Then I changed into a clean shirt and jeans, sat at the kitchen table, and shut my eyes.

Forty-five minutes later, John opened the front door. He looked tired. He immediately told me that he had wandered around the airport, gone to the lab, then to Chang Fu's, but no one was there. So he had returned to the airport where he finally found the Chinese doctor asleep in a small airline office. They bumped into Chang Fu then; he'd come looking for the man, too. The three of them went for a bite to eat—the doctor was hungry—then John and Chang Fu took him to the hotel. "What a way to spend a night." John gazed at me carefully. "How was yours? You look worn out. Is everything okay?"

"No," I said, and told him about Melissa.

He ran upstairs to see her. She lay sleeping at the edge of her bed, clutching her pillow as if it were a person. I watched from the doorway as he kissed her forehead and then looked at the stitches.

"Poor kid," he whispered as he and I went downstairs. "She'll feel better soon."

"That's easy to say now." We walked to the living room, and though I tried to stay calm, my words tumbled out. "The stitches are in. Everything is over. But you should have been with us like we planned. Nothing else is as important."

He frowned. "Calm down, Ellie. I'm exhausted, too. Do you think I like wandering around all night? I do what I have to."

"You do what you *want*. I never really saw it before. Chang Fu could have found the Chinese doctor. You made a choice. You always make that choice. We were going to spend today as a family."

"There's no way I could have known what would happen tonight." John stood beside me. "The bottom line is: Everything is okay." He put his arm around me. "Melissa will be fine. The rest doesn't matter."

"Nothing is okay." I stepped away from him. "And we're the rest. The children and me. Not just today. We're what's left after work, John."

"Goddamnit. I work to earn a living. I can't take care of everything."

"Just do your part. Can't you see what's happened to us?"

He walked away, but then he hesitated and came back. "Look. I know it wasn't easy tonight." His arms hung tensely at his sides. "We're just two people. We're like everyone else. Things happen. Come here, Ellie." He opened his arms, waiting for me.

I wanted to push him away. I wanted to take his smile, his body, his words, his promises, our whole life together, and smash it. I wanted John to stop me, to tell me he would be there for us. That accidents like Melissa's would never happen again. He wouldn't allow it. But I knew he wouldn't say that. He couldn't. And if he had, he'd have been lying. The truth was: We were as ordinary as everyone else.

I could see John was trying and that he couldn't help himself. He couldn't help me. He might never understand or change. No matter how I would try to explain or how long or patiently I would wait.

I turned to leave the room.

"Ellie." He followed me. "I love you. I love the children. That's what matters." He took my hand in his. "Isn't that enough?"

"It hasn't been for a long time, but I didn't see it."

"Just let it go," he said, his voice strained. "You're tired. I am. We'll work it out."

"We have to, but I don't know if we can." I stopped, aware of how tired I was. Maybe I'd been unrealistic about marriage, I realized, naïve. Moisture gathered in my eyes, and he hugged me. I knew he thought I was crying for Melissa, for how hard it had been tonight. For Billy and Laura, too. For how scared they had felt. And I was. But the tears were really for the broken promises, for all that John and I had lost.

"Mommy." Melissa's voice floated from upstairs. "Where are you?"

"I'm right here," I called to her. "I'm coming."

I pulled from John's arms and hurried up the stairs.

Taking Leave

They have been waiting with excitement for this moment, their arrival at Meg's dormitory room at college. She is a freshman, the first child Sandra and Mark have sent off, their only child, though they tried desperately for others. We have only one child, Sandra likes to say, and she's our masterpiece.

"I wish they didn't stretch out this leave-taking," Mark says.

They are walking in the sunshine of a cool morning toward the red brick dormitory building on this verdant New England campus.

"Deposit your kid, help her unpack, go to orientation sessions, lunch, good-bye cocktails," Mark goes on. "It makes it harder for everyone. When I went to college, my mother put me on a bus with a suitcase and I was off and running."

"The generation gap," Sandra says.

Mark shrugs. "Getting bigger every day."

She smiles. She has heard this story many times, his going to college on his own, working his way through. Like a badge of honor for him. Mark still works hard, too hard, Sandra thinks, as if he's not finished proving something to himself. His father abandoned the family when Mark was three.

"Colleges are businesses, dear," Sandra says. "They want to please their paying customers now. The parents. Times have changed."

Mark frowns, and she can see he's convinced that the times in which he grew up were the best and most sane.

"Part of me is almost happy she's leaving home," Sandra says as their daughter runs ahead, out of earshot. *Part of me,* she thinks. *As if you could chop yourself into pieces and categorize each segment.* "Relieved." She feels a stab of guilt as she says this, just as she's felt guilty when she's lusted after a man other than her husband, as if being a member of a family demanded unwavering loyalty in both one's actions *and* heart. She tries not to dwell on these feelings for long, though. She is a fitness instructor, runs a small fitness business, and prides herself on being rational, in shape, ready mentally and physically for whatever comes. With her shining brown hair pulled back into a luxuriant ponytail when she teaches her classes, and her flexible, slim body, Sandra sometimes feels younger than forty-eight. In fact, not much older than Meg.

"It's time for Meg to be on her own," she continues, to reassure Mark. "I won't miss the worry, the mess, the chaos."

"The demands," he says. He's always in a hurry and walks quickly now, nervously, and fingers the cell phone tucked in his pocket, as if he's expecting an important business call. "The abuse. All these kids feel so goddamned entitled. The way Meg talks recently, you'd think she could run my real estate office better than I can. Run the world."

Sandra laughs and slips her arm through his. It's true; Meg can be condescending and infuriatingly dismissive. Sandra feels sympathy for her daughter, though, and supposes she, herself, was much the same as a teenager. Her own mother was horrified when Sandra wore T-shirts without a bra, grew her hair to the middle of her back, talked openly about sex and orgasms, and once demonstrated to her mother how to roll a joint.

And Meg. Sandra watches as her daughter hurries ahead. Five silver earrings in each of Meg's ears, a delicate tattoo of a red flower on her right ankle. She wears a bra, but beneath a black tank top so tight you can see her nipples. The white bra straps gleam against her skin. It's the fashion, Meg has argued when Sandra protested. Meg's boyfriend last year, Josef, sported dyed blond hair, a tongue piercing and an unwieldy tattoo of a blue web that encased his left arm; the dark tendrils seemed to choke his skin. Sandra used to wonder idly how he ate citrus with any comfort with that shiny tongue ornament, and the sour taste of worry lingered in her mouth all those months because she hoped he wouldn't influence Meg.

Meg brought back tales of serial oral sex at high school parties even in ninth and tenth grades, though she swore she wasn't one of the daring ones. She had come home drunk on occasion. Once, when Mark saw her, he had been livid. "No one likes a goddamned drunk," he had shouted at her, and imposed a harsh sentence. Groundings seemed to put a stop to the drinking, but Sandra didn't know for sure, didn't know what went on when Meg wasn't home. Mark was home less and less, too, working. Sandra arranged her fitness teaching schedule as she had done since Meg was born, so she could be at home when her daughter was.

When Meg finally ended her relationship with Josef, she confided to her mother that he had an abuse problem.

"Abuse of what?" Sandra asked.

"Chemical dependency," Meg pronounced, all she would tell, and Sandra wondered which chemicals they were. Marijuana, alcohol, cocaine, speed, ecstasy, heroin, or drugs she didn't even have an inkling existed? *That* was the generation gap. How much did you really know about your own child, after all, about her world, what went on inside her? For that matter, how much did you know about yourself?

Sandra and Mark wait as Meg struggles to turn the key in the rusty lock. Room 6410, on the first floor of one of the older residential buildings on campus. The corridor is dimly lit and narrow, and just one bathroom services the six dorm rooms surrounding it. When the wooden door to Meg's room finally swings open, squeaking, Sandra looks in, aghast. The room is a cell, she thinks, a cell without bars, two beds next to each other, with barely two feet between, dirty, gray walls and a hard, faded yellow linoleum floor. A room without light or life. A musty odor rises in the air. There are no personal possessions here, no sign of a roommate's arrival.

Sandra's mouth feels dry and uncomfortable as she walks in. This is where they will leave Meg, their masterpiece, whom they struggled to conceive, regulating monthly cycles with charts and thermometers for years, the beautiful baby born on a Tuesday morning. Eighteen years, three months and two days ago. It is one of the few mornings of all of the mornings of Sandra's life that is imprinted vividly in her mind. 9:26 a.m. An unadorned room like this. At 9:15 the doctor announced, "I always sit down when I deliver." While Sandra lay on a birthing table on her back, half-naked, legs spread open wide like a hooker's, waiting for the baby to emerge, the doctor stood in his white coat like a gentleman aristocrat. A nurse ceremoniously brought a chair. Then Sandra pushed with all her strength; the pain and pressure burst inside her as if her body were splitting apart. She wondered for an instant if death felt like this. She remembered nothing else then except the baby's high, wild cries. Mark beside her. Her partner, her love. The beautiful baby with big brown eyes, who had burst from her, perfect. The girl they waited for. "Eyes with soul," Mark said. "Like your eyes," Sandra whispered.

Sandra pushes away the memory and surveys the room, considers how to rearrange the furniture. Do they wait for the roommate before deciding which bed to choose, before unpacking? What is the protocol? She flings open the curtains. Sunlight floods the room, making the space almost sparkle, possibly a place Meg could call home.

"Look," Meg says eagerly, and tugs on one of her small silver hoop earrings. She presses her face against the window and peers outside. Her black tank top strap falls to her shoulder, and her jeans accentuate her muscular firmness. She is taller than her mother, and there is a casual air of sexuality about her, though her face is wholesome, rosy, unblemished skin, the face still of a girl. "A view with trees and green. Grass." She faces her parents. "I'll bet I can see stars every night. It's beautiful. Do you like it?" she asks her mother.

"Oh, yes," Sandra lies. "Once you unpack. It's lovely." She knows Meg loves the country and has always wanted to live in the East. There are no stars at night in the city, Meg has complained of Chicago, where they live.

"Lovely." Meg narrows her eyes and jerks back her head so her thick brown hair spreads onto her shoulders. "That word is code, Mom. For boring. Ugly," she says. "You don't fucking like it at all."

"But I do." She flinches at the word *fucking*, hates to hear it from her daughter's mouth.

Meg shrugs. "Doesn't matter if you do or don't. I'll be living here. This is my home." She pushes one desk against a wall, enlisting her father to rearrange the furniture until the room feels more spacious.

"It's a great room, baby," Mark says, always an optimist. "Everything you could want, I hope you'll find."

Meg smiles and looks at him with adoring eyes, clearly pleased he's here, and he returns her affection in his gaze.

Then the three of them make two trips to the car, parked a block from the dorm, and haul things to the room: a heavy black metal trunk and suitcases, boxes, CD player, computer, sleeping bag, sheets, pillows, blankets, even a ragged brown teddy bear from long ago. They pile Meg's possessions near one of the beds, as if this is an upscale refugee camp.

"Do you think you could…" Meg lifts her hair from her shoulders, pushes it onto her back. "Can you make up my bed?" she asks softly, almost meekly. "It would be a big help, Mom. One less thing to do, you know."

"Of course," Sandra says quickly, surprised. "My pleasure to do that."

Mark shifts from one foot to the other. Sandra imagines he must think making the bed for Meg is foolish, but he is quiet. His mother sent him to college on a bus, after all. Meg's request pleases Sandra all the same; she wants to feel wanted, she realizes, still useful, still part of her daughter's world.

By lunchtime, the roommate hasn't appeared, which makes Sandra anxious, as she's eager to meet her and hopes this girl will be kind and a good influence. No female Josef. No drugs. No promiscuity. Mentally stable. Meg has tried to get in touch with her these last weeks. Jessica Hamilton. From rural Vermont. But the girl never phoned back or sent an email. It is an oddly intimate relationship, and temporary, Sandra thinks, roommates. Living with someone other than one's family for the first time. She has done this and Mark has, too, so long ago she can hardly remember the feelings of newness, excitement. Promise. Of trying to mesh one set of habits with another person's routine. Perhaps almost like a marriage, but with greater formality, and without the urgent motivation of sexual chemistry.

Meg has hung up clothing in the closet, filled the drawers of one dresser and unpacked books. Sandra has placed folded towels on top of one of the mattresses, but she hasn't spread the sheets on the bed yet. "First come, first served doesn't seem right," Meg says. "I'd like to give my roommate a choice, too." She repeats the girl's name as if trying on a piece of clothing to see if it will comfortably fit.

Sandra has repeated the name in her own mind, as if peeling petals from a daisy. Will the girl be a good influence? Yes she will be, no she won't; Sandra is gambling with Meg's future. If the roommate meets Sandra's approval, she will be confident that Meg will thrive here. She can safely let her daughter go then.

The three of them leave the dormitory, and outside, Sandra watches the students and parents who mill about the rural Massachusetts campus in front of its stately ivy-covered buildings. Yesterday, driving from Chicago, she looked with distrust from the car window at the gentle hills that surround the campus, and worried this environment might swallow Meg. Though Sandra loves to bicycle and hike, she has never felt comfortable in the country. She's a city girl and a Midwesterner. She's never trusted nature enough or other people perhaps, and feels like a stranger in the East. But Meg has longed to leave Chicago far behind, eager to shed her old life, Sandra realizes, to shed her parents.

A mix of people mingle, Asians, blacks, Hispanics among them, but some in the crowd seem brushed by the stuffy air of privilege. A few parents appear almost interchangeable with their children, and wear brightly colored shirts and blue jeans, trying to reclaim their own youth. Others look dowdy and middle-aged in khakis or skirts that fail to mask their bodies' fleshy spread. Sandra wonders if she and Mark look dowdy, too.

The college has arranged a full schedule, and Meg hurries off to lunch orientation for students. Mark wants to attend a session on academics, but Sandra prefers to go to another entitled "Taking Leave."

The moderator, a psychologist, rambles on in a soothing baritone about the need to let go of one's child. When it's time for questions, a woman at Sandra's table raises a hand. She has short gray hair, stylishly cut, almost a man's haircut, wears amber beads over a black tunic, with purple half-glasses balanced on her long nose.

The woman removes the reading spectacles with a flourish. "Do you mind if I ask a personal sort of question?"

"If it's pertinent to everyone here," the moderator says, "to other parents." He smiles. "Please, go ahead."

"Oh, it is pertinent. My question is this: How often should I call my son? After I leave him here?" the woman asks loudly. "He's very ascetic. He doesn't want a phone in his dorm room, or a computer. He's on a spiritual quest. He's not happy and I worry about him *constantly*."

The psychologist nods kindly and leans back in his chair. "That's an excellent question. Remember, it's a biological necessity to let go of one's young. For all species. Telephone calls or not."

The woman presses a hand against her heart. "But *how* can I call him if he won't put a damn phone in his room? He refuses to use a cell phone. He's got a gay mother and two biracial siblings, he's traveled everywhere and he wants nothing to do with people. Last week he stayed in bed for two days. What should I do?" Her voice vibrates with an anxious plaintive tone.

Sandra can feel this woman's tight, choking grasp on the boy. A growing dread percolates in her own chest as she contemplates leaving Meg, really leaving her. She would like to tell Mark this, wishes he were here with her at this session, but she's embarrassed by the emotion that pushes inside her.

As the psychologist assures the woman that she needs to give her son independence, and perhaps they should talk after the session, Sandra suddenly imagines danger lurking on this pristine campus. Then she senses danger back home, too. The quiet of the house with Meg gone. Mark's footsteps late after work. The silence between the two of them, thick and belligerent like hot, humid air. What they mostly talk about now is Meg. Sandra thinks of the empty rooms at friends' houses, friends with children grown and gone, rooms preserved with bulletin boards, stuffed animals and trophies, shrines of regret to the passing of youth.

After lunch, Sandra and Mark prepare to begin their drive back to the Midwest. The roommate has not yet appeared, so Meg chooses the bed farthest from the window. Together, Sandra and Meg slip on the rainbow-colored striped sheets, arrange the blankets, plump the pillows. Then Sandra crowns the bed with Meg's old one-eyed teddy bear.

Meg brushes a hand against the stuffed bear, then turns to Sandra and hugs her. Sandra clasps her arms around her daughter.

"Thanks, Mom," Meg whispers.

"Oh, honey. Daddy and I will always help."

Meg nods, then steps back and wonders aloud if the roommate has changed her mind and isn't coming after all. Her voice is a little shaky. Meg is worried, Sandra thinks, about being lonely, uneasy to stay here by herself.

"Nothing you can do about it," Mark says. He puts his arm around her. "You'll be happy at this school, I hope. Be happy and have luck, no matter what."

Then they leave to stroll around campus one more time, Sandra's sentimental request, though Mark eyes her with impatience and says, "Let's get on with it, honey. No use in prolonging the good-byes." But he joins them, and Meg walks between her parents, her arms linked in each of theirs. When they stop at the dormitory room again to deposit her for good, the space is crammed with more suitcases, boxes, blankets, pillows, and five people.

The young woman from Vermont, Jessica Hamilton, is standing next to a large bass fiddle. She's pretty in her jeans and blue T-shirt with the inscription "Keep Your Friends Close and Your Enemies Closer." No wild hair coloring or tattoos or face and mouth piercings. She has a wholesome look with her curly brown hair and freckles.

She and Meg exchange tentative greetings in the crowded room, and the girl's mother reaches to shake Sandra's hand. "How nice to meet you," Mrs. Hamilton says.

"Yes." Sandra smiles.

The woman's grip is strong and certain. She is wearing an oversize Hawaiian shirt with bright yellow flowers on it, and a knee-length knobby blue wool skirt. She has straight white hair and wears no makeup, as if she couldn't be bothered trying to camouflage her age. She looks *old,* like an odd, clumsy creature, Sandra thinks, ashamed of the thought.

Mr. Hamilton shakes Mark's hand. The man has white hair as well, a neatly trimmed beard, and looks like a newly shaven, slender Santa Claus, with a mild expression as if he might be bewildered by his daughter's growing up.

"We call her Munchkin," Mrs. Hamilton says to Sandra in a flat New England accent. She smiles at her daughter. "What will we do without our Munchkin?"

Jessica grins, an expression of affectionate patience.

"These are Jessie's sisters," the woman says. One looks in her thirties, with long curly blond hair and a willowy, muscular body, as if she has walked off the set of *Sex and the City*. She wears a short shirt, which exposes her flat, golden midriff and a gleaming belly button ring.

The second sister appears younger, but with the same long, curly blond hair and thin, solid body.

"I went to school here for two years," the oldest sister says, "then went back home to Vermont. But it's a wonderful place. You'll love it," she says heartily to Meg. "Jessica will love it. She plays the bongo drums."

"Munchkin does," Mrs. Hamilton explains with pride. "The bass, too."

"That's nice," Meg says. She eyes the set of slender wooden bongo drums amidst piles of boxes and suitcases.

Sandra fixes her eyes on the drums, too. *Noise*. The girl might be full of noise. That was for Meg and Jessica to work out.

"Last child for us going off," Mr. Hamilton says.

"Meg is our only child," Mark replies.

"Our masterpiece," Sandra laughs.

"Ah, so you're in the same boat as we are," the man says. "But I tell Mary, it's not the empty nest, but the love nest now." He winks at Sandra and chuckles, and she can't help but imagine him and Mrs. Hamilton in bed. Perhaps he comes home early from work, has a voracious appetite for sex. Perhaps Mrs. Hamilton shares that, despite her dour appearance.

"Oh, yes, a love nest," echoes Mrs. Hamilton, interrupting Sandra's thoughts.

There is an awkward silence. Then the frantic, mechanized tones of the *William Tell Overture* explode in the room. Mark grabs his phone from his pocket.

"Yes," he says after he's listened. "I can. Hold on a second." He points to the door. "Business. That real estate deal. Excuse me." He nods at Sandra and disappears into the hall.

"Pardon us, too. We've got to move the car. Illegally parked," Mr. Hamilton says. He winks at Sandra again, then he and his two older daughters sweep out of the room.

Meg points to the bed with the rainbow-colored sheets. "If you'd prefer this one," she says to Jessica, "please, take it. I don't mind switching."

"The other is fine."

Meg looks at her watch. "There's a meeting for students. Want to go?"

"Sure. Let's."

"We can come back in a bit, Mom. To say good-bye," Meg says.

"We'll be happy to walk you there," Mrs. Hamilton says.

"Oh, yes," Sandra agrees.

Meg smiles at her mother. Then she and Jessica walk a few paces ahead of the women, outside, and hurry down the stone dormitory steps, the girls' bodies moving in tandem.

Mrs. Hamilton glances at the girls. Then she looks at Sandra. "Do you think she'll be lonely?" The woman walks slowly, with a slight limp. "Meg, I mean."

The question takes Sandra by surprise. Her gaze follows the girls, and she slows her pace until she is next to the woman.

"Lonely. I don't know." *But I will be,* Sandra thinks. "I hope not."

"Oh, I hope Jessie won't be either. But I most certainly will." The woman places one foot carefully on the next step down and grasps the railing. "My children. They've been the center of my life."

"I suppose of mine, too," Sandra says, realizing this is true.

"They come into the world and you're not sure you really want them," Mrs. Hamilton goes on. "Jessie is our fourth child. Unplanned. We're Catholic. There are *no* mistakes for us. For better or worse. And they can be so much trouble. Then they leave you. And sometimes you just want to hang on."

"You do." Sandra thinks of the woman from the lunch session, with the troubled son. Perhaps she herself is more like that grasping woman than she imagined. "We wanted to have Meg so badly."

Mrs. Hamilton descends another step and stops. "And you did. You had her. Raised her. But as far as I'm concerned, we all lead a pretend life anyway."

"Pretend?"

"Oh, yes. Me, for example. I have my work on the farm, my organizations, volunteer at the hospital. I play cards. Poker. But we never talk about anything of substance at those places. That has meat. Fat." She pinches the flabby skin on her arm and continues in a high, mocking, girlish voice. "How is *this* one or *that* one? The cows? The crops? The husband? The children? Except for a few good friends, never asking about what's really on your mind. In your heart."

Sandra is silent, no longer on this college campus; she is immersed in her thoughts, at a bridge game, a social event for Mark's real estate business, teaching a fitness class, listening to the idle chatter she often hears. Mrs. Hamilton is right. In fact, Sandra realizes that sometimes she doesn't feel married. Her whole life seems pretend. Mark is away so often for business. She misses him but almost never tells him this. They rarely talk of things of substance anymore. She is on her own so much. Meg has been their anchor. Sandra hates this change, to give up being a mother in such an intimate way. She has seen couples drift apart when children leave. She's afraid, and at this moment certain, that this is the course she and Mark have been traveling on. Drifting. She can feel it. No love nest.

"I'm so happy they've found each other, Meg and Jessica," Mrs. Hamilton says, breaking into Sandra's thoughts.

"Yes. I hope they'll become friends."

"Real friends are the key to life," the woman says. "Kept me going, good times and bad." She touches Sandra's arm, and Sandra is surprised by the woman's soft, comforting grasp.

As they approach the last steps of the building, Sandra continues on, eager to join the throng of students collecting at the quadrangle. Mrs. Hamilton stops again and leans against the railing. Sandra gazes back at the woman, then retraces her steps. The two watch as students gather in the afternoon sunshine, young, strong figures converging on the appointed spot, fifty, seventy, hundreds of students now, Jessica and Meg somewhere among them, indistinguishable. The group surges into a triangular configuration as the students make their way to the grassy center, like flocks of brightly colored swallows about to take flight.

Moisture fills Sandra's eyes and she feels sentimental. A heavy, thumping sensation sweeps through her. Unexpected grief.

"My older girls," the woman murmurs. "They're not *mine* anymore." She points to the students on the quadrangle, then links her arm in Sandra's, holding her to the spot. "I'm theirs now." She laughs. "We've become friends. The time will come for you and your daughter. You'll see."

"I'd like that," Sandra says, heartened by the thought.

"But you need patience. To be lucky. You need to wait."

Sandra nods. She eyes the students with longing, then leans toward the woman, as if they are sharing a great confidence.

"I know how you must feel," Mrs. Hamilton says. "Your only child. Your masterpiece, you said. But she's not yours anymore, either. Never was."

"I guess she never really *belonged* to us." Sandra breathes in the crisp autumn air, suddenly chilled. "Maybe it was pretend that we raised her."

"Who can say? In a sense, children raise themselves, don't they?"

"Maybe Meg will live a pretend life too," Sandra says. She tries to find Meg in the crowd below. "And your daughter." If only she could warn Meg, prepare her, prevent it.

"We're all pretending. We live our lives and give them the meaning we want," the woman says. "Sometimes, in our minds, we make them better than they are, sometimes worse. Pretending about our lives suits us, maybe more than our lives do."

Sandra drops her arm from Mrs. Hamilton's and steps toward

the crowd of students again, as if decreasing the distance between herself and Meg might actually bring them closer.

"But you can't hold on. No matter how much a child fills your life. Or how much you love her," Mrs. Hamilton says and stands next to Sandra.

She feels the oddly intimate touch of the woman's fingers on her shoulder.

"Don't even try," Mrs. Hamilton says.

Intense feelings ricochet inside Sandra as she catches a glimpse of Meg. "Perhaps you're right," Sandra says to Mrs. Hamilton, and she feels a burst of optimism. "Parts of our lives are pretend. But if we're lucky, parts of our lives are authentic, too."

The crowd of students has parted, and Meg lingers in the quadrangle below, young and lovely. She turns toward Sandra, stands on tiptoes, and gives a jaunty wave.

Terminal

My mother-in-law, Sophe, watches me from the doorway of our red brick apartment building. I look back at her, and she seems to shrink as I walk away. Her gray hair curls into a hopeful flip; her red lipstick shines lustrous in the morning light. But her face is pale, a tinge of yellow on her cheeks. She's ill. Terminal.

Her diagnosis doesn't matter. They all lead to the same end.

My husband stands next to her, his feet bare like a Buddhist guru's. He's a cell biologist, precise, tall and thin, with short gray hair. When will you be back, Fran? Ed calls to me.

Soon, I say. Then I sprint away, eager to leave them both, my black Pumas squeaking against the hard New York City pavement.

I do not say when.

Sophe lives with us now in the apartment. Our three sons are in college. Our oldest had a hearing problem when he was a boy. I still worry about him. But Sophe has become my new worry. She endures chemotherapy once a week. A pill a day, a treatment a week. Her "special treatments," she calls them, as if she were going to a spa.

Last week, the apartment was crowded with old people since my parents visited us, too. They live in Florida. I took time off from my job at a small publishing company where I edit books; some I'm not so proud of. Self-help. *Women Who Love Men Who Murder. How to Expunge the Inner Alcoholic. Five Mathematical Equations That Will Save Your Life.*

My mother was heavy, her legs puffy and swollen. More feeble than I expected. I hadn't seen her for a year. She was twisted with age. When she walked up or down the stairs in our building, she grasped the railings fiercely, like a toddler. My father slept all day in the gray autumn light that trickled through our living room window, his wide body sinking into the brown sofa, a fisherman's cap perched on his head. They weren't the people they used to be, vigorous, hopeful, confident life would turn out as they planned.

No one in this apartment is the same I realized last week. Not Ed or me either.

Ed spent their visit at work or in his study at home, plotting intricate mathematical equations. He works at a pharmaceutical company and studies diseases of the heart. A + C divided by the square root of X - Y + Z, and other symbols I didn't understand. Tangential equations, confidence intervals, distance formulas, scientific principles, and so on. Numbers and letters crowded like refugees across his papers. Head bent toward the shiny mahogany desk. He studied the pages even when my mother or Sophe walked into the room.

For the past eight months, I've been a witness to Sophe's deterioration. I help her with meals. I've worked from home as much as I could. We have hired someone to bathe her. One day her face glows with color; the next, her skin is pasty, her hands tremble. The cancer is advancing. Pain in her shoulder. Pain in her legs. Her voice doesn't fool me. Voices can play tricks. When my parents telephone from Florida, I imagine they are young and strong, with a billowing future.

A hurricane damaged their apartment last month. Curtains wet. All the bridges in the area were closed. Floors in the apartment buckled. And the mold. Now that the destruction is over, my mother said, the fear of mold is terrible.

Sophe owns an apartment in Florida, too. When she is not talking about her disease or the pain, she talks about her apartment. What will happen with the mold? The decay? I won't be able to live there. This is the darkest period of my life. If I wasn't sick, I could live on my own. This is how life will be now.

I wish I could make her healthy. There is nothing I can say that will make life better for her.

There is nothing I can say to myself, either. I can't live in our small apartment with Ed and his mother. Everything has deteriorated since she moved in.

All day, Sophe paces in her pink robe and green slippers.

I have never been comfortable leaving people or places. How do you say good-bye to someone you love who is about to die? How do you say: This relationship is terminal. Do you shut your eyes and reach for what has meaning to you, a grab-bag? You take this; I'll take that; let's divide these in two. Like King Solomon did. And the dog? The children? The apartment? The memories? I don't have the patience. So I walk up Fifth Avenue now. My cell phone, money I withdrew from the bank, and my credit card burrow in my fleece jacket pocket. Perhaps I will write a letter: Dear Ed, Good luck with your mathematical equations. Good luck with your mother. She has always been good to me. I hope I have been good to her. I can't say when I'll be back, or if I will.

Is it acceptable to be mean at the end?

Anger helps you separate, my friend Susannah told me. She lives off the coast of Vancouver on a boat with her third husband. She loves the sea. It's always changing, she said. The tide, the force of the waves, the gradations of color. The sea is so fluid.

Like memory, I said.

Like life, she said.

Nothing stays constant. My brother lives in another state. He and I used to play together every day in the neat front yard of our house in Detroit. Now we rarely see each other. I can barely remember what he looks like. Ed works on equations day and night. He doesn't have time to talk anymore. We used to talk for hours. Make love almost every day. Go for long walks late at night. The last few years, even before his mother moved in with us, that changed.

Now it is difficult to relax or concentrate in the apartment. I used to read three books a week. Poetry and novels. But Ed is busy with his equations. Sophe paces in the rooms. She needs a meal or an errand run. I want to help, but I'm a stranger here. Sophe's boyfriend, Jonas, stayed with us last week, too. He's eighty-five, four years older than she is. He lives in Florida. My dashing older man, she calls him.

Will it be cold today? he asked one morning.

Let's check the newspaper, I said. We did.

Five minutes later, he said, Will it be cold today?

We looked in the newspaper, I said. Nothing has changed.

We did?

Afternoons, Jonas watched football or Court TV in our living room. Fuck, he yelled one day. At first I was frightened, worried he was sick. Fuck. Fuck. *Fuck. Fuck that game.* He pounded his hand on the sofa's armrest.

Fine wisps of talcum powder trailed everywhere in the rooms, where he showered, where he stepped. He tracked the talc as if shedding a layer of skin. Walking up Fifth Avenue, I wipe the fine white dust from my black pants and feel clean for the first time in weeks.

I read a story years ago by a famous writer about a woman who left home and kept walking. I don't remember the woman's destination or what happened next. But I remembered the idea of it. To walk. Walk away. I do this now. Fuck, I think. Fuck it all. I wander up Fifth Avenue, beneath the shadow of tall buildings, past the Korean grocer and bunches of yellow carnations gathered like a garden, with their promise of spring. I don't know where I'll go. Maybe I'll walk through Manhattan, this long island, over a bridge and disappear into the state. I don't need much money, I think. I don't even need love. I have my two strong legs, with the crick in my left knee like a lever that needs oiling. I like my body. My arms swing at my sides as if each is a person, the right moving faster than the left. My belly has softened with age. My breasts are like overripe pears. I like the way my breath roars in and out of my chest, like a gathering storm, and how my heart beats, a percussion instrument, as if I am the last Mohican abandoning the reservation.

I met Ed in Amsterdam twenty-six years ago, at a hooker hotel. I didn't know what kind of hotel it was. Susannah and I were traveling after graduating from college. She planned to return home before I did. I wanted to test myself, to see if I could travel alone. The hotel rented rooms by the hour, the day, the week. How perfect, I thought. Stay as long as you like. No strings. A man smoked cigarettes in the garden, though a sign read "No Smoking Here." One day, I banged on his door to complain. Ed invited me in. That was the end of the story. Or the beginning.

He had thick red hair then and a dazzling smile with perfectly spaced white teeth. He was American, bumming around Europe. Staying in Amsterdam for a while. Happy to have found a clean, cheap hotel. Divorced. It had been a short, unimportant marriage, a mistake to marry so young, he said. He had just finished his PhD. For me, it was love at first sight, as silly as that sounds. I told Susannah before she went home: Here is a man I could marry. He was smart, tender, a little rebellious, didn't like to follow rules. We were opposites; we each made up what the other lacked. He dispelled the beliefs I had about myself. That I was unadventurous. That I preferred to live in books rather than with people. That I was not pretty enough for a man to love.

Ed is an inventor, too, not just a cell biologist. He often stays up late creating inventions with metals and bolts. He hates to be interrupted. He has no patience for idle chatter. I have never been able to figure out what he is constructing, but I admire his creativity. Mechanisms. If one invention doesn't work, he tosses it in the trash and goes on to the next.

Walking up Fifth Avenue, I realize I still don't know who he truly is.

Last week, Ed's ex-wife stopped to visit, too. That's what life is like in New York City—people turn up, suddenly they're your best friends, even though you haven't seen them for years.

The ex-wife is a potter. Short brown hair. Thick, expressive eyebrows. Not quite pretty. She lives in Utah. I sat on the sofa in the living room. She and Ed sat on armchairs across from each other. A respectable distance between them. The old people were in the kitchen eating and worrying.

Ed and his ex-wife began to talk about when they'd visited Ethiopia. He had been working on his PhD, applying scientific principles to population studies there.

Driving through that sandstorm, he said, you couldn't see a thing, the dust so fine and thick. I had never been in anything like that.

Nor had I, the ex-wife said. They looked at each other.

I thought: I have never been in a sandstorm. Never set foot in Ethiopia. Never wanted to.

The oasis, they said in unison.

I wondered if Ed had regrets about getting divorced long ago.

Green, the ex-wife said.

Yes, the oasis was so green, he said. Never saw anything so beautiful.

They spoke to me now, explaining fiercely. As if they could pull me into their memories. The car ran over a rut and wouldn't go further, Ed went on. They had to abandon it. They rode a bus back to the town that no longer had a name in their minds. The story spilled from them both: the bus, the crush of tall, thin Ethiopians with gleaming dark skin. The smell of live chickens and vomit. The unscheduled stop at a village where every passenger disembarked and two men lifted a coffin from the top of the bus, a plain pine box, then disappeared into the landscape.

I listened to the volley of memory. I had never seen Ed talk so much, with such animation. He knew the landscapes, the geography, even the names of some towns. His ex-wife's images were fuzzier, but he pulled recollection from her brain.

You were always adventurous, she said to him.

He smiled, clearly pleased.

I left the room. The cords of the past still bound them. Early love and its failure. I wondered if the past still bound Ed and me.

The last few years, everything has seemed to crowd in bed with Ed and me. Crowd out tenderness, crowd out sex. It's been worse since his mother came to live with us. Worries about the boys, especially our oldest, Nick. And now the troubles with Sophe, my parents.

When Nick was a child, we discovered he didn't always hear what we said. Ed and I consulted an audiologist. The man helped Nick cope. They say if you temporarily lose hearing during childhood ear infections, you can forget how language sounds. You don't just remember again after the infection passes and hearing returns. There's a delay. Something is lost. You have to relearn. Nick has always been behind other kids.

What will Nick do after he graduates college? I asked last month as Ed and I were going to sleep.

Ed sprawled on his back in bed, eyes shut, the blanket pulled to his neck. He didn't so much answer as grumble. He'll figure it out, he said.

There was so much I wanted to talk to Ed about. From the very first. And now. Our future, the boys, the parents, the visitors, and, last week, the ex-wife. My work. His. But each night as I began, he fell asleep. I realized I was talking to myself.

I walk up Fifth Avenue on the hard gray pavement in a dwindling drizzle. There is no sun today. Clouds stretch across the sky like gauze. Cars rumble past, their horns shrill. Everything is like a muscle, Nick's audiologist had said. You use it or lose it. Or have to relearn.

Hearing. Tenderness. Hope. Love.

I stroll through the Twenties and Thirties and into Midtown, past the glittering shops. A black man with dreadlocks wears a white shirt and red tie. He leans against a building and holds a sign: "Help Me Get On My Feet Again." I drop a quarter in his cup and think: I could use the help myself.

A block later, I take a detour to the East River. Smoke rises like dragons' breath from the white chimneys across the water. Lights flicker: *Long Island.* As if one did not know this was an island.

I was here last week in a building that overlooks the river. Up the elevator to visit the dermatologist, to be certain the blemishes on my skin aren't terminal. There is the possibility in this life for most everything to be terminal. A pain in the arm. A mole on the cheek. Blood in the veins. Maybe mold. How can one keep track? After Sophe got sick, I made a promise to take care of myself. First the skin doctor, then the internist, then the cardiologist, the gynecologist. And tests—colonoscopy, mammogram, blood panel.

I read a poem in a magazine while I sat in the doctor's waiting room. The poet wrote about her ex-husband. He had said of poetry, "I never understood the point." How could he not understand? The point of poetry, of words, was expression. He didn't understand the need for this, as if the need to communicate were a foreign language. In the poem, the ex-husband was a dentist. He knew the language of the mouth: molars, incisors, crowns, and gums. Like the language the dermatologist knows, of skin and medicine. Or the language Ed has mastered: square roots and fractions, tangents, cells, and diseases. Not the words of feeling or thought.

My reflection stares at me from a GAP window. Tall and thin, a woman who knows what she wants and where she is going, no-nonsense expression, middle-aged. A little bedraggled. Not fashionably dressed. Pants a little baggy. Hair streaked with gray. Walking with a mission through the crowds, past Central Park, an oasis of green and golden fall colors. The fancy buildings and limousines, fancy people.

The reflection appears a little dour, I think, not like I looked in Amsterdam, when I was bold and happy. Then, the future was a dare.

The mechanized notes of Beethoven jar me from my reverie. The phone screen reads "Home." I push the phone into my pocket and wait for the sound to stop.

All day I walk, all the way to the Bronx, one foot in front of the other, which is how one has to travel through life. Finally, I reach a neighborhood with small houses and neat front lawns. A place Ed and I discovered years ago. So much like the neighborhood where I grew up in Detroit. An oasis of green and quiet.

I stop and stare at the houses. A man with long curly sidelocks and a tall black hat emerges from a house. I am the owner, he says to me. Do you want something?

I am standing on the sidewalk that snakes to his door. I shake my head. What could I want? Foolish tears suddenly fill my eyes. He sees I am troubled, and he says, Stay here as long as you care to, but I cannot have you inside. Then he walks to a car parked on the street and drives away. He can see I am not a thief.

The sky is white, so thick with fog now, like dust from a sandstorm, and I cannot see what is behind me or ahead. The houses, identical in their modesty and age, sit like relatives, one next to the other.

They say during a near-death experience, your life flashes before you. I am not near death, but life in our apartment is. Now a rush of memory races through me like a river, dammed up long ago that suddenly bursts. The bright pink kitchen, the white living room sofa, the stain on the rug like a half moon. My father, tall and thin, rushing home from work, the strong steps, his eager tales about the insurance he had sold. The promise of a bonus. Blue apron wrapped around my mother, as if she were a present, slim, confident hands shimmering with *schmaltz.* The scent of onions and her sweet orange perfume. A smile, a kiss on my father's lips, her words for me: Why don't you sit down when you eat, Franny, tell me why? Why can't you act like a lady? Look how well-behaved your brother is. Books can't teach you how to live. What will happen when you grow up?

Nothing will happen, I told them and laughed gaily, with great confidence. Didn't they know? The future was a blue moon, hanging in the sky. So far away. There were books to read, places to travel to, people to meet, men to love. I didn't understand there was always something to be afraid of. Mold or illness or memories or change. Love and its failure.

Memories barrel through my mind, the lush garden of the hooker hotel, the hotel that no longer has a name, Ed's dazzling smile, our kiss in the small, dim room there, love at first sight, talking with him into the night. The boys when they were young. The silence in the apartment between Ed and me, how it's grown, like a cancer, since Sophe moved in. My mother tottering. My father asleep. Jonas shouting: Fuck, fuck, fuck. Sophe's illness, the terrible pacing.

I feel tired and hungry, like an old person myself. I sit on the front step of this house. Old people look backward, I think, because they can't bear to look ahead anymore.

The ground here is parched and brown. Winter hovers in the air but has not yet arrived. The season is a train pulling into the station; we are all sitting in the terminal, have heard the announcement, the blare of the horn, but have yet to see the train itself. The wind blows, leaves of a tall oak tree shiver. I try to think of a mathematical equation that will save my life. Nothing comes to mind.

A woman emerges from the house. A black hat sits on her head; the full sweep of her black coat grazes the ground. She looks at me with surprise, but almost recognition. I can tell she is religious, a woman of God. By the covering on her hair. The length of her skirt and coat. The bulky black shoes.

You can sit here, she says. But this is private property. You can't go inside. Her face softens. What is it you want?

She resembles my mother when she was young. Tall, slender, crow's-feet pleats stretching across her skin. A kind, assured expression. I imagine the inside of her house is identical to ours long ago.

Just to sit, I say.

She nods and goes back into the house. I envy her, the confidence, as if she is not afraid, not of the past or of the future. Envy how she defers to a higher force, gives herself over to a power she allows to shape her life, the power she believes created the seasons, the horizon, light and darkness.

My cell phone rings. I pull it from my pocket. "Home" flashes across the screen again. Everyone there needs something.

How foolish, I think. To walk away. When I have made no provisions for the future. Not for the children or Sophe or my parents or myself. I pat my pocket; my credit card and cash are still crumpled there. The cell phone rings and rings, a frenzy of sound. I toss the phone into the bushes; it makes a soft thud as it lands, like dirt hitting a grave. I will plan for provisions now. I think of all the misbeliefs I have about myself, what I can and cannot do. I cannot leave my family. I cannot leave Ed. I wouldn't survive without him. I am scared to be alone.

Daylight slowly disappears. A cool wind slaps my skin. I don't want to walk anymore. I stare at the house. I want these people to invite me inside, ask me to join their circle, give shelter to the stranger, but the curtains are pulled shut. Loss creeps in the air. I can't stay here forever. But I won't go home. So I pull up the collar of my jacket and wrap my arms around my chest, bracing for night's damp chill, waiting for darkness to surround me like a gathering storm.

2.

Matters of the Heart

1

Denise wasn't looking forward to the *shiva*. *Shivas* weren't something to enjoy. After all, someone had died; more grief had washed into the world. The mourners sat, and visitors paid their respects; these were often awkward gatherings, events she felt obligated to attend. Although she wasn't observant, she believed in doing a *mitzvah*. Comforting the grieving was a gift in itself. But this one would be more difficult than most.

Two weeks ago, Neil had told her that he planned to leave; he had found a temporary apartment. Now, with one week to go before he moved there, Denise couldn't bear to be with people. But a man she'd worked with years ago had died, and she couldn't stay away. Even attending a *shiva* seemed preferable to wallowing in despair.

She and Neil had been married for twenty-three years and had three children, twin boys and a girl. The marriage was like most Denise had seen, not all good or all bad. After Neil told her, she begged him to stay. She was still in love with him. But Neil said he'd fallen out of love with her. In the last months, she had witnessed a relatively happy union disintegrate into bickering and silence. She had tried to be sensitive to his complaints. She switched off the radio when he was home; he liked quiet. She stopped nagging him about household chores. She was never late. She didn't know what had happened to their marriage.

In a desperate attempt to save the marriage, she had telephoned counselors and carried the list of therapists in her purse, like a good-luck charm. Tonight, after the *shiva*, Neil would be home from a business trip. Stay, she would say, and come to a counselor with me.

It was true, she'd had doubts about Neil from time to time; years ago, she'd even had an affair. Now she was overcome with unexpected grief.

Why weren't there *shivas* for the death of relationships? she wondered as she trudged in her black down coat in the windy January chill to the apartment building where the *shiva* was being held. She had once asked an Orthodox rabbi's wife what Judaism postulated about divorce. "Everything is God's will," the woman had replied. The rebbetsen shook her plump head, and her shiny brown wig slid slightly to one side, revealing scraggly gray hair. Then she leaned toward Denise, so close Denise could touch the rosy cheeks and smell mint on her breath.

"But when a relationship crumbles," the woman had whispered, clutching Denise's arm, "the stones of the *chuppah* weep."

Denise was a photographer. Grant, the man who had died, owned an advertising agency. He believed in her work and encouraged her. This was one of the reasons she had decided to attend the *shiva*. It was a way to show respect, a kind of debt she wanted to repay. He was also the man with whom she'd had the affair.

Neil had always been the main breadwinner. He worked in his family's retail men's clothing business. He had studied to be a climatologist and still relished talking about the gloomy future of the planet. He taught at a small college now in New York City, too. She and Neil shared a curiosity about the world and loved to travel. He was interested in climates, Denise in people. Neil had been married once before, but had no children then. His first wife was a cellist. When Denise was honest with herself, she knew his ex-wife had been a ghost in their lives. The woman sent notices of concerts and tours to him. Neil still listened to her old demo tapes.

Denise photographed for low-budget catalogues and for weddings and bar mitzvahs, work she squeezed in while raising the children. Now that they were in college, she volunteered at a city school, helped immigrant children with reading, and also did photography projects with them. This was another kind of *mitzvah*.

Her true joy was to photograph objects. She wanted to capture a moment of beauty, in time, to pretend this could extend indefinitely, not just in photographs but in lives.

In college, her real love, before she met Neil, had been archaeology. Now she photographed objects discarded on the street. Found objects. On garbage days the sidewalks of New York were a museum of social history. Denise snapped photos of cracked mirrors, chairs with springs bursting out. She photographed in attics, too, in her parents' home in Iowa: the old oak rocker and her grandmother's bleached, warped mahogany hope chest. How many hopes remained buried there? Denise had wondered. How many secrets?

Neil had never really liked her photography. In a hidden part of her heart, she had understood this, but couldn't bear to face it.

She had always longed to do something pure and artistic. Last year, she had learned about cyanotypes in a class. She loved the process and worked on it in the room she claimed as her studio in the apartment. She used a heavy piece of paper, watercolor weight. She combined iron salts with water and applied this mixture to the paper. When Denise found the perfect combination, the salts turned the paper a glorious azure blue. She placed an object on the paper—a square of lace, a flower, a leaf—then pressed a piece of glass on top. When the paper had dried, she removed the glass and object. The image appeared white on a blue background, like a painting. Sometimes she placed the specimen on dark paper and painted everything blue so the image became blue as well. Her designs were a puzzle, like a Rorschach test. Everything depended on how she chose to look at the world.

She rode the elevator to the twentieth floor. In Grant's apartment, a wall of windows opened onto sweeping views of the city. The dark expanse of Central Park stood like an ancient forest. The lights of the

Empire State Building—tonight red, white, and blue—glittered. The bright beams of cars below sparkled like showers of stars.

She had never been here. The room was filled with people, but she felt lonely walking in. She felt uneasy, too; she had never met Grant's wife.

Denise left her coat in the den, smoothed the front of her slim black A-line skirt, and tried to tidy her short, silky brown hair. She missed Grant, and she missed Neil. She felt like a planet forced from its orbit, as if she were spiraling alone in darkness. Panic rose in her as she walked into this room of windows.

The widow, June, was fifteen years older than Denise. Her soft gray-blond hair curled limply to the middle of her neck. She was, thought Denise, a handsome, hardy woman, and she wore black—a sheath dress, hose, and shoes, and a black velvet cord around her neck with a shiny gold charm of a heart. Her face crinkled into a sad smile.

"So, you're Denise," she said. "Grant talked so much about you. He admired your photographs."

Denise nodded awkwardly, suppressing her own tears for Grant. She had been jealous of the woman years ago. "He gave me my first job," Denise replied. "I've always been grateful." Her heart twinged with affection for Grant, then with guilt and shame. Did June know about the affair?

"He was like that, wasn't he? Generous." Tears swam in the woman's deep-set brown eyes. She and Denise chatted for a moment, then the widow wandered off to talk with others.

Denise was relieved the conversation had ended. She'd accomplished her mission. She had seen where Grant lived and had paid her respects, but it seemed rude to leave so soon. Since her marital troubles had begun, she felt unanchored. Now she couldn't decide whether to stay or go. She studied the room, as if to take photographs in her mind of the neat rows of books on shelves: Edward Steichen, Weegee, Ansel Adams, Diane Arbus. Black-and-white photographs of landscapes hung on the walls, and brightly colored woven pillows graced the sofa. She wandered to an oblong table covered by a white linen cloth. Blue china platters sat heaped with rugelach, brownies, cookies, bagels, lox, and breads.

Three women stood talking. Denise joined them. One, a stunning redhead, had a face so smooth Denise envied it. Clearly a facelift or Botox. Denise lingered at the edge of their circle and brushed her hand against her own face, imagining its web of wrinkles. Denise knew one of the women, Pauline Silip. She had worked at the advertising agency with Grant. Pauline hugged Denise and introduced her to the others.

"Brenda was telling us about her great luck," Pauline said.

The three women laughed, and though the air of gaiety felt inappropriate for the occasion, Denise was attracted to it. Her life felt like a *shiva* now, with Grant gone and Neil on his way out.

"I was so tired of going places alone," Brenda, the redhead, said. "I met Bill on an airplane."

"Now they may get married," Pauline explained.

"It's destiny," said the woman named Liz. Her face was smooth, too, and her smile stilted. The skin had been pulled so tight her teeth seemed to bulge from her mouth as she smiled. "Everyone is marked by fate," she went on. "Life is predestined."

Denise wondered if she had talked to the Orthodox rabbi's wife.

"My husband and I divorced," Brenda told Denise. She spoke with a delicate drawl and said she was from Tennessee. "Of course, it took a while before I realized our marriage was over. I had hope. I teach theater arts and direct regional theater. The hard truth is: I was too successful for my husband. He started to undermine me."

The others nodded.

"My father told me to get an education and have a career, so you're prepared when husbands leave home," Brenda said. "I think most people live between marriage and an arrangement."

"Three days after my husband left, I began to date," Liz said. "I told June this. Not to be crass. Oh, she's dealing with a death, but her husband is not coming back. I joined It's Just Lunch. You meet a guy for lunch. What can you lose?"

They all nodded again. Denise felt as if she had walked into a taping of *Oprah*. She noticed her head was bobbing vigorously, so she stopped herself.

"I like to meet one new person a day," Brenda said. "You can always learn something."

"When I started to date, my husband wanted me back," Liz said. "Men are hunters. They love the chase; they want what they can't have."

"Human nature." Brenda shrugged. "Bill was sitting across the aisle from me on an airplane. Can you believe it? He's wonderful."

"Yes," Pauline said wistfully. "You'll have to meet him, Denise."

Denise looked from Pauline to Brenda.

"I've lost years since knowing him." Brenda blushed in anticipation of what she would say next. She glanced around to be sure no one was eavesdropping. "All day long," she whispered, "we fuck like teenagers."

Denise inched away from the women, to the table, wondering if it was good luck or bad to eat at a *shiva*.

"Everything okay?" Pauline asked, following her. "With Neil, the family?"

When people asked, did they really want to know? "Yes," she said. "Good." When did you share what was on your mind? Denise couldn't talk about Grant, and she didn't want her marital problems to be fodder for gossip.

"Everything is…" Denise stared at Pauline blankly. "Not so good. We may separate," she blurted before she could stop herself. *May*, she thought. "Neil and I, we…"

"Oh, no," Pauline grasped her arm. She was divorced. "I'm sorry. That must be tough."

There was silence.

"We'll try counseling," Denise whispered, which was not exactly true. She hadn't brought this up with Neil yet.

"You'll have to stop wearing your wedding ring," Brenda said brightly, joining them. "If your husband leaves. Remember, It's Just Lunch." She pressed her business card into Denise's hand. "Call me. When you're ready."

Denise felt queasy. She wound her plain gold wedding band round and round her finger while clutching Brenda's business card. She excused herself to search for a bathroom. In the hall she thought about Grant. They'd had a relationship ten years ago—well, an affair. She'd ended it after a few years; she wanted to put her energies into her marriage. But she'd seen Grant again two years ago, too, after his first heart attack. Denise hadn't wanted to become involved with him at first. They were married to other people, after all. She believed in old-fashioned values, like doing a *mitzvah* and obeying the Ten Commandments, virtues her grandmother Bertha extolled in Iowa. Bertha could be stern but was lavishly loving. She freely imparted her wisdom to Denise in a thick Russian accent: "Everything takes a toll," she'd said in a shaky voice when she was ill and confined to bed. "Old age takes a toll, my Denisenik. Sometimes it's worth it, sometimes not."

Grant had been persistently seductive, and the truth was, Denise couldn't resist. He had never had an affair, he said, and she believed him; they clearly shared a connection. He had been tall, with auburn hair and hooded brown eyes. She marveled that she could love both Neil and Grant. Perhaps Neil's leaving was punishment for her actions. Why had she come to this *shiva*—because of prurient interest, self-punishment, or real grief?

She stood in the hall, staring at the landscape photographs on the walls. She had once been dazzled by Grant and his *things*. The beautiful photographs he took on his own after work, the books in his office, his great knowledge and appreciation of art. Like she had been dazzled by Neil when she'd first met him. She had fallen in love not only with Neil, but with his whole family. Their intellect. The order. They were German Jews. Her own family was Russian and sprawling. Her grandparents had escaped from pogroms long ago; their house and village had been ruthlessly destroyed. There were family squabbles and gyrations, fallings out and reconciliations. Neil's family was quieter, more dignified.

She and Grant had always made love with an abandon that felt like play. As if they were teenagers, like Brenda had said about herself. Even two years ago, although Denise hadn't seen him for years. "You like to fuck," Grant said as she sprawled on top of him in bed, gazing into his eyes that were glassy with pleasure. "Don't give me that other shit."

"It's true," she whispered. "I love to, but only with you."

Their coupling had been a mystery. Was it pure physiology that had caused her pulse to soar and her body to shimmer with such delicious sensations that, try as she might, she couldn't recreate in memory? Or was it love? Or an illusion? Together, she told Grant, they were acrobats in the art of making love.

"Of fucking," he'd said.

Acrobats of the soul, she'd thought naïvely. She had been so smitten at first that she imagined one day they would run off together. She hadn't allowed herself to think about the pain and distress this would have caused their spouses and children.

Now she had seen the wife, and now Grant was gone. It seemed unreal. How could something that brought shame also bring joy? How could a marriage that once brought joy now bring shame?

Instead of finding the bathroom, she wandered to the den to retrieve her coat. The door was mostly closed, and she peeked into the room. A man in his twenties with wavy auburn hair—Grant's son, she surmised—sat hunched over a computer. A small piece of torn black fabric, like a mourner's badge, was pinned to his lapel. A black yarmulke lay on the desk. He didn't acknowledge her. Today was the fifth day of the *shiva*; Denise supposed he had taken refuge here, tired of company. She tiptoed in, not wanting to disturb him, rehearsing in her mind what she would say to Neil about a counselor. The son was intent on the computer.

She gazed from him to the monitor. On it were photographs. She grabbed her coat and slid Brenda's business card into her purse. Then she said quietly, "Excuse me."

The son didn't reply. He sat transfixed. Denise stared at the screen, too. The photographs, she saw, were of men. Men who were clothed. Men who were naked. A penis—an erect, engorged penis—glowed on the screen. There was another image, an anus. She blinked and read the words: "BIG MUSHROOM. *Call me.*" She felt as if her eyes might pop out of her head, but she said, "Sorry to disturb you." The son quickly jiggled the mouse. The window on the screen disappeared. The new one read: "SILVER DADDIES." With one stroke, he closed that. Up popped a weather site. He mumbled with embarrassment, without looking up, "No problem. You didn't disturb me."

She walked out in a daze. She was in Rome before its fall; she was hurrying into the outer hallway now without saying good-bye to anyone, astonished by the ways people dealt with or avoided grief.

"Denise," June called. "I wanted to say good-bye to you." She stood at the doorway to the apartment, escorting a man out.

Denise retraced her steps.

June hugged her. Denise's knees felt weak.

"Thank you for being here tonight." She glanced from Denise to the man to Pauline Silip, who had joined them. "All of you meant so much to Grant," June said. "He was the love of my life."

Outside, the chilly night air burst against Denise's face. She breathed it in with gratitude. At least she was done with the *shiva*. She thought of the photographs of men with wonder and disgust. What kind of world was this where people were dispensable, like objects? Perhaps this was how Neil felt about her. Perhaps this was what she tried to do with her photography, to capture that impermanence. *He was the love of my life.* One could laugh at such sentiment or weep at it. Denise envied the widow and Grant; they had shared such a grand love. Or did it seem so only in retrospect? He had cheated on his wife, after all. Denise remembered the night at a work party when he'd approached her in an upstairs room and kissed her.

Denise believed in the difference between sex and love. Pauline Silip had once confided that, after she divorced, she learned she could enjoy sex and not be in love. Denise had experienced this in college, a few one-night stands and brief relationships with men in whom she had no interest for anything lasting.

But when she had been with Grant, the sex had felt like love, emotions entangled like their bodies, and when they rose from bed, she wanted only to be in his presence. Just as she had felt about Neil at the beginning.

Grant, on the other hand, admitted his marriage was an imperfect arrangement, but he wouldn't walk away from it. This was what he offered Denise, too, and she had accepted it. She didn't want to leave Neil or her family either. She had come to the *shiva*, she supposed, to see what Grant hadn't wanted to leave. She had never asked how he felt about her; he had never asked about her feelings for him. Unspoken bonds, secret ones. In the end, his wife had been at his side to take care of him. Denise pulled up the collar of her coat, buffering herself against the night wind, feeling a pang of envy.

She rode the subway, then ambled past Washington Square Park. Years ago she had strolled gaily from her assignations with Grant past the park; every person she saw then glowed with promise. Now the landscape looked bleak. The snow was dirty and encrusted with litter—a Starbucks cup bent in two places, a black hair band, cigarette butts, a beer bottle peeking out from a brown paper bag. Everywhere, she saw neglect and ruin. Even the white marble

Washington Square Arch. At one time, she and Neil had walked past the Arch, holding hands, and admired it. The Arch stood bare and gray now without the forgiving gleam of daylight. She squinted to see the words engraved on the stone; they stared down at her, barely readable in the thin thread of moonlight: "Let us raise a standard to which the wise and the honest can repair/The event is in the hand of God."

The hand of God. God's will. The stones of the *chuppah. The love of my life.* Let people live with their illusions, Denise thought. She imagined Neil in better days, when she'd first met him, playful, sexual Neil.

She left the park and hurried up Fifth Avenue. What's public is private, she thought. What's private is public. She tried to clarify this and realized that what she meant was: What is *public*—a separation, a divorce—concerns the most private of matters, matters of the heart. What is *private*—sexuality and sexual habits—had become public. Like the porn and dating sites Grant's son cruised. His behavior had shocked Denise. She imagined the stone tablets with the Ten Commandments crumbling into dust.

She had always wanted to create what she hadn't had, a close family, with a mother and father who lived together. Stability. Her father had left her mother when Denise was nine. Hers was the only family that faced divorce in their neighborhood. Her father quickly remarried and moved to Seattle. But he telephoned her mother every week for the rest of his life. Denise hated him for this. Her mother welcomed the calls. He had never released Denise's mother to love anyone else.

Carpe diem, Denise told herself as she trudged in the cold. What other choice did she have?

She stood in front of the apartment building, collecting herself. Heaps of brown snow sat hard as stone on the sidewalk. She would be reasonable and convincing with Neil. Loving. She would banish Grant from her mind. She had telephoned several marriage counselors but wondered now if she had done this because of a nagging, unrealistic hope—like Brenda, the woman at the *shiva*, had felt about her marriage.

The woman's card sat in Denise's purse, propped against the list of counselors. Denise pulled out the list and stared at the names. Geography was important. She and Neil wouldn't consult with a counselor in Brooklyn or the Bronx or even the Upper West Side. Too much time spent in transportation. Neil would never agree to that.

George Stefaninie was the first name on the list. Italian, she'd thought, when she had called. Would he ooze Mediterranean charm? His voicemail message sounded expansive, gave her hope. She had left information. "We're interested in couples' therapy," she'd said, beginning a quest for truth with a lie. *I* am interested, she thought.

Glenn Jones had a flat affect; Sevana Miller sounded no-nonsense. Robert Pataki charged $525 an hour. Denise had crossed him off the list. Steven Donaldson. He was located on the Upper West Side, but his voice and manner had cheered her, as if she wrestled with a terminal illness and he offered the promise of a cure.

"I do a lot of consultations with couples," he'd said. "Whether I'm the right person for you or not, you'll have to see. It has to feel right, be the perfect combination."

"Yes," she said. "Like a marriage."

"If it's not, you can't make it right," he had agreed. "That can be like pushing a square peg into a round hole."

He didn't ask personal questions, but said, "I'm not surprised you made the call and your husband didn't. Women usually call first."

All she could manage to reply was, "Yes."

"In the world of couples work," he said, "some therapists have every degree in the world. Degrees mean nothing. Even the best therapists have strengths and weaknesses. You can tell the moment you're with them."

Like dating, she had thought.

"Don't worry," he said. "I'll take good care of you."

Neil was sitting at the kitchen table, reading the obituaries in the *Times.* He always read the obituaries first. His tortoiseshell reading glasses made him look scholarly.

"Hey," he said offhandedly as she walked in.

Denise slipped off her coat and sat across from him. He didn't ask where she had been. She was astonished by how uninterested in her he seemed recently. His smile looked as seductive as ever, and she was ashamed to admit to herself that when he smiled, her heart gave way. Yet he planned to leave and didn't seem inclined to change his mind. She felt dizzy as she considered this scenario. She was on the wrong airplane, traveling in the wrong direction, to a strange, foreign land. All they had done together seemed to shrink away—all those years, the children, a bundle of nothing, wasted time.

This was the kind of despair she wouldn't talk to friends about. They had their own sorrows. Many had been divorced and told her about the grief they'd experienced. Pauline Silip had once confided that, for years after her husband left, she had not slept through the night. They'd fought bitterly when they were married, but his presence, a familiar human being, had soothed her.

"I think we need to see a counselor," Denise began. "I've made some inquiries." She laid her list on the table. "If you give me times that work for you, I'll make an appointment. Before you leave or do anything you can't undo."

There was silence.

"We don't need a counselor," Neil finally said. "We need to communicate with each other."

"You can't communicate by leaving." She bit her lip. She would not beg.

"I haven't been a model husband," he mumbled.

"I haven't been a perfect wife. No one has to be perfect. But let's not throw our marriage away. Neil. Please. Listen to me."

He frowned and glanced at the newspaper.

"Are you having an affair?" she asked.

"Huh? I'm not leaving because of anything like that. I told you we need some space. I *have* to do this."

She waited.

"What has gotten into you? It's just a trial. A trial separation."

"There are no trials." She cautioned herself to be calm. She dug a fist into her thigh. "Yes, yes. No, no."

There was more silence.

He drummed his fingers on the table. His nails were bitten down. "I've had…" he stopped. "I've had several long relationships with married women. Not now. The last few years. That's where I've been."

Denise stared at him.

"I'm being honest," he went on, as if she had made a comment. "You wanted to know what I was thinking."

She clutched her stomach as if she had been hit. She had asked him before about an affair, and he'd denied it. Images of Grant fell away. All she saw was Neil. Here but not here. All those years. How many? She felt as if she would break in half.

"That's not thinking, that's, that's…" Her words sputtered and then she yelled, "You bastard." She was aware of the irony, her own double standard. "I want you to leave now." Tears filled her eyes. "I can't bear to see you. This is a slow death. I don't want any part of this. It's over."

"Dennie," he called, his footsteps coming closer to the bedroom where she had run to. She locked the door. Locked herself in.

"I was trying to be honest," he said. "I want us to be honest, I want…"

She didn't reply.

He pounded on the door and when she opened it, he smiled like a boy who had been caught by his mother doing what he was not supposed to do.

"Leave right now," she said. "Go to your apartment, your new life."

"The apartment isn't ready until next week. It's a separation, to see what we really want. We have the children, we—"

"To see what *you* want." Her voice had no vibrato of anger in it, she realized, just the dull, deep sound of sadness. "Get out now."

She walked past him and yanked open his dresser drawers. She began pulling out his possessions. Hanes white jockeys, torn blue-and-white-striped boxers. The white undershirts, crew-neck and V-neck. The pile of mismatched socks he kept surrounded by a rubber band in case the missing socks magically turned up. Business cards, a black bathing suit. She hurled them to the floor.

"Let's handle this like adults," he said, his voice a soothing murmur.

"Lies, lies," she shouted, opening another drawer. "Get out of here."

He watched and did nothing to stop her.

Finally he left, pale and trudging out of the house, carrying a small duffel bag with a change of clothes. He moved his neck in such a way that she knew his nervous crick had reappeared, the pain that emerged when he was anxious or unhappy. This pleased her. Then he slammed the door. She usually worried about him and had suggested he go to a doctor, but now she felt no worry.

Only panic. What had she done? Too many things to remember: all the omissions and petty unkindnesses of marriage, coldness, impatience, her relationship with Grant. Too many things to unravel. What had Neil done? The same but with more bravado, daring, and pride. They were both responsible for the tensions in their marriage, but he had bombed the marriage. A pogrom.

She wandered around the apartment like a sleepwalker. The only objects she could focus on were ones that belonged to Neil. Clothing from his drawers littered the bedroom floor.

Then the anger began to dissipate. She felt, instead, a great sadness, something so large inside her that she felt swallowed by loss. All she could do was to try to make sense of the feeling. But there was no sense to it.

The children's rooms seemed empty of human warmth, as if no one had ever lived in them. The spirit had seeped out of the rooms. Like when her grandmother had died, and Denise sat in the bedroom with the body in Iowa. She hadn't wanted to let go of her grandmother; she wanted to say good-bye, to tell her how much she loved her. But Bertha's body was flesh without a spirit, without those attributes that made Bertha live and breathe.

The rooms in the apartment felt the same now, too. Physical accoutrements remained but the life force was gone. Each room seemed more lifeless than the next—the kitchen with dishes piled in the sink, the living room with the most recent family photograph displayed proudly on the mantel. Denise flung the photograph on the floor, and the glass shattered.

In the bedroom, she threw off her clothes and slipped into her nightgown. Then she lay on the mattress. No matter how she arranged her arms and legs or the blankets, the bed begged for another person. She thought about Grant's widow. June was in bed alone tonight, too; millions of people slept alone, lived alone. How did they manage?

An African saying she'd read somewhere flitted through her mind: If you die alone, no one escorts you to the next world and you wander between this world and the next. Would this be her fate? Is that why Judaism required someone to watch the body?

Denise couldn't sleep, jumped out of bed and yanked open Neil's dresser drawers. She pulled out his black V-neck sweater. Then she searched for a scissors in the medicine cabinet. She snipped the sweater's fine, soft wool on the bottom, at its front, then ripped the wool all the way to the V-neck, until the two pieces of the sweater dangled, like twins, like the cloth the rabbi rends in two for a mourner.

She dropped the sweater on the bed. The pall of depression fell over her. She could fake a smile but her insides were weeping, like the stones of the *chuppah*. She didn't know anymore if she loved Neil. How could she have feelings for someone who treated her so coldly, shabbily, whom she had built her life around in good faith?

All around the apartment were the artifacts of their life. She didn't think she would be able to rid herself of his presence. She wandered again from room to room. Intimacy was buried deep, beneath these objects.

The only room that welcomed her was her studio. It was dawn by now, the sun just peeking above the horizon. Denise knew the times of day when this room was bathed in light. She often felt here as if she were an angel fluttering in heavenly light; she'd told Grant this. Here she created her photographic collages and cyanotypes. Here she dove into another world.

Grant had replied that this wasn't only because of the actual light, but because of the feeling inside you when you worked. "I am most myself when alone," he had told her, "when I work."

She found herself collecting odd possessions from the apartment now, possessions of Neil's that he would have wanted if he hadn't left in a hurry. His office key. A photograph of the children. A square of lace that had belonged to his mother.

The studio was the one place where Denise felt calm. She had the patience to let her hands work at their own speed. She lived inside of time here, instead of fighting time.

As a child at summer camp she had gotten lost with another girl in the woods. At first, they had been afraid and tried without success to retrace their route. When it was dark, they built a bed of leaves. Denise hadn't been frightened anymore, certain they would find their way or someone would come looking for them. She had learned her first lesson in patience then. In the morning, they had found their way back, greeted by anxious counselors. Her studio was the one place where she duplicated that feeling of patience.

She arranged Neil's possessions in a neat row on the table in the studio, as if they were companions at a *shiva*. She wasn't sure what she was doing, but she began shuffling them. She would make a cyanotype of their married life, she thought. She gathered more items. Neil's spare car key. His sock. A stiff white collar stay from a shirt. Then she returned to the bedroom and grabbed the black wool sweater she had cut in two. Her thoughts were clearer now, and her body no longer felt rubbery but was rigid with purpose and focus.

She studied the objects as if seeing them for the first time, as if they were found objects, thoughtlessly discarded. Then she slid off her gold wedding band and set it on the table. Grant had told her that in art you use illusion to create truth; she would try to do this now. She pulled the list of counselors from her purse, laid that on the table, too, and set Brenda's business card for safekeeping on her desk.

She wished she could talk to the rabbi's wife about the stones of the *chuppah*. How did you know what was true in life and what was an illusion? What could you really hope for? How long should a person weep, how long should you mourn? A month, as if a spouse had died? For a year, as if you had lost a parent? What were the requirements of the heart when you mourned for someone who was still alive?

Denise snipped a small rectangle of soft wool from the bottom of the black sweater. She cut the rectangle almost in two, so the ends dangled and were just the size of the mourner's cloth Grant's son had worn. She pressed the wool onto a piece of paper and rearranged it again and again until the wool lost its original shape and no longer appeared as what it had once been.

She carried her bottles of iron salts to the table and slowly mixed the chemicals until they turned a glorious blue. She would apply this mixture to a heavy piece of paper, place the wool there, and then put a piece of glass on top. When she was done, the black wool would appear as a stark white image against the beautiful background. She slid her wedding ring, the list of counselors, and the other objects closer to her. She would create image after image until she could quiet the ache inside her.

She lifted her paintbrush and began to work.

2

It was October. Neil had moved out nine months ago. He said he still didn't know what he wanted to do about their marriage, and there were times Denise wasn't sure either. She was more devastated by the separation than she'd expected. Some women hated their husbands. Denise understood restlessness, boredom, or anger in a marriage. But hatred? Was she one of those women?

When she was honest with herself, she knew that she and Neil had problems in their marriage, but she'd always believed the tensions would subside. "The wrinkles press out," her grandmother Bertha used to say. "Life is full of wrinkles, and one way or the other, they fall away."

A friend of Denise's confided she had begun to hate her husband before she left him. Another friend was abandoned by her spouse. Yet at lunch last week, Liz had said, "When he walked out I was in shock, but even so, I felt free." She said she despised how sloppy he was. He complained about money but never altered his extravagant habits. After they argued, she sometimes feigned a headache and refused to have sex. "I suppose I chased him away," she'd said.

Denise envied the clarity of these emotions. In her own case, during the separation, she had met a man named Nathaniel Green. She knew she could love him, and she loved to have sex with him, but felt cautious. He was salve to the wound of being left. She'd gone out with a few other men before she met him and slept with one, although she didn't enjoy this casual freedom. Neil still dipped in and out of her life, like a yo-yo or a chronic ache. And while Denise had no concrete thoughts of reconciling, she sometimes wavered.

Her emotions skidded about, even affection for him rising when she remembered the happy moments they'd shared.

Besides, she and Neil needed to discuss issues regarding their three college-age children. There were money matters and mail. And matters of the heart. How, she wanted to ask, did our life come to this? What happened? What did I do wrong? Who are you now? Sometimes she wept. She imagined it would have been simpler if he had died—a clean, if shocking, break. She imagined the warm rally of support for a widow instead of the tepid concern for and fear of the separated or divorced.

She had struggled to adjust, to move on, although these words conjured images of barreling ahead with vigor, like characters on a TV sitcom. "When you mourn," her grandmother used to say, "you have to walk the world." In her worst moments, Denise could barely trudge into the world and felt panicked—about money, the future. She kept busy with her photography business, volunteer work, and with her friends, or she worked on her cyanotypes, which she did on her own, striving to create art. Bent over her worktable in her apartment, a paintbrush in her hand, the hum of New York City traffic seeping in, she thought with astonishment about all that had happened in the last months. Twenty-three years wiped away in a single slam of the door.

"It's hard to disassemble a marriage," Neil said. "And life is short. Seems shorter all the time."

Denise nodded. She'd agreed to meet him in the small one-bedroom apartment he'd rented on the Lower East Side. He'd invited her before and she'd always refused, but curiosity had finally gotten the best of her. The place was grim and she was eager to leave. Thin gray carpet, bare white walls, newspapers and mail cluttering the kitchen table, plates and bowls crusted with food piled in the sink. A spindle-backed kitchen chair from their apartment stood there, a relic from the past. Greasy scents of fried food wafted in through the opened window. This was, she thought, a hotel, not a life. No plants, no joy.

"I call the kids every day, honey. I try to reach out to them," he said. "They're my kids too."

"They're busy. They're in college." She held the plastic bag filled with the mail and nervously smoothed her white blouse and navy pants with her other hand. She stood a few feet from him, which made the conversation seem oddly formal. There was nowhere to sit. Stacks of newspapers were piled on the two kitchen chairs. The apartment was stuffy on this warm October evening, and she felt uneasy. Her pants and blouse hugged her slender body, and her silky brown hair fell almost to her shoulders now. He seemed to be talking to her as if she were his friend or mother, as if he wanted approval. *Honey*, he'd called her, like he used to. The word made her shudder.

"The twins never have time for me," he said.

"When they were here for a few weeks in the summer you weren't at home anymore. They're upset about our separation and they don't want to talk about it."

"Once we split up the holidays, it will be good. Would you like water? Wine? Something to eat?"

"Split up the holidays?" Her arms tensed and she clutched the mail she'd brought. "How could that be good? We're a family."

He smiled weakly. His shoulders looked thin. Two black hairs, coarse as straw, jutted from his right nostril. She thought to mention this, as she would have in the past, but reconsidered. Let him look neglected. Let him take care of himself. He looked like some of the men she'd met through the dating service. The collar of his blue Oxford shirt was frayed and missing two buttons. His shirt bunched out carelessly from his khakis.

"You break an arm and the body heals," he said.

"Is this what you wanted to talk about? Clichés? You break a life and the people heal? You left your first wife. Now you've left me. Who do you think you'll find out there?"

"If there wasn't healing, there wouldn't be hope. You have to hope for the future."

"Well, I just wanted to…see how you lived," she said, trying to make sense of his words. She dropped the mail on the table. "We don't have anything to talk about." She felt confused. What did he want? It was her own fault. She still hoped he would transform into who he had been, or maybe who she *thought* he had been, a man with one marriage behind him, eager to climb into a future with her. She had loved him. He was a different person now. He was no longer tender but desperately plunging back into his youth, searching for illusory happiness, she was sure. Self-absorbed. Sexless. She hated him for this.

"You came here, to my apartment, because you're nosy," he said, as if he could sense the shift in her thoughts. "I won't live this way forever. I don't have to explain myself to you."

"You invited me. What did you want?" She walked to the door. "I've got to go," she said.

"I want to tell you some things," he said evenly. "I need to get used to living on my own. I quit teaching at the college. I'm still working at the clothing store, but I'm cutting back."

She swung around and stared at him. What about his income? Their expenses? "We have kids in college, Neil."

"I hate the fucking retail business. I'm tired of academics. I've decided to take time to write a novel. If I don't try now, when will I? I've always wanted to."

"A novel?" Her eyes widened in panic.

"I want to do something that has meaning." He walked toward her, to brush his cheek against hers, this new sexless ritual of greeting and parting. When for much of their twenty-three years together, they had kissed with passion, or in bed she had taken his cock in her mouth. Eagerly. Lovingly. The thought disgusted her now.

She charged out of the apartment before he reached her. Then she stopped and faced him. "I never thought we'd be living like this," she said. "Getting divorced. I've always loved you. But Neil, I think that's over. Fucking, fucking over."

"Wait."

"Man plans and God laughs," she mumbled to herself. She slammed the door. "My grandmother was right."

"I shouldn't talk to him or see him," Denise said. She was at a restaurant in Midtown two days later at lunch. She and her friends sat at a table in the back. She hardly ate her tuna melt. "I'm losing it. I'm quoting my grandmother. Talking to myself. I feel like killing him." She tapped her fingers in agitation on the table. "I never wanted a splintered life. That's what I've got. Pure aggravation. I'm not going to answer his phone calls. E-mail is out."

"No question, aggravation takes a toll," Brenda said. "Total elimination of contact is the solution. That's what I've found."

Brenda had problems herself. The woman had divorced her husband and then fallen madly in love with Bill, the man she met on an airplane, then weathered a breakup with him. Now they were back together.

"Everything is fluid," Brenda went on. "I don't look at Bill as the love of my life, but the love of *now.* It's self-protection. Talk about aggravation. My son punished me for leaving his father. He didn't speak to me for two years. But now he realizes he needs two parents."

"Someone in a family is always punishing someone else, divorce or not," Pauline said.

"Everyone I know has aggravation," Liz said, slipping a green bean into her mouth from her salad nicoise. "It's a midlife thing. In your twenties you do drugs and sex. In your forties and fifties and after, you wish drugs and sex could wipe away the aggravation." She laughed. Her smile was still lopsided from her facelift. The skin pulled too tightly. "The doctor says the nerve in my lip will go back to normal," she said, as if one of them had asked. "I'll be able to smile." She pressed a hand against her lips. "It's a complication and happens to a statistically insignificant portion of women. Well, it happened to me."

Even with the lopsided smile, she looked pretty with her bouncy blond hair, Denise thought.

"But I'm ready for an adventure," Liz went on. "It means more debt, but I don't care." She was a high school history teacher and had paid for the facelift with her credit card. "I'm going on a yoga retreat and to Mexico to study Spanish. I'll go during winter break and in the summer. I've always wanted to. When I was married, my husband never liked to travel. Now he lives in Serbia. Go figure."

"I'm going to Mexico with Liz," June said. She was still handsome and hardy. Her gray-blond hair was wound in a neat knot at the nape of her neck. "Grant hated to travel. But Mike is coming with us," she added. Mike was her new "friend."

"That's a way to deal with aggravation," Denise said.

"It's a way to be happy," said Pauline.

"I've got to talk to a lawyer again," Denise said, "hire one, and move ahead with a divorce. Neil told me he quit his job. I hate to be dependent on him, but I am, financially."

"I'll bet he hasn't quit. He wants to scare you," Brenda said. "You're not *dependent.* He has responsibilities. He doesn't want to fulfill them. Absolutely, get a lawyer. I have the best. But happy?" She sipped her cosmopolitan and enunciated each word, as if she were teaching a theater class. "At our age, happiness is: If you have your health and so do the people you love, your kids. If you have a way to support yourself. I used to worry about money, but I stopped. Do I want to live or be an accountant?"

They all laughed. Denise gazed at her friends. No one seemed humiliated or devastated by divorce.

"You can't dodge aggravation," Brenda went on. "My ex came over to talk with me last week. Bill was at my apartment. And my ex was jealous."

"That's the unexpected gift of being a widow," June said. "No ex. Just memories and grief."

"None of it is easy," Denise said.

"My news is: I'm doing a tummy tuck." Pauline patted her generous belly and sat straighter. "I have to do *something*—there's so much competition. I just did speed dating. It was jammed with women."

"I've only tried online," said Denise. "I've been lucky so far, but…"

"Oh, you're the novice," Brenda said. "You and June. And besides, you're still in limbo."

"You're lucky you haven't been single long, Denise," Liz said. "People think you're contagious and that you'll infect *their* marriage. There are plenty of bad marriages around." She sighed. "Thoreau was right. But there are times I feel unquietly desperate. I just bought a thong. My new friend likes that kind of thing. I met him through a matchmaker." She frowned. "If my students knew. Talk about fiscal responsibility. But don't judge me."

"You're no different than any of us. Fifty years old. We're still slaves to men," Pauline said. "As if we're in high school."

"No," said Brenda. "We enjoy men."

"I was involved with a married man once," Pauline said quietly. "I vowed I wouldn't be. I loved him but it ruined me. It was like being abandoned again and again."

"We've all been there," Brenda said. "It's a shame how practical you have to be." She took a last gulp of her cosmopolitan.

"You're looking well," Liz said to Denise. "How's your new friend, Nicholas?"

Denise felt herself blush. "Nathaniel," she corrected. "Good. I'm seeing him this weekend."

"The antidote to rejection is a lover," Brenda laughed.

"Or a vacation," Pauline agreed. "Maybe they're the same."

All around New York City, Denise saw what seemed like stable marriages, as if two countries existed side by side. More like a million countries, she thought; but she focused on two: people who seemed content with stability and those who faced ever-changing liaisons. She stared at the women who wore shiny wedding rings, who linked arms with a man as they traversed the city. She envied what she presumed was uncomplicated happiness.

She glanced in a window at her reflection as she made her way to work after lunch. The sun's bright glare emphasized the wrinkles on her face. She would never try Botox or a makeover like her friends had. Her head was spinning with their conversation, as if they warned her of what was to come. June's new paramour, a man in his late sixties, had separated from his wife twenty years ago. Never divorced. The wife had dementia; he moved her into assisted living. "He's not a marriageable prospect. I've had the love of my life with Grant," June had told Denise and the others. "What I want is companionship. Fun."

Married, separated, divorced, never married, widowed—ways to categorize the indefinable permutations of fate and the heart. But companionship was at the core of life. Denise would tell her children this. What you need is a companion of the soul. Her grandmother had spoken of this when Denise's grandfather died. "I lost a companion of the soul. That's what you hope for in this life, my Denisenik. But such a companion doesn't last forever. Nothing does. So you have to be strong as stone."

Her parents' divorce when Denise was nine had been the great ache and shame of Denise's youth. Had her parents' troubles shaped her so she was predisposed to love Neil, a man who wavered, who could not commit his heart? Neil's parents had divorced and each had remarried twice. Who knew the right history and formula to protect you from grief?

At home that night, Denise found a message on the answering machine. "Hi, Neil. It's Cindy. I gather it's late. I'm returning your call. Call me back at your convenience. That would be great. Can't wait to talk. Take care. Bye now."

She sank into a chair and checked the caller ID. Cynthia Finnerman. Denise didn't know the woman. She wasn't one of the colleagues with whom Neil had had an affair. Denise could hardly breathe. Someone new? She played the message again. "Take care. Bye now," said the voice in a breathy, hesitant lilt. Disgusted with herself, Denise sat at the computer, Googled the woman and found a photograph of her flanked by three other women on a Walk for the Cure charity website. The woman was tall and reed-thin, with long, straight dark hair, and she wore a colorful clinging dress, what looked like a Pucci design. She reeked of the worst of singledom: work on her face, sessions with trainers and love coaches, ready to pounce on the competition.

Denise hated the woman and she hated Neil. All she could think about were her childhood bouts of anger. She'd hurled herself on the floor and hit her head against it. "Tantrums," her mother said. "Stop those tantrums."

"Listen to me, listen to me," Denise cried then, as if she were no longer Denise, but a thing made of skin and bones and anger. Her parents began arguing and didn't stop to hear her. Listen to me, she wanted to shout to Neil. What are you doing to our life? Why is this woman calling here?

Denise raced wildly around the apartment, grabbing his books and clothing, the work papers he'd left behind. She hurled them into garbage bags. This kind of stress was not good. Her heart thumped. Sweat pooled on her forehead. The stress of letting go. Not just of Neil, but of their life together, the comfort, the web of hopes. People her age got cancer and had heart attacks, broke bones and even died because of stress. Stress could kill. Separation could kill. Matters of the heart. Love gone sour could do you in.

She hauled the bags to the garbage chute and crammed them in. She left a phone message for him, screaming, "I've thrown out the crap you left in the apartment. And Cindy Finnerman called you here."

She and Nathaniel were on their way to an opening on Twenty-Second Street in Chelsea. The photographer—a brother of one of Nathaniel's childhood friends—had a thing for church spires, luminous steeples pitched against vacant night skies. It was a mild evening, the kind Denise loved, before the chill of fall set in. A make-believe night with perfect weather. An evening to feel alive.

She held Nathaniel's hand. His presence calmed her and helped dissolve her anger. Nathaniel was a journalist, with chestnut-brown eyes, a receding hairline, and a handsome, full smile. He was an inch shorter than she was, and although she had been self-conscious about her height when younger, his height didn't bother her now. He'd been widowed once and once divorced. "I wanted to try everything," he joked.

When they turned onto Twenty-Second Street, she blinked. She couldn't believe what she saw. Young, trim, beautiful men and women in stylish clothing crammed the sidewalk. A woman with bright-orange hair, the color of a pumpkin, strolled past. Two men, handsome as models, with sculpted beards and blue eyes, cigarettes dangling from their hands, spoke animatedly in accents. French or Italian, Denise thought.

"This is like a movie," she said.

"New York is a twenty-four-hour movie," Nathaniel said. "They have a bunch of these openings on Thursdays. Everyone preening, like birds trying to attract a mate." He gestured to a slim woman with curly red hair who was wearing a tight black dress with a scooped neck. Her shapely legs wobbled as she walked in shoes with heels at least four inches high.

"But what does it matter?" he said. "You fix yourself up, do yoga, make yourself over. We're all broken in the end and we all die. Maybe we should live for pleasure."

"Maybe we should." She inched closer to him. He was a real human being, she thought, without pretentions. He said what he meant, and she could believe him.

She didn't tell him about her latest encounter with Neil. She wanted to leave the aggravation behind. Neil had left four phone messages in response to hers; she hadn't called back. Last night she had blocked his e-mails. Total elimination, like Brenda suggested. The woman who telephoned, Cynthia Finnerman, whoever she was, had done Denise a favor, had squashed any remnant of love Denise still felt for Neil.

In his messages, Neil said he needed to talk to Denise. "Talk" seemed an odd word to use, implying an exchange, a dialogue. He seemed to want to *tell* her what was on his mind, not listen.

Nathaniel had recently gone out of town on a magazine assignment. She missed him more than she'd expected to. In one of their many phone conversations, they laughingly stumbled into phone sex. She had never done this but was determined to try something new. "Talk" was what they named these faceless, breathless, titillating encounters. *It was nice to talk.* That kind of talk was finished forever with Neil.

In the gallery they wandered, admiring the photographs, some like science fiction landscapes and others like the dark, sloping craters of the moon. Denise hoped one day her photographs and cyanotypes would be good enough for display. But time was passing, passing, ephemeral as a kiss.

On the way back afterward, Nathaniel stopped in front of a red brick building. "I haven't seen this place for years," he said. "When I was young, I used to write poetry. I took classes in an apartment here. It was cheaper than a psychiatrist," he said and laughed.

"Do you still have the poems?"

"Those notebooks are buried in bookshelves someplace at home. Filled with half-finished hopes. It was a time in my life, that's all. You can't create things again."

At Denise's apartment they tumbled into bed. With Nathaniel she felt pure need. Skin next to skin. His lips on hers. His hand roaming the soft hair between her legs. Her hands on him. It was never just sex, she thought. Oh, with a casual encounter, yes. But something more existed with him, something real—she was sure of it, whether or not the relationship led somewhere. Nathaniel tasted of coffee and sweet mint. She could live for pleasure.

Afterward they lay in each other's arms.

"I've been thinking. I don't want to be in your life on the rebound," he said. "Your transitional object."

"You're not."

"Don't do anything because of me. Of course, I'd like you to be completely free, divorced, not partially married. But you should see a lawyer because you have to."

"And what I do is separate from..."

"Us. There is an 'us' now, you know," he said.

"Yes." She held his hand and smiled into the darkness. It was all discovery with him.

"And I know none of this is easy," he said.

She sighed. Nathaniel had once told her to drop the Jewish-mother shit. To stop pretending everything was all right. Stop censoring what she said, stop believing in uncomplicated happiness. "You're right," she said. "Really, it's tough. But with you, I'm more than all right, I'm—"

The telephone interrupted. The answering machine in the kitchen switched on. Neil's voice reached the bedroom. "Dennie. I need to talk to you. Please pick up. Dennie, are you there? I've been calling you. I've made a huge mistake. The biggest mistake of my life. I want to come home. I've decided. Call me. We're a family. We belong together. Please. I'm..."

Hearing the click as he hung up, Denise shuddered and squeezed her eyes shut. Her knees weakened.

"You can't control these things," Nathaniel said quietly. "Do what you need to."

What would she have done in her grandmother's era? Was there really such a thing as a companion of the soul? Denise laid her head on Nathaniel's shoulder, eased her body into his. Had she become like Brenda and Liz and the others? Is that what happened at the end of a marriage? Did even hatred fall away until all that was left was a void, an ache, an absence, in the place where love had been? She didn't know.

She didn't care. She brought Nathaniel's hand to her lips and kissed his fingers one by one. Then she reached across him to the night table, lifted the receiver from the cradle. A simple, uncomplicated gesture. She set it on the table and waited until the beep of the dial tone finally stopped.

Foreign Lands

This is a story I have wanted to tell. When the events occurred, I was traveling. I never traveled when the children were young. Now I have no roots, not the kind I had years ago, that bind you to people or a place. My husband allows me to come and go as I please. He's busy with his work, just as I am with mine. He owns a jewelry store in Queens, though in his heart he's an historian, loves the history of a particular precious stone and stories of the past. On weekends he sits bent at the dining room table in our apartment, writing his treatise on gems in the Middle Ages. I work for the United Nations, in a minor but responsible position, preparing reports on climate and world hunger. On occasion, my job involves visits to foreign lands.

When the opportunity to travel to Poland came up, though, I hesitated. At work, most everyone covets junkets to Paris and London. Eastern Europe has a reputation for being colorless, claustrophobic. Once, my husband joined me on a visit to Rome. It was like a second honeymoon for us, and I often think of that week with surprising longing. Although I've learned to navigate the world on my own, I had hesitations about how I'd fare in Poland.

Of course, the association with the war and Nazis was in my thoughts. I wondered, perhaps irrationally, if I might be snatched into a cauldron of anti-Semitism, might even disappear. I didn't tell my husband. He would have dismissed my fears as ludicrous. But I remembered stories I'd heard about foreigners who had been murdered in Guatemala, South America, Serbia, the Middle East. Accidents of fate that in retrospect seemed like destiny.

I accepted the assignment, though. The trip began in Krakow, a city that had the feel of a village, with winding cobbled streets and old stone churches. Like the place my ancestors might have lived or the town in Austria where I was born and that I left when I was a girl. Or the village in Germany where my husband's parents had grown up. I didn't mind the lack of sunshine, the April dampness, or the gray that hung like soiled sheets across the sky. My business took much of my time. I might have felt perfectly content had I not always been aware of the presence of Auschwitz kilometers away.

At the last minute, I rode a bus with other tourists and visited the concentration camp. How could I be so close to this place that had changed the history of Jews, of the world, and not visit? I wandered around the grounds and entered a state of numbness as I saw with my own eyes the site where so much cruelty had occurred. The camp was a plain expanse of land, like any other, and this fact chilled me.

The next morning, early, I boarded a train traveling north, relieved to leave behind the camp's images of death, hopeful that Warsaw, where I had more business, would provide an antidote. On the train, though, the spirits of the dead seemed to be with me, and as the cars sped along the tracks, I imagined the pool of ashes and crumbling crematorium, as if they were beckoning me, too. I tried to study surveys and reports, but felt so far from home, from my husband and children, anything familiar, that I wondered in panic if I would ever return.

I am not a person who dwells on the past or easily gives in to whims of imagination. I was able to calm myself on the journey. What's past is gone and done, I told myself. Though I suddenly wished my husband had joined me here. Then I remembered other travels we had shared, his impatience to see as much as possible. He would dart across a street in the middle of traffic, yell to me, "Hurry, Julia. Can't you hurry for once?" I would run, dodging cars, trying to keep up with him. It wasn't until I began to travel alone that I wondered why he always rushed, why he didn't have time to cross with the lights or have a moment for simple human consideration.

I expected Warsaw to be bustling and vibrant, like the city I had heard about in my youth. Now it was filled with cars and crowds, the foul smell of automobile exhaust. It had none of the glamour of London or Paris.

The guidebook had raved about the charm of my hotel, but the Elektra was a small establishment with a faded elegance. The lobby was furnished with dusty green brocade armchairs and lit by a dim chandelier. Breakfast was served in a tiny room. Starched white tablecloths covered the few round tables. Each morning, the room was empty. No other people, no laughter, no voices. Only the scent of strong coffee and the distant rumble of traffic. I sat by myself in my beige wool business suit, my nylon stockings and heels, pearl earrings, preparing documents, working on the day's schedule. There were no slim, chic women here sparkling with jewelry, or handsome men in suits, the smell of their aftershave wafting through the air. Sitting alone, I realized I felt neither feminine nor masculine, but rootless, genderless. I thought of the years when our children had lived with us, when my life felt as if it had a higher purpose. Sunlit mornings in the kitchen, the meals I cooked, smells of onions, garlic, and chicken, the soft faces of the children, the touch of my husband's hand.

In recent years, my husband has said I am domineering, but sometimes I have talked just to catch his attention. I considered this as I ate breakfast at the Elektra. What did I want from him? I wondered. I wanted him to respond to my words. No. I wanted to just *hear* him, hear what was inside of him. That was all. My husband is a product of the war. Perhaps "product" is the wrong term. He would be taken aback if he knew I described him in such a functional way. His family fled from Germany and his thinking is often so shaded by the shadow of those years that he sometimes seems like a stone with an imperfection. When the children were young, if they wanted new shoes, he insisted that they *need* them and purchase nothing superfluous. If an appliance was broken, or a table worn out, he demanded an accounting, to be certain this was a matter of *need*, not of desire. I had always thought ours was an "old" marriage from another generation, when marriages lasted forever, without shame or excuses.

Each morning during breakfast at the Elektra, I thought about him and then my mind returned to my visit to Auschwitz. In my own way, I am religious, but my reverence has been in nature and people, not in a God. I'm most comfortable with facts and figures, but there on the plains of the concentration camp, I had felt the dead everywhere, and was moved. A restless spirit seemed to wander in spaces between the barracks, sit on cold cement floors, rest on hard wooden slats of beds. I went to the camp searching, as one might go to a cemetery to find communion with an invisible presence. My husband would say, "Nonsense. When you're alive, you're alive; when you're dead, Julia, that's the end." But I have always imagined that one might find some elusive *thing* at a gravestone, and feel a great centering. I might feel at one then. With whom? I wondered as I sat in the Elektra. With my mother, I thought, my grandmother, my sister who had died as a baby during the war.

I notice almost everything, both a blessing and a curse. I noticed the woman behind the Elektra's front desk immediately. She seemed older than I, and she was the one note of life in the drab hotel. She had a high, round bosom and wide waistline, but she had the manner of a girl, a girl with melancholy eyes. She was dressed like one, too, in a soft gray sweater and black pleated skirt. As I looked at her, I realized the bleakness of Poland had intruded on my mood. I imagined my husband again, bent over his tools with a loupe or magnifying glass pressed against his eyes or looking through a magnifying machine, working on watches, settings, diamonds. Paying attention to tiny details, as if he were seeing the world from a distance, through the thick, distorted lens of glass.

I was in this mood when I went to the desk to inquire about an English newspaper. The woman flashed me a smile and ran her fingers through her limp blonde hair colored by dye. I stared at her white teeth and the lines that lay like crinkled cloth in the corners of her blue eyes, at the sides of her mouth. I suddenly felt my age, my station in life—mother of grown children, grandmother, career woman traveling alone, married to a man who is a perfectionist about settings, jewels, life itself. I felt colorless next to this woman.

She spoke in a thick accent and gave me directions to where to purchase the newspaper. Then she said, "You are Jewish, yes?"

I looked into her light-blue eyes, surprised she would ask, especially here in Poland. But I replied simply, "Yes, I am."

Her expression relaxed. "You don't find many Jews here," she said. She thrust out a callused hand to shake mine. "I'm Katia. Oh, you see visitors, but always this trip or that trip and the children come for a look, gathered around a guide like scared sheep." She leaned toward me. I smelled rose perfume. "They want to see where people lived and died. I'm a Jew, too." She sighed, as if this was a great burden. "It's been a long time since I've had a visitor. Would you like to come to my home for tea?"

We arranged a visit for the next evening. Perhaps I was lonely. I thought of my mother, ill, in a nursing home now. In her middle years, she had been a member of the *chevra kadisha*, the society to dress the dead. She said the last act of kindness one can perform for another is to set dirt on a grave. An anonymous act. Perhaps this was an act of kindness to visit this woman who might have no friends, no living relations. I thought of myself. Where were my friends, my relations? Still, I felt unaccountably drawn to this woman, the way I'd once been drawn to a palm reader on the streets of New York, a man who claimed he could see the future in hands.

I met Katia in the lobby of a building on Marszałkowska Street, a wide, proud boulevard lined with trees and tall buildings. Hers was a weathered structure, the light brick a dirty brown in need of cleaning. We walked through the dank lobby up three flights of stairs. On the landing stood steel bars, as if the doors on the other side were encased in a large cell. Katia must have had twenty keys on a metal ring, and she opened the barred steel door as if she were a prison guard. Then at her apartment, she unlocked the six deadbolts that secured her door, pushed open the door, and disarmed a burglar alarm. She laughed nervously, glancing over her shoulder as if she expected someone else to appear. "Russian Mafia," she whispered. "You must lock everything up or else all that is precious will disappear."

In her dining room, I felt oddly at home, as if I had re-entered the era of my childhood, when I lived in the small Austrian town. The room had the same musty smell, in desperate need of fresh air, that my grandparents' apartment did. They used to sit at a long wooden table much like this, where Katia and I sat, with lace doilies and white china teacups. Crystal figurines of dancers and a silver menorah sat on their breakfront mantel. How I had wished then that I would grow up to wear fine silk dresses and sweet jasmine perfume, live with a husband whom I would adore, in the very same apartment with china and lace, be the lady of the house, like my grandmother.

Katia and I sat opposite one another. I set my black wool coat on the chair beside me as she poured steaming tea from a china teapot into my cup and hers. After we'd engaged in small talk, Katia said, as if to explain why she had invited me, "I would like to tell you a story. It is always good to hear one in foreign lands, don't you think?"

I needed to work on a report for the next morning and make this visit brief. But I nodded, curious.

"Good," she said, as if we had been bartering and had finally settled on a price. "This is the way it happened. In 1923, a young woman, Jewish, and her family went to a performance at the Stadt Opera in Wein. Vienna. Do you know it?"

"I was born in a town nearby," I said, though I am usually careful not to talk about my past. I took a sip of tea and felt myself beginning to relax, as if my mother were about to tell a bedtime tale as she used to long ago.

"Then you will understand," Katia said. "The young woman and her family were citizens of Czechoslovakia. Perhaps it was by chance that Fräulein Brick met Herr Veroberger, an Austrian man. Is not all of life chance?" She leaned closer to me. "Don't you agree?"

"I suppose," I said, and thought of sitting with this woman now by chance, and of how I'd met my husband. By chance, too. In Chicago, on the streetcar. I'd told myself then that meeting him was an accident of fate, an act of divine providence.

"They kept in touch, visited one another, and the next year they were married," Katia said. "They lived in Graz, then were joyful at the birth of a little girl. Lily."

I watched the woman as she spoke. Her chest seemed to heave in satisfaction at telling a tale. I was distracted by my thoughts. Lily. That had been my younger sister's name. She was hidden by peasants during the war. We never learned what became of her, but my mother felt certain she had died. I was a child then. This was my mother's greatest sorrow. She used to drink vodka in the morning, before dinner and bed. "Then the world looks happy," she would say to me and smile. "Everything is as it should be."

"But the young mother of the infant Lily died," Katia said. "Infection. The father remarried, a daughter of Catholics, and the next year their daughter Celia was born. The girls were raised as sisters. In four years, the father was dead as well. Such is life."

I sipped my tea and thought of the twists of life that force you to act in ways you can't anticipate.

"The mother," Katia went on, "Mutte as she was called, wanted to raise Lily, but the family forbade her to raise a Jewish child. Lily went to live with an uncle and aunt in Vienna." The light in Katia's eyes that had been so striking in the hotel was gone. I glanced at the dusty crystal chandelier, at the dining room walls, bare except for a cheap etching of a cathedral and an old black-and-white snapshot of a man and woman, from decades ago. This is a home without joy, I thought.

"Vienna was nothing like the child hoped," Katia said, and waved a hand. Her fingers were slender, her wrists delicate, one encircled by a small bracelet with a charm of a gold heart. "The aunt and uncle spent days and nights at the jewelry shop they owned. They sent the girl to live with another family, outside the city. Every week, they visited. But the visits became less frequent. In the early years, Mutte sent cards, a charm of a heart for a bracelet. Lily would write, thank her, and write to her aunt and uncle, begging them to visit. They didn't. She wrote again and again. How many times can one ask? Eventually one loses hope."

I nodded to encourage Katia to continue, though I wanted to tell her that a child's perceptions are full of expectation; often even an adult continues to have hope. I thought of the hope I had had even during the war, for a better life, the hope I have always had that my husband and I would find time for each other.

Katia left no room for a response. "One day, Lily was called from the classroom," she said. "Her uncle and aunt were there. 'You bother us,' they said. 'Do not write or call. We will see you when we can.' The girl cried bitterly. She ran away from home, was sent to still another family, then to a home for Jewish orphans."

Katia stared at her teacup. She looked frail, with her thin arms, her gray sweater with its sleeves that hung listlessly above her wrists. Orphans. I felt surrounded by the invisible presence of my past now, too. I remembered myself as a girl, when my breasts began to bud and soft dark hair grew in secret places. I used to imagine myself as a woman then. I would be nothing like my mother, wouldn't drink vodka or dwell on the past or rebuff my husband. I would be happy in the arms of a man. I recalled, too, now, a girl, older than me, who had stayed with a family for a season, then was sent to an orphanage. I remembered how she had walked close to a boy, whispering as if they shared a secret language. Would I know a secret language someday, too? The family she lived with dealt in diamonds. Could this be the very same girl Katia had described? As she talked, I imagined my husband again, bent over his stones, perhaps like the aunt and uncle, with no time for anything but their store.

"When the Nazis came, the world changed," Katia said. Her expression tightened, and the light in her eyes flickered, then was gone again. Her expression had a heaviness I felt in myself now.

"The orphanage where Lily lived burned to the ground." She looked beyond me, as if staring at the ruined building. "Lily was put on a transport to Palestine. She married; the marriage floundered. Years later, she found herself in Munich, near Graz. Always, she had thought about Mutte and Celia. Were they alive? But in the strange way prisoners love their bars, she was afraid to inquire." Katia rose abruptly and said, "Lily stood on the platform to catch a train to Graz. In the last minute, she did not go."

The woman flashed her smile, and went into the kitchen. She seemed to float from the room. The chandelier cast a faint light. I sat thinking of Auschwitz and of the fate I had been spared, then of my childhood in America. The second part of childhood. The cramped apartment, and my parents who spoke in accents of deep sorrows. I had believed they were peasants from a foreign land and had been ashamed of them. Now in their old age, I was taking care of them. I visited them in the nursing home, arranged for doctors and medicine, but with regret for my youthful arrogance. There was nothing I could do to right that wrong.

I remembered now, too, something I knew by heart, but did not allow myself to think of often. I felt my face grow hot and my heart pound. I had been in love with a young man my parents disapproved of. His family was not religious. He was a socialist, brash, and I adored both his nature and his views. My parents forbid me to see him. In a moment of weakness, I consented. I have always wondered what became of him. It is as if the earth swallowed him up. When I was forty, my mother gave me letters he had written to me fifteen and twenty years earlier, telling me he would wait for me, no matter what. By then, I didn't know how to find him. More than twenty years have passed since that time. I keep the letters wrapped in an old towel in the bottom of a drawer, and even now, the few times I have allowed myself to look at them, I feel longing in my heart. Occasionally, at the theater near where I live, I see a woman who resembles his sister. Thinking of Katia's words, I wondered if it was too late to find him. If he was even alive. I wondered if *I* was a person who loved her bars. Bars of loneliness, of duty. Perhaps I had created them myself. A chill crept through my body, and I struggled to dismiss my thoughts as if they were a swarm of pesky flies buzzing in my ear.

Katia returned with hot tea and thin wafer cookies that had the fresh almond aroma of home-baked sweets. "Please eat," she said, then launched again into her tale. I was content to listen, and she seemed to want no other connection than this.

"Lily survived on the sheer force of her will," Katia said. "She found a second husband. They settled in Vienna. No one was left of those she knew before the war. But the husband had friends, and Lily asked one if it was possible to find someone in Graz. Why she changed, I cannot say. 'What is the name?' the man asked.

"'Veroberger.' The friend found a telephone number. In the evening, Lily telephoned. A woman answered. 'Is anyone here named Veroberger?' Lily asked. The woman replied, 'Yes.' Lily whispered, 'May I speak to Frau Veroberger?'

"'She is not here now,' the woman said. Lily could have hung up, but she replied, 'It is private.'

"'I am her daughter,' the woman said." Here Katia paused again, as if reimagining what had happened next. "Lily found her courage, and asked, 'Celia?' The woman said, 'Yes, who are you?' For a moment, Lily could not find her voice. Finally she told the woman.

"'You are still alive,' Celia gasped. 'We thought you had died.'

"'And Mutte?'

"'Do not call her; the shock will be too great.' An hour later,"

Katia said, "the telephone rang. Lily heard an old voice, 'My child, you are home now. I have two girls.'

"Mutte had saved a piece of crystal, a wedding present given to Lily's mother and father. After Lily's father died, Mutte kept the piece of crystal. She wanted to give it to Lily when the girl grew up and married. But Mutte did not have the opportunity to raise the child. Even so, she saved the crystal vase." Katia pointed to a tall vase on the breakfront. "Of course, this story is mine," she said. "In Poland I use my middle name. Those were my happiest days. I moved here with my husband. He died, and here I sit with my memories." She placed her hands on the table, tapped her fingers against one another as if they were knitting needles. Then her face took on the aura of a girl's again, as if this unburdening had made her feel lighter. "For my soul's sake I needed to find them and remember." She rose, signaling that our time together had come to an end, and she pressed her slim fingers on mine. "I have seen with my own eyes more than enough for a lifetime. I can see in your eyes that you have seen the same. Perhaps you will stay here, too, and find that a foreign land can be like home as well."

"That isn't possible anymore. Too much of my life is over." I slipped on my black wool coat.

On the landing, she unlocked the steel gate and escorted me down the stairs. Then she handed me a miniature crystal figurine of a young girl, the size of the palm of my hand. "Our lives are filled with stories," she said, "without pattern or repetition. Don't you think?" She stepped toward me and kissed each of my cheeks.

The night was windier than when I had arrived at Katia's apartment, and I clutched the crystal figurine, careful not to break the delicate arms that seemed to stretch toward the sky with joy. I could still smell the scent of Katia's perfume.

Perhaps she had done me a kindness, I thought, and I felt an odd, great centering now, as if I was at one. With whom? Perhaps myself. With my memories. The cold air pinched my skin, and I suddenly understood the world as it was: a vast cauldron that sucked in people and souls. I envisioned with piercing sorrow ghettos, people living and dying, losing track of one another's lives.

A light snow started to fall, as if a God exhaled these tiny, pure flakes. The snowflakes looked like diamonds as they spun beneath the streetlights, and I thought of my husband. I looked at the wide, proud boulevard that glistened in the snow. That's how I had wanted my life to be, wide and proud, glittering, seemingly without end. I wondered if this independence I'd so carefully crafted was a facade. For what? *Profound loneliness*. Just as Katia's smile was her facade.

I had always believed my work sustained me, but now I felt a hollowness inside, as if the work hadn't fed me at all. I had always believed I had fashioned my own happiness. Did I even know what happiness was? Perhaps I had locked myself away.

As the wind pushed into me, I realized living with my husband was like living in a foreign land, one I'd never become accustomed to. My husband is a decent man. Perhaps I have been at fault for having so many expectations. For not following my heart long ago. Or perhaps all of life is like light. A string of moments when a certain light gives the stone of your life extraordinary color or sheen. When I was a girl, my life was blue-white, like a diamond, like Katia's life had once been. "There is no blue-white," my husband has said. "A trick of the imagination."

I walked against the wind and searched for a taxi, but none were in sight. Katia's building disappeared behind me. I imagined my husband bent over his stones. He has spent a lifetime certifying diamonds. "You can tell the highest grade," he has told me, "when a stone is the purest white." He used to spend weeks appraising jewels and made his judgments then based on the image he saw with his eyes. Now he uses a different procedure. "Sometimes you need machines," he has said. "The human eye isn't enough."

I have often deferred to his opinion. But with that I disagree. When I return home, I will tell him so, tell him he is wrong. He has taught me about stones. I know a setting can change its color in light. I know our marriage has survived on the sheer force of my will, that for my whole life I have doubted myself, and the time has come to stop. I know that as I gazed onto the fields of Auschwitz, I realized that I'd always been terrified of dying. But walking into the damp, glistening snow, away from the light of Katia's apartment, I understood I had been afraid to live as well.

I vowed to tell my husband this when I returned home. I didn't care what his answer would be. I knew at that moment on Marszałkowska Street that he would not change. As I hurried toward my hotel, I felt a sudden surge of vitality. The energy of a girl. I wanted him to take me in his arms; I wanted to feel the warmth of his touch. But even if he didn't hold me, I would tell him: I see what I see, and I know what I know. The human eye is always more than enough.

Relocation

Ellen's Volvo sedan smells like a classroom on the first day of school. Scents of cardboard boxes and pens—fine points, Sharpie markers—swirl from the back seat. She is used to these smells, comforted by them. Each time she inhales the scents, she feels optimistic and imagines new beginnings and the pleasure of creating order out of chaos.

A relocation expert, she makes house calls, ministering to both the house and its occupants. She loves going from place to place. She comes armed with box cutters, labels, tape, and scissors. Her cell phone is a Rolodex of resources: Salvation Army, Goodwill, moving companies like Graebell and Golan's, and miscellaneous providers—appraisers, stores that buy pianos or jewelry, people who refurbish wood, and laborers who do hauling or shredding.

She's aware of the irony. Her own world is changing; she's getting divorced. She helps people relocate and cope with change, yet she hasn't been able to do this herself.

The divorce was Todd's idea. The process is proceeding in the usual way, she supposes, with lawyers, aggravation, and bitterness.

Six months ago, in May, they were going to go for a walk after dinner. They lived in an apartment near Lincoln Park, with a view of the lake, where Ellen still lives. It was the kind of evening she loves, warmth in the air, a new growth of leaves dangling from trees. Spring, delayed as it often is in Chicago, had finally arrived.

Just as they left the apartment, Todd stopped and looked at her evenly. "I'd rather talk here." He walked back into the apartment, and she followed. He shut the door. "I want you to know something," he said, standing in the living room. "I've had a secret life."

"What?" She was thinking of their two daughters, one in college and the other in graduate school. "What are you talking about?"

"I've had a girlfriend for years."

Ellen felt weak. *Had,* she thought. Was he telling her about part of his past? "I don't understand." To her surprise, tears filled her eyes. "What are you saying? Are you upset about something?"

"I want you to understand," he said. "I want you to understand why I want a divorce."

She knew something had been wrong, but she didn't know what. She had been worried about him and had tried to talk to him about this. He had been distant the last few years, and he'd started drinking too much, lots of wine with dinner and more before bed. "All this time, you've been lying to me?" She stared at him with shock and disgust. "You wouldn't talk about what was bothering you. I asked you so many times. Who is she?"

"It doesn't matter who. I want things to be open between us. No more secrets. I'm sorry."

"Of course it matters. You're sorry? That's a lie. The biggest lie of all. Get out."

This morning before work, Ellen sits at her desk in the living room. She lives by lists. She compiles lists of what needs to be accomplished for clients, and creates lists for clients of what they need to complete. She believes if she writes down tasks, she'll gain control over them and clear the clutter from her mind.

She writes a list for work now, and then one for herself:

What I miss about being married:
The sex
Companionship
Having a common vision for the future
Someone with whom to share my life
What my life used to be like! Or what I thought it was like.

She reads this, satisfied, and sets the paper in the desk drawer.

Out of sight, out of mind. That's how she feels about Todd. How she's trying to feel about him. Still, she misses him when she thinks of the good years they shared, and the years she imagined they would have in the future. She is still struggling to come to terms with what's happened to her marriage.

She boots up the computer and reads her horoscope. Capricorn. The goat. The plodder. She is cheered by the words: "Let loose. What better time than now?"

Yes. That's the advice she needs. That's what she wants to do—put the divorce behind her and embrace life. She grabs her purse and dashes out to her car.

What she loves about her work is this: She can forget her own life and dive into other people's worlds.

She is meeting her new client in Skokie. It's a mild November day. Skokie isn't a glamorous suburb with substantial homes like Winnetka or Highland Park. She's worked in those neighborhoods and also in Lake Forest, far north of the city, a village populated by sprawling fenced mansions. Skokie has a different feeling. Everything is small, the streets and houses. Years ago a controversy had erupted—Neo-Nazis demanded to parade with songs and swastikas. There was an uproar in the largely Jewish community, but the Neo-Nazis were allowed to march.

Ellen is Jewish, though not observant as her parents were. She grew up in Evanston, not far from here. Her destination today is on Crawford Avenue, a main artery.

A "For Sale" sign sits on the front lawn. The small beige brick house stands on a modest plot of land, near the railroad tracks.

The woman who opens the door thrusts her hand forward to shake Ellen's hand. "Glad you could make it. I'm Charlene James."

She is tall, leggy, and middle-aged, with dyed black hair. She has a slender, pretty face, a teenager's figure. She must work out with a vengeance, Ellen thinks.

The woman ushers Ellen into the kitchen. A man stands up.

"This is my brother, Gregory," Charlene says.

"Greg," he corrects.

Ellen sits across from them at the table. She can't tell who is older. They both seem to be in the vicinity of her age, early fifties. Greg has thinning brown hair. He has a round, boyish face, a pleasing one, with a scattering of freckles and eyes so blue she wonders if he wears contact lenses to amplify the color.

She hands Charlene a yellow folder stamped with the words "Ellen's Relocation Service." She wishes she'd brought two. "I can do almost anything for a move. Plan the move, sort, deal with donations, or sell furniture. The information is in the folder. I can be as involved as you want or help with occasional tasks."

"That sounds greaaaat," Charlene says, stringing out the word so it sounds twice as long. "I live in LA. You'll work mostly with Greg. He's local. This is our parents' house. Daddy is in a senior community near me now. And our mother…" She stops, then whispers, "She died five months ago. A stroke." The woman eyes her brother. "Will you have the time, Greg?"

"I told you, I'll make time," he says. "This has to be done. You'll come back as soon as you can, Char. If I clean out the house, I don't want complaints. No *kvetching* after the fact about what I do or don't throw out."

"This isn't about *you*, Greg. We have to decide together what to do with Mom's stuff."

"And it's not about *you* either."

Ellen looks from one to the other as if she's stumbled into a domestic argument.

"We have our disagreements," Charlene says to Ellen, then turns to her brother. "Look, Greg, sweetie, if you have a question, call. I'll answer right away. The relocation lady will help."

"She's in publicity and marketing," Greg says to Ellen. "She doesn't waste time."

"I don't want to waste your time now," Ellen says. "Why don't you show me around? Then you can decide the kind of help you need."

She follows them, carrying a pad of yellow lined paper on which she jots a description of the rooms, estimating the time she will need to sort items.

There is a striking absence of clutter. No photographs sit in the living room, no *tchotchkes* on the coffee table. A tall wooden curio cabinet stands empty. The kitchen counters, yellow Formica from another era, are cleared of possessions. Not even a toaster or microwave graces the countertop. Only a silver menorah sits on the kitchen table.

The house is a bi-level, three bedrooms on the second floor, similar in size to the house in which Ellen grew up. Upstairs, Charlene pulls open a closet door. The closet is crammed with clothing encased in plastic bags. Ellen's mother kept clothing in the same way. Boxes are haphazardly piled on the shelves and the floor. Paper bags are squeezed in.

"So that's where everything is," Ellen says.

"She liked the common areas neat," Greg explains.

"Mom was very attached to this house," Charlene says. "Now we're getting rid of it all. I know we have to. We've sold it. The closing is in seven weeks. But she's going to be blotted out—everything she collected and everything she built, our father built." There is an edge of stridency in the woman's voice.

"You're lucky you sold the house," Ellen says soothingly. "But you're not getting rid of your memories. You'll keep what's important here and discard the rest."

"Keep whatever you want," Greg says to Charlene.

"I wish I could help," Charlene replies. "You know that, Greg. My work is very inflexible. The company is laying people off left and right."

"I've got a tight schedule, too," Ellen says. "Let's finish looking at the house."

She continues on her rounds, opening drawers. They are filled with tangled support hose and women's cotton underwear, scarves, and colorful T-shirts. Tops of red plastic medicine bottles peek through the clothing.

After work, Ellen sits at her desk to call her lawyer. The tension between Charlene and Greg reminds her of when she and her sister sorted through their parents' house. Two years ago, their mother had been rushed to the hospital after she fell. Miriam lived for only two terrible weeks after that. Ellen was shocked by her death, the sight of her mother so pale and silent in that garishly lit hospital room. She waited helplessly by the bedside, in case, by a trick of fate, her mother would revive. When the nurse left to give her a moment alone, Ellen whispered to Miriam: "I know you can't hear me, but I love you, I love you, I love you." She touched the cold, lifeless hand.

She and her sister moved their father into an assisted-living apartment and brought some of his possessions there. Ellen knows how to clear out a house efficiently, coldly even, but she was surprised by how emotions had ambushed her then. She and Sally found a rectangular white china bowl decorated with a delicate strawberry pattern.

"Oh, I love this," Sally said. "I want it. Remember how Mom used to serve strawberries in here?"

Ellen remembered. *Milkhik* dinners around the dining room table in the humid summer heat, her mother ebullient and smiling, serving strawberries and lavish heaps of whipped cream, the crown of the dinner. Their father, even-tempered for the moment. Idyllic slices of time, those moments in childhood.

Later, Ellen lifted her mother's brightly colored muumuu from a closet, surprised by the lump of sentiment in her throat. "She used to wear this to Ravinia. Every summer. She loved those concerts."

"I want the dish and the muumuu!" Sally said.

"That's not right," Ellen said. "We should each take one."

Sally finally relented and kept the strawberry dish. Ellen still has her mother's muumuu, encased in plastic, hanging in her own closet.

If only she could talk to her mother about how life has evolved, Todd gone, a divorce, the relocation business surprisingly thriving. Miriam often said about the unexpected, "It just goes to show, my darling. Life is so strange and uncertain. I suppose it's a good thing we can't foresee the future." Ellen wonders if the ache of missing her mother will ever completely disappear.

She sighs and reads an e-mail from the lawyer. Then she places the call.

Ellen thinks of Melvin Davis as a New York lawyer, although he lives in Chicago. He speaks fast and has an aggressive edge. He grew up in Brooklyn. But aren't all divorce lawyers New York lawyers?

"I'm glad you called," Melvin says quickly, as if aware every second costs Ellen money. "You need to get everything for the document request. Did you read the material I sent?"

"Yes. I could barely understand it."

"Don't be compulsive," the lawyer says. "Gather all the documents you can. Bank statements, credit card bills, etc. It's all there in the request in black and white. Make copies and bring them to my office. What you don't have, you don't need to find."

"Like what?"

"Let's say you don't have the January bank statement from a year ago. People lose things. It's no crime. Don't spend time tracking it down. If your husband's lawyers want the missing document, let them spend the time getting it."

The next week, Ellen begins her work with Greg. They split up tasks. Charlene hoped to be here to help, he says, but there was a crisis at work. Ellen is relieved; the woman would be a handful, emotional and defensive. Greg telephones his sister to tell her the plan for the day: the basement and kitchen. "The relocation woman says to do one room at a time," he explains.

Ellen wears black jeans and a long-sleeved gray T-shirt to withstand dirt and dust. She carries in cardboard boxes, markers, Bubble Wrap, packing tape, labels, scissors, and garbage bags. The scents from her car rise in the house, competing with the musty, close odor. She sets her coat on a chair, stations herself in the kitchen and sorts items, an easy, though grimy job, pulling pots and pans, half-filled boxes of Chanukah candles, trays and appliances from the cabinets. Some pots are bent and rusted; others have caked-on food. Most need to be discarded. There are just a few traces of Jewish life here, she thinks as she tosses the candles into the trash. She will never know much about Greg's parents; though she works in an intimate way in people's homes, she rarely learns the stories of their lives.

While she works in the kitchen, Greg does the "heavy lifting," he jokes, and hauls newspapers, tangled extension cords, and rusted cleaning supplies from the basement, near the old broken incinerator, to the trash cans outside.

Maybe this job will go quickly, she thinks, like the one she completed last month. The man's wife had died; he told Ellen to throw everything out. He seemed harsh to her, unsentimental, but she knows people cope with loss in different ways.

"This is going fast," Greg says when she goes downstairs to see if he needs help.

"It's the easy stuff," she says. "The junk you know has to go. No decisions. Here, let's take this out together." She points to a tall white metal cabinet, rusted and bent at the sides. "I'll bet a scrap metal guy will pick this up in no time."

"You think if we put this by the street, someone will take it?"

"Guaranteed."

They haul out the cabinet. He carries the bulk, out of solicitousness, politeness, she supposes. As they walk back to the house, Ellen hears the screeching of brakes and looks at the street. A white Ford pickup stops.

"Trash?" the driver, a gray-haired man, calls out.

"It's yours," she says.

Each night after work, she gathers materials for the document request. She makes a list of what she has accomplished and what still needs to be done. Papers sit everywhere on the floor where she does her organizing. She's sorting through another life and home, just as she does at work. This time, they belong to her.

She has always had so many desires. She tried to teach her children the difference between needing something and wanting it. She still struggles with the concept of wanting. Why couldn't she have what she wanted? She wanted to be an artist and a lawyer when she was young, but she dropped out of law school when she met Todd. In Wisconsin, where she and Todd used to live, she taught high school history for a while, and then did calligraphy for invitations, some graphic design, and taught calligraphy at a community art center. When they moved to Chicago eight years ago, the family needed a steadier income from her. Ellen started the relocation business, though Todd objected. He wanted her to have a regular job with a regular salary. Even when her roster of clients grew, he never had a word of encouragement for her.

The next time she works with Greg, two days later, Ellen is conscious of wanting to look more presentable than she did on her last visit. She chooses a new white T-shirt, a Petit Bateau with a V-neck, and a pressed pair of blue jeans. Instead of sneakers, she wears black flats, leaving the sneakers in a tote bag in case she needs to change.

She likes the rhythm of working in this house, likes the feeling of cleansing. She wants to cleanse her own life, and she is eager to finish gathering the documents and give them to the lawyer.

"We'll make five stations," she says to Greg. "One is for giveaways, one for items you want to keep, and another for Charlene. A fourth if you can't decide. And a fifth is for papers to shred. I'll keep a list of donations. That way, you can itemize them and get a tax write-off."

"Sounds like a plan." He's wearing jeans, too, and a long-sleeved pale blue polo shirt that mirrors the lovely blue of his eyes.

"Let's work in the basement first," she says.

Greg has cleared the incinerator area. They still must tackle the crawl space, his father's office, closets, and bookshelves. She eyes many loads for the Salvation Army here.

"I can see you can't get attached to anything." He pulls open a closet door. "We might as well give all this away."

"You should be in the relocation business," she says.

He laughs.

"Are you a Buddhist?" she asks, half-seriously. She arranges boxes for the five stations. "You sound like one."

"No. I'm an atheist. We go from dust to dust. There's nothing more, no afterlife. I believe in cremation. You go back to earth. The ultimate recycling."

Ellen nods, though she doesn't share his belief in cremation. That's not the Jewish way of dealing with the dead. She still believes in rituals like *shiva* and burial. She doesn't mention this. Instead, she peers in the closet, which is filled with dresses, men's coats, and garden tools. An odd triad of things, she thinks. She pulls out a long-sleeved purple chiffon dress. The fabric smells musty, with the hint of something sweet—perfume, perhaps his mother's scent.

"I almost forgot," Greg says. He hands Ellen a list of items he and Charlene will divide.

> Paintings, photographs, glassware (Charlene
> can have it all)

Clothing (hers, if she wants)
Silverware, Rosenthal China (I'd like)
Tablecloths
The rest (to be decided)

"You're prepared," Ellen says.

He eyes the pad of paper she carries like another limb. "You're pretty organized," he says.

"I have to be. That's the part of me that comes out at work." She thinks of the disorder at home: her desk, the floor, her life. "I really shouldn't tell you that. You're supposed to think I don't have another life."

"Do they teach you that at relocation school?" Greg jokes.

"They teach the secrets of the trade." She laughs and blushes, despite her effort not to.

"I'll bet it's a lot of psychology. You're in people's homes. It's an intimate space. I guess you never know what you'll find."

"No, you don't. Sometimes I've gone to a house and the client has been in her pajamas. It happened in one of those huge houses in Lake Forest."

"What do you do?"

"First, I make sure everything is okay. The people are usually elderly; I want to be sure they aren't ill. Then I go about my business. That's what I like about this work. I go about my business." It's a relief, she realizes, to be telling someone this.

"So you're a democrat." He smiles approvingly. "You've worked in mansions. Now you're helping us in this crappy little house." He stops. "I'm wrong. We moved here when I was four. Forty-nine years ago. I lived a lot of my life here. I was ashamed of this place when I was growing up. Now I'm not so different from Charlene. I hate to let the house go."

In the afternoon, Greg looks over Ellen's shoulder at the list of donations.

"This would have killed my mother," he says. "She liked order. She had so much...*stuff.*" He pronounces the word with part disdain, part amazement.

She and Greg read silently together. So far they have set aside to give away: twenty-five pots and pans, a child's wooden sled, twelve packages of playing cards, eight blankets, fifteen glass vases, seven photo albums still wrapped in plastic, a bowling ball, eighteen unopened packages of Rosh Hashanah greeting cards, a torn High Holiday prayer book, and forty 33 rpm records, including an unopened boxed set of Mozart's *Symphony No. 40 in G Minor*, Columbia Records, Sir Thomas Beecham conducting the London Symphony Orchestra.

Black garbage bags lean against the wall, bulging with trash. Boxes contain stacks of papers for shredding. Objects sit scattered on the floor.

"There's a lot of space for storage here," Ellen says. She is careful not to judge or at least convey her judgment to a client. She has, in fact, never seen so much paper as in this house: in Greg's father's basement office, in closets, in the shoe boxes on shelves. Some shoe boxes contain old letters and cards. Others are crammed with donation requests in envelopes, only from Jewish organizations, she notices: Hadassah, American Society for Yad Vashem, Jerusalem Orphan Fund, Save Ellis Island, and ones she has never heard of. She has discovered two Israeli art calendars for 1996-1997, from nine years ago, and a magnet wrapped as a gift that reads: "Praiseworthy Are Those Who Dwell in the House of the Lord."

Greg sifts through a box of donation requests. "Why would she keep this? Did she donate to these places? Or did she want to? Or did my father keep this? No, I think it was my mother."

"We'll never know," Ellen says. "Unless you find the canceled checks."

She slides open a door to a wooden cabinet in his father's office. The shelves are packed with liquor: Gilbey's vodka, Gordon's gin,

Cutty Sark whiskey, Madeira, Kahlúa, Grand Marnier, Baileys.

"These are old," Greg says. "My father brought out the liquor when friends came over. Maybe he drank here alone. I don't know. I'm sure Charlene doesn't know."

"There's always something unfinished when someone dies," Ellen says gently. She thinks of her mother, the notes she and Sally found, diaries of Miriam's travels, and the note about Miriam's feelings for the lake. Ellen keeps these in her desk drawer. The note about the lake made Ellen wonder if her mother had really loved her father. When Miriam was ill, she wrote not of her love for him, but her love of the lake.

She and Greg are working at breakneck speed. He won't be able to take off from work too often, he's told her. Ellen has other jobs to attend to as well. Still, they are making good progress. They work well together. At some point, she will be alone in the house with the decisions. She often works alone. Her colleagues are the movers, shredders, and haulers.

That night, Charlene telephones. "Greg says you've been great. I feel a little guilty. A lot guilty."

"Don't worry; we're getting a lot done," Ellen says. "The house will be cleared out before the closing."

"No, I meant I can't help Greg. He's doing this alone."

"I'm there, organizing everything. That's why you hired me."

"Of course," Charlene replies doubtfully.

Ellen waits to see if the woman will add anything specific. I'm not a psychiatrist, Ellen thinks. I can help you get rid of possessions, but not your guilt.

The next week, Ellen takes stock of what she and Greg have accomplished. The give-away area has filled the basement. There are no clear surfaces and there is barely room to walk. The house is weeping, she thinks, and she and Greg are witness to it. The house is weeping from the disorder, the dizzying pace of breaking up a life.

Greg lingers over the charity requests. He finally throws them into a trash bag.

"My mother had a number on her arm," he says.

Ellen faces him.

"That's probably why she kept these. She wanted to help Jewish charities. She was in a concentration camp. 1942, she went in."

"That's terrible." Ellen doesn't know what to say.

"She was beside herself when the Neo-Nazis marched. They marched here in Skokie, years ago. She marched in protest. Now you're going through her things. You're a stranger. She would be ashamed. I wish you'd known her. She was proud and tough as nails. She was a translator in the camp. She spoke four languages, so she was spared the worst of it; they put her to work in an office. She said when she was liberated she weighed a hundred pounds. Her parents…" His voice trails.

"What a nightmare for her," Ellen says.

"Well, that generation is dying out," he says. He throws the last of the charity requests into the trash. "Soon all the witnesses will be gone. But I lived with it. This house lived with it. If your parents suffered, you do, too, whether they tell you or not. You know. You understand they suffered and that it wasn't fair. My grandparents died in Auschwitz."

"I'm really sorry." Ellen clutches her pad of paper to her chest.

"There's nothing to be sorry about. It happened. It's a fact. My mother was a fighter. And she was grateful for what she had. Her life was hard, but she said to me, 'I've had such a good life, Greg, so full.'"

Ellen nods, touched. She is trying to learn gratitude, despite the divorce, which seems trivial compared to Greg's mother's experience. Ellen is grateful for her work, her friends, her children. So far, she's healthy. That is enough. Her mother was an optimist, but her father was relentlessly negative. If she received an A- in class, he demanded, "What happened? Why didn't you get the A?"

She tries to imagine what it was like to grow up in this house, with this history. She has learned to listen to clients and not ask questions. But she wants to question Greg. She doesn't even know what he does for work. She tells herself this is as it should be. She's hired to be an efficient guide. The less she knows about a client, the easier her job, the more businesslike she can be.

In the den on the second floor, Ellen sets up the five stations.

Greg refers to the room as "the third bedroom." After Charlene left for college, his parents used the room as a den. Bookshelves line the walls.

He reaches for a book, *All Rivers Run to the Sea: Memoirs*, by Elie Wiesel. "Have you read this?"

"No. I am Jewish, though. My father liked to read religious texts." She suddenly misses him, misses her mother. This house reminds Ellen of where she grew up. She misses the Jewish life of her youth. She has regrets about all she discarded from the family home, as if she'd thrown out pieces of her mother. She was overcome by the cleansing feeling of clearing out the house, as if this would clear away her grief. "I don't read religious texts." She laughs, inappropriately, like a schoolgirl. "But I do read a lot. I was trained to be a teacher. High school history and then I went to law school, but dropped out."

"You might enjoy this." Greg hands her the book.

"I can't accept anything from a client," she says, touched. "I appreciate it, though."

"Another rule of relocation school?" He drops the book into a box.

"More secrets of the trade," she jokes.

"I like to read, too. I'm an accountant." He pulls his business card from his pocket and hands it to her. "I also play the piano. I was always good with numbers and music."

"That's nice," she says, realizing how lame this sounds.

"It's not 'nice.' It's what I do. I wanted to be a musician. I stopped when I had a family, three kids."

"Do you still play?" she asks, curious about his family.

"Yeah. Accounting gets a bad rap. I enjoy the work, but people hate their accountants almost as much as their dentists."

"I guess everyone tries to blame someone—the accountant for problems with taxes."

"Relocation experts for glitches in a move."

She laughs. "Yes."

He eyes the bookshelf. "You know, my mother—the thing that saved her was a new life. She studied art and design here." He turns to face Ellen. "My mother said 'a new life' brought her back to life."

"It must have been hard," Ellen says. She needs a new life herself. "To hear about her experiences, her…"

"No." He frowns. "She was the only mother I had, and loving. I can't imagine anything else."

"I suppose not." Everyone has burdens, Ellen thinks. You can't quite understand how it feels to bear someone else's. She imagines her mother, an observant Jew, observant because of Ellen's father. He ruled the house with his temper. Like Todd did; he had a temper, too. Her mother would say softly, "Oh, Stan," when her father yelled, but this offered little protection for Ellen and her sister. As soon as Ellen left home, she ate shrimp and lobster uneasily, knowing this was forbidden, and then relishing the freedom. Relishing the forbidden. She fell in love with Todd, admiring his disdain for religion. This all seems foolish in light of Greg's family. It seems foolish in the context of her life—her mother is dead and her father is ill, on dialysis, and failing.

"I'm the child of a survivor," Greg says. "That shaped my life. My mother saved all this stuff so that we'd have everything we needed in an emergency. She probably wanted to take some of it with her if we had to flee. She couldn't have brought much. My father escaped through the sewers in Warsaw. Everybody survives something. What life does to people. You can't imagine it when you're a kid."

"Let's look at the clothing," Ellen says a few minutes later. "That's a huge job." It's getting late, but she wants to assess what needs to be done.

"That's Charlene's department," Greg says.

"You and I can do this."

He stares into the hall closet. "These jackets," he says. "How many will we give away?"

"All of them." She counts. "Fifteen. Unless you want to keep some." She realizes how cold she sounds. "They're in good shape. Someone can use them. You're doing a *mitzvah*."

"I haven't done enough of that. I got caught up in the wrong things."

Ellen lifts a dress from the closet, black, knee-length chiffon, pearls inlaid on the bodice. Long-sleeved. All the dresses have long sleeves; now she understands why. "What were the wrong things?" she asks.

"Who knows?" he says wistfully, as if talking to himself. "Making money, getting ahead, working day and night. I did the usual crap." He eyes the dress. "She must have been young when she wore that. At the end, she couldn't walk. She fell at night. Once, we had to bust down the door to get in. My father has Parkinson's. He loved her, but he couldn't help. It wasn't safe for them here. What good is love at that point? Oh, I know it brings comfort. And I work. I couldn't run to the house every minute, even if I wanted to."

"And your wife?"

"She and my mother didn't get along. A woman should be doing this, sorting through the clothing. It's too personal." He pauses. "I'm divorced," he says.

Ellen is tempted to ask about his marriage and divorce.

"I don't want to know this about her, my mother," he goes on. "It feels like a betrayal, throwing out her clothes."

"I can do this myself. I do it all the time. Or I can bring team members in."

He shakes his head no. "Doesn't seem right."

She nods. If he were a friend, she would hug him, comfort him.

"This is up to me," he says. "I want to see it through."

"I know it's tough. I felt the same way when I threw out my mother's things," she says.

"Look, you take care of the clothes. I'll go through the books."

"Do you want me to make the decisions?"

"Charlene says to throw out whatever I want. She's worried about blotting out our mother, but she's not sentimental. She has no interest in the past. No respect for history. She's a goddamn bundle of contradictions. She always has been. So yes, decide. If you think something is worth keeping, save it. I trust your judgment. You're the expert."

Ellen appraises the closet. Dresses, how many? She counts quickly. Maybe sixty. Flowing evening gowns. Suits. Styles from twenty and thirty years ago. Each piece is covered in plastic, as if the owner will return to wear the dress again. This seems poignant to her. She drops the black chiffon dress into a donation box. This act seems almost a betrayal to her, too. Is the first betrayal the worst? She thinks of Todd. Is the first loss the worst? She thinks of her mother. Will the losses become easier? How will she trust another man?

She and Greg work in silence. This feels like a deep silence, without a need for conversation. Not a total silence. As she peels plastic off clothing, the plastic makes a crinkling sound. Greg tosses books into boxes. They land with a heavy thud.

This is what it feels like to be married, Ellen thinks, to have a companion. How foolish to fantasize in this way. She remembers when she and Todd worked side by side, how happy she was. That hope.

When she's emptied the closet, she goes to the master bedroom. In a dresser drawer, she finds piles of garters, pairs of shoulder pads, and a Ziploc bag containing thirty perfume samples. Did Greg's mother save these to use if she had to begin yet another new life? Ellen feels like she's digging through the remains of a dead culture.

She knows it will be difficult when Greg walks through this house for the last time. There is a sweetness to him, she thinks, a kindness. The emptiness here will trouble him. She remembers her parents' empty house: the echo of her and Sally's footsteps. Everywhere Ellen looked she saw absence then: no piano, no couch, no more childhood, no mother. Everything solid was suddenly gone. Todd and her children were her one other anchor; he's gone now, too.

Anchors are dreams, she thinks, illusions. We're all tethered to this world by stuff that doesn't matter. She throws the contents of the drawer into the trash.

She knows when the movers arrive, the house will feel invaded. Four or five hulking men will scatter to pack and haul away possessions. They will be immigrants, from South America or Mexico or the Islands, with names like Antonio or Jacobo or Cipriano. She has worked with them on other jobs.

When the men carry out the furniture, the house will fill with dust, the dust that was hidden for years beneath beds and dressers. The movers will haul out boxes, and the dust will rise. The house will become a cave, a tomb.

She is sure this will trouble Greg. She is aware suddenly that he is a man, of his maleness, and she imagines the tilt of his head, his large hands and lovely blue eyes. She thinks of Todd who looked only to the future, who was unsentimental.

She remembers the unexpected tears as she walked through her parents' empty house. She felt as if she had disappointed someone, disappointed the house itself.

Todd used to say that she collected a glass menagerie, her memories of the past she liked to talk about. He was wrong. It wasn't a glass menagerie. She has reverence for history, like having respect for a person. Ellen liked to reminisce about when she grew up, when she and Todd were happy and lived in Wisconsin, when the children were young. How could someone go forward in life without touching the hand of the past?

She remembers the closing for her parents' home. She wasn't there, nor was her sister or father. She recalls the lawyer's jubilant phone call: "The house has a new owner!" A shudder of relief, like an earthquake, heaved inside her. Then an odd, vacant feeling followed—there was no one she could reach, no one who was part of the original constellation of the house. She absorbed the news herself and felt strangely alone. Her own family, the one she thought would extend into the future, was shaky even then. The moment was filled with absence and a sudden jolt of grief.

It is a silly thing, a house, but a house contains lives and hopes.

She wants to spare Greg this grief. She doesn't know if his feelings mirror her own. He seems to be a decent man, and what he says seems deeply felt.

She pushes her hand through her hair and feels the sweat accumulating, the proof of her hard work. If only she could have brought this to Todd to prove to him that she did something of use.

The thud of books stops. She looks up. Greg stands in the doorway, watching her.

"You look intent," he says. "Lost in thought."

"I was thinking about what your house will be like when everything is gone."

"I'll be glad when it's finished." He pauses. "You're just the kind of person my mother would have wanted to sort through her things. She knew character."

Ellen feels herself blushing. "Maybe she can see us now."

"I doubt it. When you're dead, you're dead." He clears his throat. "You know, you're a beautiful and remarkable woman."

"I'm not really, but it's nice of you to say." Don't flatter me, she thinks. I can withstand anything except compliments. Something rises in her. "I'm just a relocation expert. Middle-aged and getting divorced. I'm a hired hand." She is shocked by her words.

"You've done well. It seems that way to me."

"I'm sorry." She frowns and shakes her head. "I shouldn't have said that. I guess I'm disappointed. I wanted to be a lawyer and an artist. And this is what I do, relocation."

"I wanted to be a composer," he says kindly. "I wanted to be married to one woman for my entire life. It didn't work out. I didn't want my mother to die. I didn't want my father to be ill. Everyone has so many wants."

"They do," she says, embarrassed.

"I could have done a lot better. My marriage, my profession. My life. Everyone wants something."

He has a handsome face, appealing and vulnerable. Her heart gives, and she reaches to put her hand on his arm. She has vowed never to mix business and pleasure.

"I want to kiss you," she says, surprising herself.

"So we share that."

He steps closer and kisses her. The taste of him lingers, like sea salt and mints. This eases her need for laughter or coldness or caution.

In his childhood bedroom, next to the dresser where his old swimming trophies and baseball cards sit, he unbuttons her blouse. She helps. It's clear to her that to do this in the master bedroom would be an act of desecration. He hurries to the bathroom and returns with a package of condoms he discovered while cleaning. Then he slips off his shirt, jeans and jockeys, shoes and socks, while she unhooks her bra and steps out of her black flats, dusty now, that were foolish to wear to this job. She strips off her pants and cotton panties, throws the clothing on the floor, an act that is a rebellion against her strict work rules, as if these items, too, should be discarded.

His cell phone rings in the third bedroom. He climbs into his narrow childhood bed. "It's probably Charlene."

Ellen joins him. What would Charlene think of this? she wonders.

Finally, the ringing stops.

Beneath the sheets, Greg's skin is warm against hers. When he is finally inside her, it feels as if he is burrowing into a place so deep, burrowing into her past and discarding what she no longer needs: her marriage, dashed hopes, and fears. With each movement they make together, all this disappears. She doesn't know what she needs or wants anymore. Yes, she does, she realizes, kissing him. She needs this and only this: Greg inside her, the slow raspy rise of his breath, of hers, and their wails of pleasure that echo in the house.

Is this real, this feeling for him? She doesn't know. What's real in life anyway?

At home later, Ellen sits at her desk, opens the drawer, and takes out her list of what she misses about married life. Beneath this is an unfinished note of her mother's.

> Written while recuperating from pneumonia, May 1983:
>
> The Sea Has Ever Been My Love
>
> It's true, I adore my children and I do, in a fashion, love my husband. But my most enduring romance has been with Lake Michigan. Although I confess to have had many infatuations over the years with other beautiful bodies of water, particularly the most seductive Caribbean and Mediterranean water, and even other men. Nonetheless, my dearest recollections have to do with my beautiful Lake Michigan. It is soothing, nurturing and protecting. It captivates, it

Like love, Ellen thinks.

Beneath the note is a letter her mother wrote and apparently didn't send. Or is it a draft of a letter? She doesn't know. The paper is yellowed and creased. Miriam addressed the letter to her own brother after their father's death:

> Bobby dear, I am reading the story of Sigmund Freud and have found something that may help us with Pa's death. He wrote in reference to his own father. Freud says: "By the time he died, his life had been over, but at a death the whole past stirs within me."

Ellen thought she was finished with the whole sorry mess of loss and absence. She thought this was almost behind her: her mother, her father's illness, Todd. She should have known better.

She studies the neat slant of her mother's handwriting and sets the pages in the drawer. She will show the letter about Sigmund Freud to Greg.

She lifts Greg's card from her purse and places the card on the desk. She will see him tomorrow and for the next five weeks. And then? Her mother was right. Of course, no one can foresee the future. It's better that way. Ellen will find out in time.

She gazes at the papers on her desk and scattered on the floor. More useless stuff, she thinks. She scoops up most of the papers she has gathered for the lawyer. She piles them neatly in the living room fireplace. She collects some of Todd's possessions that are still here: two neckties—blue-and-white striped, a red one—a pad of graph paper, and books. She brings these to the fireplace, too.

Then she sets the list of what she misses about being married on top. She doesn't need a list to remind her of what she wants from life.

She finds a matchbook in the kitchen from Il Mulino, where Todd surprised her with dinner years ago when they visited New York, an extravagance. She lights four matches and throws them onto the pile.

Melvin Davis, the New York lawyer with the incongruously

melodious name, said if she didn't find every document, it wouldn't matter. Ellen will tell him she couldn't find many. If this causes problems in the divorce, she will find out in time, too.

Ellen has always been adept at sifting through the minutiae of life and separating items of value from those that are worthless.

She has so many wants.

She lights match after match. She has never believed in cremation. Now she understands its place.

The papers burst into flames. Ellen watches the heat devour the history of her married life. Books crackle and burn. Smoke clings to her hair. She thinks of the heat of Greg's kiss. Then a sound, like a hiss, rises from the flames, like a wail. Soon everything transforms into dust and ash.

Nine Facts That Can Change Your Life

The first letter from my husband's lawyer arrived two months ago, in mid-September, and worried me the most, more than the other letters I've received since then. I live on the first floor of a brownstone in Greenwich Village. I rent the apartment—really, my husband and I do. Thomas moved out five months ago. Our two children are away, in college. It's too expensive for me to live here alone. But I want to stay in this brownstone for as long as I can—until I can't bear to accumulate more debt on my line of credit or until the divorce is final.

The day the lawyer's letter arrived, I came home in the afternoon to retrieve papers I needed for work. I teach kindergarten in a city school. That day, I hurried past the mail carrier on my way to the house. She has beautiful dark skin and wore the coarse blue uniform of the Postal Service. The cut of the pants is masculine; the pockets bulged. The woman has soft, pretty features. Her thick black hair was pinned back with a barrette.

That September afternoon, she wasn't bending to gather envelopes from her canvas satchel or slipping mail into slots or boxes. She stood on the sidewalk next to her bundle of mail in the warm fall breeze, staring at the ground and crying.

I knew how it felt to cry like that. I'd cried when Thomas left.

"Excuse me." I stopped. "Are you all right?"

She looked up, startled. "I'm okay." She wiped her eyes with the back of her hand. "It's nice of you to ask."

I didn't want to pry. I told her if I could help, she should let me know.

She nodded.

I went inside and found my papers for work. Then I peeked between the slats of the blinds. The woman was crying again. I grabbed a bottle of water and went out.

"Take this, please," I said, as if the water could ease what troubled her.

"Thank you." She wiped her tears again. "It's my son," she said, as if she owed me an explanation. "He's seventeen. He's in trouble. Oh, I try to be a good mother, I do. I work so hard. He has no father. But I can't be with my son twenty-four-seven. I just can't."

"Is there anyone who can help you?"

She gulped a breath and seemed to compose herself. "My mother, she used to tell me there's a problem every Monday and Thursday. You know, I thought that was so stupid then. What a stupid thing for a mother to say. She was right." The woman frowned. "I've got so many problems every day of the week. It's not easy when your husband has left."

Toward the end of our marriage, Thomas and I still had sex. Sex was one of the pleasures of our relationship. One of the few times he wasn't counting. He's a mathematics professor at a college and does mathematical consulting for companies. He's terrific with numbers. When we made love, he didn't care whether the bills were paid on time. He didn't care that one of our kids had stayed out too late and come home a little drunk or that our younger son struggled with learning disabilities. Thomas and I were in the moment when we had sex. Was sex Zen? I wondered. A few nights before he announced he was leaving, we were making love. Ribbons of moonlight floated into our bedroom. I slid on the bed toward him and took him in my mouth, just the way he liked.

"Grace, honey," he said suddenly. "Don't."

"Why not?" I looked up.

"That doesn't turn me on now."

"Oh." I thought he was having a bad day or a bad night, not that he was having a bad life.

The last year and a half of our marriage, I've had a lover. I'd always been faithful to Thomas until then. I didn't approve of sleeping with anyone outside of a marriage. It wasn't just the fact of having a lover that I was ashamed of. I was ashamed of the lies. Of the need. Paul was the father of one of my students; our friendship started innocently. His son was having problems in school, and Paul arranged meetings with me to discuss this. He was separated from his wife. He isn't classically handsome, but is just my height, with a long nose, light-brown hair, and dazzlingly earnest brown eyes. He invited me to have coffee, and I suggested ways he could help his son, techniques and books. Paul listened eagerly.

Thomas had become irritable, and worked later and later on complex mathematical equations. He had too many deadlines, he told me. He checked e-mail at midnight and often went to bed at one or two in the morning. I was weak. I was drawn to Paul and relished his attention.

One thing led to another. He and his wife eventually reconciled. They moved to Atlanta seven months ago for his work. He and I are adept at what we do. We still meet from time to time. I don't know all the details of his life. He doesn't know all the details of mine—how I once told my husband I was going to a conference on battered women, would stay overnight in Connecticut and return two days later. I didn't tell Thomas that Paul would be in Connecticut; there was no conference. I didn't mention Paul and I would share a room at a Comfort Inn. I didn't tell Thomas that Paul is married, yet when I take Paul into my mouth or he kneels down and puts his mouth on me or straddles me or we kiss, there is no such thing as good marriages or bad marriages or marriages at all.

The first letter from the lawyer was unexpected. I had prevailed on Thomas to see a counselor and had great hopes we could patch our life back together. The day the letter arrived, the mail carrier finally stopped crying and slid the mail through the slot of our front door. I was about to go back to work. The mail landed on the floor with a thud. I ran to retrieve it—a habit of childhood, this exuberance about the mail. My anticipation stemmed from a time when mail meant something, when it wasn't just a collection of bills, appeals for money, and flyers for cheap contact lenses or discount cruises. It used to be that a letter from a friend or relative appeared, like a treasure. "A letter was really a letter then," my father used to say, like a dollar was a dollar, and a commitment really a commitment.

I flipped through the envelopes and found one with a return address I didn't recognize. It seemed to be the name of a company or a law firm, engraved in graceful italic script: *Goldfarb, Himmelstein, Jones & Weatherby.* The envelope was a fine beige; the paper heavy and smooth. Crane's, I thought, or William Arthur. Typed above my name were the words: "Personal and Confidential." At first, I couldn't imagine who would send me such a formal letter. Maybe this was a scam.

A sinking feeling crept over me. Had Thomas really hired a lawyer? The envelope filled me with dread. I didn't open it for two weeks. I placed it on the bottom of the pile of bills to pay, next to the large black vinyl notebook where I write lesson plans. I would read the letter when work was less hectic, I decided, when I was able to collect myself, and I didn't feel so raw about the unraveling of my marriage.

After Thomas told me he didn't know if he wanted to be married anymore, my therapist, Flora Morningside, said, "I think you should come to see me twice a week. We have to get you through this."

I felt devastated, in a daze. I sat across from her on a white armchair in her white office. I didn't know what day it was or month. The only place I could think clearly was in my classroom. I had been sure Thomas and I were heading for a good stretch of years together. Our younger son had just gone to college. Although I was drawn to Paul, I would stop seeing him, I'd resolved. Thomas and I could luxuriate in each other's company.

He'd told me his plans last April at dinner at home, the night before I sat in Flora's white office. Thomas is taller than me, with a receding hairline, black hair peppered with gray, and narrow, intense brown eyes. His body is solid and broad from swimming.

He carried his salad dish to the sink, turned to me, and said, "Grace, I don't think I want to be married anymore."

"What?" I said distractedly. I set a platter of baked salmon on the table. "We are married." I laughed. "We love each other."

"I mean, I want a divorce."

"Honey, what's wrong?" I faced him. "Is this a joke?"

"I've never felt you were a partner to me. I don't." He said this with surprising conviction and shook his head. "I would never want to hurt you. But I don't think I actually loved you."

I stared at him. I loved him. How could this be happening? Was it my fault?

Just the week before, Thomas had told me he loved me and we were partners for life. We'd planned a vacation in Mexico over spring break. I loved how he spoke Spanish. He was a genius with numbers. We swam laps together on weekends. All our married life, we spent as much time as we could together at the ocean. We met in college and moved from Boston to New York for his job. We loved each other's families as if they were our own. We loved our children. We had planned our future, until we were 120, he liked to joke. I was confused. If you fear a thing, does that make it come true?

"You're my family," I said to him. "What about the children?"

"They're in college. Grown up. They have lives of their own." He seemed to be waiting for me to say something more, but I couldn't speak.

I wasn't perfect, I thought. I had too many imperfections to list. And I had a lover, but I wouldn't leave Thomas for him. Thomas wasn't perfect, either. He was absentminded. He wasn't good about giving gifts, and he spent too freely. He often seemed to prefer numbers and equations to people. He was moody. We didn't have a perfect life. We had a good life.

"You should hire a lawyer for yourself," he went on. He told me to expect a letter from his lawyer.

"Is there someone else?" I asked weakly.

"Maybe. I'm not sure." He tensed his jaw. "Yes."

I slapped his face.

When the therapist said, "We have to get you through this," I didn't ask who she meant by "we." But I thought: Did she mean she and I would get me through this? Or she and someone else? She and Thomas? Who was going to help? I wanted to get through this.

"You like to please people," she said ominously. "That's your problem."

I even wanted to please her. I agreed to see her twice a week.

I ride the subway and a bus to her office. Thomas used to say, "Why can't you find a therapist who has an office closer to us? New York is all about logistics. Look at me. I walk to work. I don't waste time. All you have in life is time and energy."

I didn't tell anyone about the letter from the lawyer—not a friend, not Paul, not the therapist or our kids. I was too upset, afraid of the future. I didn't open the envelope either.

This was an inauspicious time to get divorced. There was never a good time. The economy was going to hell, unemployment was rising, and I was lucky to have a job. There were rumors of teacher layoffs. I told Thomas all this on the telephone in September. He had moved into a studio apartment on the West Side. I wanted to convince him to come back. I knew couples who had reconciled, like Paul and his wife.

"No time is right," Thomas said. "Every time is inauspicious. Have you gotten the letter from my lawyer?"

"No. It hasn't arrived yet." I slammed the telephone receiver into its cradle and wept.

I'd started consulting with the therapist after we'd discovered our younger son, Ethan, was dyslexic. He had difficulty with reading and numbers. Thomas was too busy to help him, too impatient. I accompanied Ethan to tutors and consulted with the therapist. She helped me learn how to best work with Ethan and how to deal with the unexpected in life.

Flora Morningside tells me again and again, as if she's never told me before: "My first analyst said: 'Miss Morningside, develop a relationship with yourself.'"

I'm trained to teach middle and lower school, but a few years ago, the principal needed a kindergarten teacher and chose me. I've come to love these children. With them, I feel young and useful. The principal tells me he's pleased with my performance, though recently, he's talked vaguely about budget problems and layoffs. I try to push those words out of my mind.

I know I'm good at my job. In my classroom, it doesn't matter which politician is in office, who is having an affair with whom, or what the latest political scandal happens to be. All that matters is this: what a student's home life is like, whether he or she earns a gold star in class for good behavior, and if students master reading and team skills. I teach them about sharing, honesty, and loyalty, solid values that will help them lead good lives.

Last year, I painted the classroom yellow. I display colorful posters and aphorisms on the bulletin board. I print the sayings in big black letters: "A PENNY SAVED IS A PENNY EARNED." Or: "HONESTY IS THE BEST POLICY." I draw pictures on the blackboard. I want the room to be bright and hopeful and full of laughter.

This year, there are twenty-six students in my class. Students or their parents come from Puerto Rico, the Dominican Republic, Korea, Haiti, Mexico, Colombia, the United States, Rwanda, and Tibet. The kids are full of energy. Some parents are unemployed or ill or divorced or don't speak English well. Everyone has his or her share of troubles. There are the difficult students who should be in a special class but are mainstreamed. They can't sit still.

After lunch each day, I dim the lights. "It's time to rest," I say. "Lie quietly on a mat." I play a CD of classical music, usually Mozart.

One day, while the students napped, I sat at my desk and finally opened the letter from the lawyer.

> PERSONAL AND CONFIDENTIAL
> Re: Weston vs. Weston
> Dear Grace Weston,
>
> As you know, I am writing to you on Thomas's behalf. He wants to proceed to formalize your separation and has asked for my help. By way of this letter, I am asking you to find a lawyer and to have that lawyer call me so we can come to terms in as speedy and amicable a manner as possible.
>
> I look forward to hearing from someone on your behalf.
>
> Sincerely,
> Duncan R. Weatherby

I didn't check the brand of stationery. I decided to let the kids nap all afternoon, but a few students sat up and kicked each other.

At home later, I looked through the mail to see if I'd find another letter from the lawyer. After all, I'd received the first one two weeks ago, and I'd only read it today. There was no new letter. I felt a fleeting surge of joy, as if the absence of another letter would delay a divorce. Amidst the bills, I found a pamphlet that caught my interest. "Nine Facts That Can Change Your Life," from the pages of the Next Generation Institute for Biomedical Studies *Better Health and Wellness Letter*. You could get twelve issues for twenty dollars, I read, which seemed a bargain for life-changing facts.

I sat on my bed and perused the pamphlet. Since Thomas had left, I'd begun to take an interest in the mail and self-help offers on the Internet. I started to write long letters and e-mails, too, to our sons in college, not about the marital issues, but about the world in general. And I wrote to my father, who has Alzheimer's. This newsletter was dedicated to in-depth coverage of important subjects, the pamphlet explained, such as "Little Problems, Big Stress." If there were big problems, I wondered, did this create bigger stress?

When articles in the professional-education literature I read mention stress, authors often begin the list of major stressors in this order: death, a divorce, a loss of a job. The *Better Health and Wellness Letter* rated stress in a similar way:

> The greatest impact from stress may not come from death, divorce, loss of a job, or other traumatic changes or misfortunes, but from the minor yet common frustrations we all experience every day—gaining weight, standing in long lines, getting stuck in traffic, having an argument with a spouse or a child or friend. These relatively small hassles often have a greater impact on us than major life events do, and can increase the risk of high blood pressure, cause back or neck pain, and even increase the risk of heart attack. These were the conclusions of Dr. Zachariah L. Joseph and his colleagues at the Next Generation Institute for Biomedical Studies. Dr. Joseph and his team conducted extensive research on stress. What is intriguing and encouraging about their results is this: Although stress and frustration are an unavoidable part of everyday life, we *can* do something about them and the negative impact they may have on health and psychological well-being.

This was something to remember. This was encouraging. Divorce is considered a traumatic change and misfortune. However, I reminded myself that millions of people end marriages, and divorce may have less effect on my health than the hassle of riding the subway and bus to get to the therapist. Or the aggravation of dealing with students who won't sit still or shout out: "Mrs. Weston, you didn't tell me what to do! What should I do?" Or the tension of talking to a parent and explaining that a child may have a behavior problem, and the parent spitting back, "There's nothing the matter with him. He behaves at home. What kind of teacher are you?"

The newsletter was just what I needed to consider after reading the letter from Thomas's lawyer.

I could use the newsletter's concept in my classroom. "Nine Facts of the Day." This seemed a productive idea and cheered me up. I would create nine important facts of the day or the week, like: "The Best Way to Read." Or: "The Purpose of Winter."

The newsletter promised articles that guaranteed a true epiphany. I read the titles, hungry for knowledge about life:

Aluminum and Alzheimer's
The Best Way to Warm Up
Focus on the Positive
Never Too Late to Get Fit
How Far to Trust Food Labels
Can Anything Slow Down Aging?

There were also articles about family quarrels and lie detectors, about complaining and exercise, about vitamins for cancer and eating soup to lose weight.

The first letter from the lawyer arrived two months ago, and this week, I finally consulted with lawyers of my own.

"This is a fact," one said. "The first letter from your husband's lawyer will be the nicest. They will keep sending letters. This won't go away. My feeling is, why wait? Get on with your life. Just fuck the guy—sue him right now for divorce."

Her office was beige and serious-looking. There was a large wooden desk, file cabinets, and bookshelves. She was young and attractive, with shiny shoulder-length brown hair and an hourglass figure. Her hips were a little wide. She wore a tight, short skirt and David Yurman jewelry, a ring and a necklace with a flashy charm of a gold heart. She told me she had gotten divorced. Her marriage just wasn't working out, but she was shocked by how much the divorce affected her. "I do this for a living, and my feelings took me by surprise. It was harder than I imagined, the feeling of failure. It just won't go away." She shrugged. "But don't deny yourself," she said. "Take a vacation. Buy nice clothes. Let him pay."

The night before the appointment with her, I'd tried to talk to Thomas on the phone about our marriage. Why hadn't I seen this coming? I thought. Why hadn't I paid more attention to him? Had I been thinking too much about Paul?

"Maybe our problem is that we have to be more direct with each other," I said. "Maybe we've each been too immersed in our own worlds."

Thomas didn't respond to this. Instead, he recited his litany. After twenty-five years of marriage, he didn't think he loved me. "I don't want to live that way for the rest of my life. Maybe I never loved you. I'm not sure."

"I don't believe that," I blurted out.

He didn't reply.

In the lawyer's office, I remembered how tender Thomas had once been, all the nights we slept together, our arms around each other. How many times had we had sex in our married life? It boggled my mind to calculate. I was sure Thomas, with his genius for numbers, would have no trouble figuring this out. The lawyer was talking, but I wasn't listening. Fifty-two weeks in a year, I thought. Thomas and I had had sex twice a week on average. Maybe a hundred times a year, for twenty-five years. That was a conservative estimate, but I'd use it. That was 2,500 intimate encounters during our married life. Could you pretend to love someone 2,500 times? And there were even more occasions if I included sex at the beginning, when we indulged all the time, and our beach vacations. Or was sex just sex? Even with your husband? Did 2,500 times have nothing to do with love?

"I just want to try something different," Thomas had said on the phone. "I want to try a different life."

When I spoke to Paul later that week, I told him I was just okay. As okay as I could be. "Thomas is really moving toward divorce now," I said.

"So you're not okay," Paul said. "You have to protect yourself. Financially."

"I can't talk about it. Do you understand?"

"Then don't talk about it. But get a lawyer. Someone to help you, protect you. You can't trust Thomas."

Paul had been divorced once, a brief first marriage.

"Remember, Grace, this may not be what you want," Paul said. "But I'm telling you, the only way out of it is through it."

Paul sometimes speaks in platitudes. I accept this. Appreciate it even. He owes me nothing. He gives me friendship. Thomas owes me more—he is my husband, after all. He gives me nothing now.

You can talk to a lot of professionals and each one will give different advice. I've spoken to three divorce lawyers. I had to take personal time and sick days off from school. At first I debated if I should wait to talk to the lawyers during the Christmas holidays so I wouldn't need to take time off. But the holidays were months away. The lawyers might be out of town then, I realized. Or I could consult with them on a school holiday, Martin Luther King Day or Presidents' Day. I knew I couldn't wait that long.

One lawyer charged $300 an hour, one charged $500, and one wanted $650—when I first called him his fee was $600, but by the time I went to his office, the fee had gone up.

"I'm a schoolteacher," I told him.

"Divorce is expensive," he said. "Your husband will pay. Of course, the woman's standard of living goes down in divorce. You'll have to get used to it."

He advised me to sue for divorce right away. Another lawyer said, "What's the hurry? The more time that goes by, the more money your husband puts in the marital pot, into his retirement."

The second letter from Thomas's lawyer arrived two weeks after I read the first one.

> PERSONAL AND CONFIDENTIAL
> Re: Weston vs. Weston
> Dear Grace Weston:
>
> I have again spoken to Thomas, who has reiterated his intention to proceed to formalize your separation. Please have the lawyer of your choice call me within one week so that we can discuss moving forward in hopes of reaching a prompt accord. Please give this letter your immediate attention.
>
> Yours,
> Duncan R. Weatherby

This time, I was familiar with the fine paper. The legal language. The imperative. I told myself the kinds of things I tell parents when I'm trying to soften unpleasant news. I told myself: This was something I didn't choose. But it wasn't heart disease or cancer or brain surgery. It wasn't a seventeen-year-old son in trouble. It was a letter from a lawyer telling me what I knew: My husband wanted a divorce.

I told myself the pain of this would get better. Maybe someday the pain of my split with Thomas would completely disappear.

I read about trauma in a book I received at a workshop for teachers. There are all kinds of trauma. Someone who experiences trauma may need to talk about what happened over and over. As a teacher, my job is to listen. This can be the case if students have behavior or learning problems or if parents have problems with their spouses or children. The best approach is to listen, try to calm anxiety, and, if necessary, enlist professional help.

Sometimes when I sit in my lawyer's office, reviewing finances and the changes that will come, I think about the *Better Health and Wellness Letter*. Today it is hard for me to concentrate. The first letter from Thomas's lawyer arrived three months ago, and I've finally hired my own lawyer. I listen to the woman's deep, authoritative voice and admire the shiny gold heart on her David Yurman chain. I stare at it, as if she can hypnotize me into acceptance. Her office is so different from the room where I teach. There are no bright colors or posters or childish laughter here. There are no aphorisms on display about honesty, loyalty, and sharing. The lawyer's office is filled with the serious paraphernalia of grown-up life.

"The law doesn't care about emotion," she says. "Facts and numbers. That's what counts."

I nod. I tell myself I had twenty-five good years with Thomas. Maybe until the last three. Still, that's twenty-two good years, even if he didn't think so. Then was then, and now is now. I wish I could shake away this feeling of failure.

"Do you have questions?" she asks. "You look like something is puzzling you."

"No. I understand." I jot her words on a piece of paper: *The law doesn't care about emotion.*

"When you go home, look at those notes. Get the financial information and make a budget, or I can't help you. I need a detailed list of everything you spend, even for the dry cleaners. Once you're divorced, the small expenses become important. You have to think about your future."

I nod again.

"Don't you want the help?"

"Of course I do."

In this office, I feel like one of my students who can't sit still, who has a learning disability. It's hard to think about budgets and health insurance, retirement and Social Security. It is hard to think about the future. Hard to think. I lay the letters from my husband's lawyer on the woman's desk. I have received five, a new one yesterday. She barely glances at them. She's probably seen this all before. I imagine nine facts that might really change my life:

What to do when you aren't prepared.
It's never too late to enjoy life.
The best revenge is success.
The right way to deal with a marital breakup.
Alzheimer's and divorce.
A vitamin for despair.
Can you trust your spouse or anyone?
Does denial work?
How to tolerate loneliness.
The best way to develop resilience.
Is adversity ever useful?

I know these aren't really facts, but ideas. I've thought of eleven. I'll tell Paul about this when we next talk. He's told me that teaching kindergarten makes me soft, like a kid—in the best sense. He's an architect, and philosophical. He likes to say, "It's not what happens to you, but whether you rebound—if you have resilience. This is the key to living." He tells me this on the telephone. When he says something quietly, I know he believes it's true. "Everyone experiences traumatic events in life," he told me last night. "You have a good marriage, and your spouse dies. You have a bad marriage, and you muddle along. You *think* you have a good marriage and your spouse leaves. You're healthy, until you're not. Or your parents die when you're young or they die when you're older. Either way, you're an orphan. No matter what age you are, you want them around. You pine for them."

I have learned the meaning of the word "pine" from Paul. I pine for the sound of his voice, the smell of his skin, the quality of the connection. I pine for *him*. And sometimes I pine for Thomas, for who he used to be, who we were together.

I pine for when my life was normal.

"It's just a new normal," the lawyer says cheerfully. "Oh, it's hard," she admits. "No getting around that. But you have to get used to it."

Later, I set the forms she's given me on the kitchen table and begin to gather the information I need: credit card statements, insurance, receipts, checks. I sift through piles of papers and folders and try to list figures for a monthly budget. The numbers confuse me. Papers are strewn everywhere on the table. I set my lesson planning notebook on top, like a paperweight. In my search, I come across the subscription form for the *Better Health and Wellness Letter*. I meant to subscribe, but I haven't. The pamphlet is still on my night table.

In the kitchen again, I print on a sheet of three-ringed, wide-lined paper, the kind with the large margins I use for school:

> I have decided to subscribe to your newsletter. What about an article on Big Problems, Big Stress? Do your articles contain facts or just ideas? I suppose ideas can be useful, too. I guess I'll give the newsletter a chance. I hope you'll come through for me—I need you to.
>
> Sincerely,
> Grace Weston

This is useless. I really want to write a letter protesting divorce. To whom could I write? I scribble a check, enough for a two-year subscription, and stick it and my letter in an envelope with the subscription form. After I collect everything for the lawyer, I'll write to the *Better Health and Wellness Letter* again with suggestions for other practical facts and ideas.

Out the window, I see the mail carrier. Though it's late in the day, the woman is still delivering mail. She's dressed in her official blue uniform and a blue down jacket, and she pulls her wheeled satchel bulging with envelopes. Her pretty face has a hard edge to it. She's not crying, but she's not smiling either. I fasten a stamp on the envelope, throw on my wool coat, and hurry outside in the cold December air.

"Oh, hello," she says brightly. "You were so kind to me a few months ago." Then she flings her arms around me, as if we are old friends, conspirators in adversity. "I've wanted to thank you." She steps back.

"I didn't do much," I say awkwardly, surprised by this odd moment of intimacy. "I wish I could have done more."

"I didn't mean to…" she says, embarrassed by our hug. "You okay?"

I nod.

"It's the small things in life that count. You know, my son is a little better. Not as much as I'd like. Guess I'm better, too. I mean, I'm dealing with it, you know? Sometimes that's all a person can do. At least he's back in school. You tell me if I can ever help you."

She sees the envelope in my hand and reaches for it. "I'll send it priority." She flashes a smile. "On my dime."

She sticks the envelope in a pocket of her satchel, and I thank her. I'm glad she's doing better. I walk toward the brownstone, feeling an inexplicable optimism.

Then I stop and retrace my steps. "Do you want to come in for coffee?" I ask.

"Oh, thank you," she says with surprise. "That's really nice." She checks her watch. "I can't today. Maybe another time?"

"Great. I'll look for you tomorrow."

We smile before we part, and I make my way back to the house. If I can help her, maybe I'll know how to help myself. She's dealing with her problems. Sometimes that's all you can do. I'll have to deal with mine, too. I'll order the newsletter for her, I decide, and if it's useful, order one for Paul and recommend it to the parents at school. Surely in the newsletter, there will be one fact that can really change a person's life.

Adjustment

August 20, 2002

Dear Aunt Z,

I read once that the Chinese say one move is like two house fires. This I know: Leaving a solid old house in a small Michigan town and moving to the city is a kind of trauma. There is an odd quality, as if I've been in a Rip Van Winkle sleep until now. Lewis, the children, and I are crowded into a small New York apartment. I sit in our kitchen as I write this. Two windows open to an expanse of city. Our vista is not of apple trees but of tall buildings, cars, young people with piercings, tattoos, and fuchsia hair. Women wear tight cotton T-shirts, their nipples exposed like young buds. I want to cover my children's eyes.

There's been a long hiatus in our letters, and I'm pleased we will start to write to each other again. I was nine when you sent me your first note. Do you remember? Almost forty years ago. The West, across all those mountains, seemed like another country then. We've lived so far apart.

You asked how I am adjusting to life here. To be truthful, I often feel lonely here. The boys are teenagers and absorbed in their new world. And Lewis. I love him. He's a good husband, considering the pulls on his time as dean of an engineering school. When I tell him of my battles with the canvas to try to establish the right quality of light or color, or my frustrations about finding a job, he says, "I understand. It takes time. To adjust."

"I want us to have a good life here," I tell him. "How much time?"

"Who can say?" He shrugs. "Don't be impatient. That's the only answer I know."

We see little of each other now. A million thoughts in my head, and I cannot talk to him about any. There is none of the intense interaction we had when we met. Before children.

You and I have never corresponded about the state of our marriages. What can one expect over the long haul? You're in the long haul now. Is it fifty-nine years with Uncle Sidney? Your last letter was poignant: *Uncle Sid and I have no family close-by. We have five grandchildren and nine great-grandchildren who really don't know us. All of our friends have passed away.* I try to imagine your life. When one is surrounded by strangers, marriage must take on new importance. That artificial union. Based on promises kept, no matter what the secret twists of one's heart.

Yes, it was a miracle that my father—your brother—survived. He received a death sentence with his cancer. "He will not live six months," the doctor said. I did not let you know. I believed this would be too great a shock for you. I was in shock myself. Now a year and a half later, my father is thin and tired. But alive.

Three weeks have passed since I began this. The days speed by. There is hardly time to adjust. We've been here almost two months. The children are settled in school. Zach has the moody outbursts of a fourteen-year-old. "I hate you," he screams when I impose a curfew or request a chore.

"Please be home by 10:30," I told him last week. "We live in the city now. If you'll be late, call and let us know."

"You don't trust me. I'll stay out as long as I want," he yelled. "You're not the boss of me. You and Dad made us move here."

The apartment is filled with boxes. I've found a job at a school in Brooklyn. Lewis works longer and longer hours. The distractions in life overtake us.

Yesterday, we went to Rabbi Levinovich's grave. A shrine, supposedly, to a great sage. An aunt of Lewis's made arrangements to pray there for her husband's health. She invited us. We drove to the edge of Queens, to a tiny house where we met ten men who wore long beards and dark fedoras. A sign instructed us. Women must cover their heads. One must write prayers on a piece of paper. At the grave, you read these prayers, rip the paper, toss it onto the dirt.

A rabbi accompanied us. He said, "Miracles happen here."

The grave was surrounded by four walls. Like a house that had no roof, just an open view of the heavens. The air was chilly. Lewis stood on one side in a group of men. I huddled on the other side with the women, in a space so small our bodies touched.

After I whispered my wishes, I tossed the paper. I tried to keep my eyes focused on the grave. The others stared at it, too. Young women with skin like silk. Old, bent women. Some clutched prayer books. A few wore wide-brimmed black velvet hats. Some hugged themselves and hummed. Our souls seemed naked there, Aunt Z. Our fears. Of illness. Suffering. Death. Not just the fear we all live with now, that connects one person to another like terrified puppets. Fear that's risen since the attacks here last year, in that terrible September. I saw in those women's faces a fundamental terror about the nature of life itself, though I had not exchanged a word with them.

At that moment, I wondered about the direction of my own life. About the future of the world. The ambition of my husband. The idea of home seemed more elusive and important than ever.

Aunt Z, you have been like a second mother to me. *How is your mother?* you asked. *It seems a lifetime since I've visited with her.* She is a stranger now. She has faded with old age. She doesn't recognize people anymore. Last summer, in the retirement home, she held my hand and said to me in a high, thin voice, so unlike her, "You seem like a nice woman. I'd like to be your friend."

"Oh, Mother," I said, holding back tears. "I am your friend."

When I write to you or read your letters, Aunt Z, I begin to catalogue my thoughts. These are some of the few times I feel the lightness of being a girl again.

October 3

I have met a man. A month ago. At a party. He wears a navy wool coat with brass buttons, double-breasted, and has black hair that falls in waves on his forehead. He has a handsome, compact nose and wide gray eyes, and he gazes at me when we talk. About what? Politics and Greek mythology, the meaning of life. "The meaning of life is what you make it," he tells me. Make it. The lilt in his words when we sit in a café captivates me.

He is an actor. I have never trusted actors or writers. They seem able to adopt different personae at will. Slip into personalities that mask their true nature. Though I find this man, this actor, charming, I am wary. Is he playing a role? Is he real?

He is not famous, but he makes a living at his trade. He does readings for audio books. Appears in roles in small theaters. Volunteers and reads to the blind. He teaches an acting class for children on Saturdays.

When we met at the party, it came up in conversation that I am an Aries. My actor friend said, "I'm a Taurus. All the important women in my life have been Aries." He named them. Friends. His sister. "And my own mother," he said.

My own mother. He is middle-aged. I found this endearing. The affection in his voice.

"She died fifteen years ago," he said. He looked into my eyes. "She had a lovely, intelligent face like you do. Astrology may be bullshit, but it's a way to start a conversation."

"A point of connection," I said. His words were shopworn. I felt absurdly pleased by his attention, though.

He is not like other male friends. There is the beginning of an odd emotional connection with him. An affinity. We have visited the J. Pierpont Morgan Library and he has told me about plays to read. I've gone to small productions he's recommended, alone or once with Lewis. Last night I took the boys.

My friend is an actor and he lives a life of art, of the mind. He makes no excuses.

To be truthful, this appeals to me.

November 2

Last week, on the subway on my way to the doctor, I read a short story in a book. The main character wrote letters to her ex-fiancé. We don't know if she sent them. I found this an interesting approach, because one feels as if one actually *knows* the narrator. A reader understands the woman's life through the filter of her words and observations. There is the *illusion* of intimacy. As happens in letters, I realized.

I read years ago that every letter has two lives. One in the writer's mind, and the other that the reader gives to it. Perhaps I haven't been able to finish this letter, knowing that once I send it off to you, I will give it a second life.

I thought you'd appreciate the device in the story since you are a reader. A letter writer. I always believed you could have accomplished great things in your life. Of course, you have. You've raised three children, you have been the wife Uncle Sid needed while he practiced law. You've had grace in your voice and words. Feminine, always, with your turquoise eyes (like my father's, the most beautiful blue I've seen), your blond hair with its soft curls. Your dress. Simple gray or blue with a turquoise medallion. Nothing flashy like the New York women with their blood-red nails, glittering gold jewelry, and a manner so impatient and aggressive that I am often intimidated when I talk with them. Even in conversation, they seem to elbow me away.

Not you. Thoughtful, well-read. A dancer. Artistic. Your photographs of people are beautiful. How I admired you when I was a child. You once wrote to me about the grace of Isadora Duncan, who you saw perform when you were young. How she created miracles of dancing on the stage. *Isadora Duncan was perfection in my child's eyes. I imagined that she might dance, young and strong, forever.* Why did you only compose letters?

Perhaps I'm like the woman from the story. Will I send this letter? Censor parts of it? I do not know.

The man I met is married. All the attractive ones are, says a divorced girlfriend of mine. He has a ten-year-old daughter.

He told me that his wife travels for her work. "She's gone so much that I could have another life." He paused. "In addition to the one I have."

"Why would anyone *want* another life?" I asked, then stared at the floor. I realized I didn't need an answer. Perhaps I might want another life, too.

When I glanced at him, he shrugged. He has a neatly trimmed dark mustache. Like my college history professor. I was in love once with my professor, a schoolgirl crush, a secret feeling I never admitted. My friend reminds me of him.

November is speeding by. I was happy to receive your response to my hurried card. You've already replied, while I am still composing this.

Days disappear: dishes and grocery shopping, curfew struggles with the boys, who want to stay out until three in the morning, as everyone else in New York seems to. A job where I help teach social studies to seventh graders in Queens. I am an assistant to a teacher; there were no full-time teaching positions available, but, still, I want to make a difference. The students are Russians, Haitians, Chinese, Croatians, Nigerians, Bengalese. I take a trip around the world in that hot, stuffy classroom.

There are social obligations where I appear as the dean's wife, as if I am dressed in a veil that covers the true shade of my hair, the most expressive portion of my face. *Acting.* Perhaps I am an actress, too.

We walk on a street at midnight in the cold air, and a crowd hurries along as if it is noon. I can buy detergent or sushi at dawn, or bring my dry cleaning in at three in the morning. Does one live longer if one sleeps less?

I told my friend about my art. "I'd love to see it," he said.

"Cartoons," I told him. I blushed. "Attempts at painting. Hardly a place to do it in our small apartment."

"No. Don't denigrate it. Don't dismiss your art." By the expression in his eyes, almost tender, I knew he was thinking: Don't depreciate yourself.

I have not mentioned my friend to Lewis. I am not sure why. It is a burden to live with secrets.

Aunt Z, I must write this, but do not know if I can send it. I am hopeful a letter can relieve a burden. This is what I need to say: On the twenty-second day of November, I go to my friend's apartment on the West Side for the first time. The very upper part of Manhattan, a handsome brown brick pre-war building. I am learning about the neighborhoods here, and buildings. Pre-war, doorman. Post-war. Upper West Side, residential, progressive. His building does not have a doorman. The lobby is dingy. But the apartment is shining. It is small, the white kitchen the size of a closet. At the back of the building. With a view of the river. High, airy ceilings. Sunlight creeping in. Clay pots of coleus and bright green ferns. Old leather books on shelves. Volumes of Shakespeare. The scent of lemon. You can hear a whisper in this space. The breath of a soul.

After a while, we both take off our clothes. This is awkward. But not unnatural. I am shocked that I do not hesitate. I lie on the carpet and let him touch me. I touch him. We are looking at one another. Lips, chest, thighs, muscles, penis. Touching. We kiss and do not stop. We make love and there are great gasps of pleasure.

When we are satisfied and quiet, he tells me that his wife has taken his young daughter and left him.

"Oh no," I say. "I'm so sorry."

He wants to tell me every detail. "I'm confused," he says. "I don't know. Maybe it's better they're gone for now. I think I may be beginning to love you."

"Don't," I say, afraid of his words, of his feelings, of mine. "I have a family. I'm married. You are. You need to bring your wife and daughter home. Maybe we want different things."

"What things?"

Things. The wrong word. The future. I realize there is no way I can know what he wants without asking. But I do not ask. I realize I may have caused his wife pain. I don't ask about this either.

Later, when I leave, I wander the streets like Lewis does. He adores New York. "I am a street rat," he says. "I love to put on my sneakers and walk." When he can, he walks for hours.

"This is a bigger job than I thought. Harder," he said to me yesterday. "Being a dean."

"What exactly do you do in a day?" I asked.

"A million things." He pulled piles of papers from his leather briefcase. A packet came unclipped and typed pages scattered on the floor. "I don't even know myself."

On occasion, I have gone to visit my friend on the Upper West Side while my husband is out walking and the boys are away at friends' apartments or in the library, doing research projects for school.

"Research," Zach laughed tonight. "Did you ever do research when you were younger, Mom?" Code: smoke marijuana, do drugs, have sex.

"A bit, when I was in college." I cleared dishes from the table and avoided his eyes. Half the story. Before I was twenty I had tried them all. How much do you tell your child about your past? Your present? How much do you tell a dear aunt?

There has been a long hiatus between the time when I loved the world and set out on my own, full of great hopes, teaching in the ghetto of Detroit, and now. Teacher, wife, mother. Roles imposed, accepted. You wrote when I was twenty: *These are the best years, when you have the most energy. How many good years does a person have? We can fool ourselves. Really, we have forty, fifty years.*

To be productive. To grow. Then the energy wanes, the body goes. I have kept every letter of yours, brought them to New York in four large manila envelopes. I thought then you were overly pessimistic. But my energy is waning. My resolve. With this act, this first transgression, I have crossed a border, entered another country, accepted citizenship. The land of desire. I have sold my heritage and birthright: upstanding, considerate, honest. I hate myself for this. I feel shriveled and small. Hate the secrets. I do not tell lies easily or casually. I would never want to hurt Lewis. I have given up my values. Nothing is left in their place. Only a deep ache of longing for lost innocence.

What I am sorry to tell you is that having done this once, I would do it again and again. When I am with my friend, I am giddy, like a girl. My skin and senses are alive. My energy is back, and we soar.

Aunt Z, this is a true story. This morning, mid-December already, as I walked in the lobby of our building, the doorman smiled and said his usual greeting. He has deep-set dark eyes, a high forehead, thin lips. Friendly. He likes to talk.

"Your husband is a very important person," he told me, as if he were sharing a confidence. "You and I both know that."

"Thank you," I said, and buttoned my coat to signal I had to get going.

And then he asked, this man in the white shirt and navy suit with its stripes of authority and brass buttons, "Do you have a minute? Would you mind doing me a favor?"

"Of course not." The man has done favors for us, been kind.

He looked to his left, then to his right, as if worried someone might overhear us. The lobby was empty. He stepped closer to me. "I'm going to dial this phone number," he said in a low voice. "Can you take the phone? Just say 'hello' to the person who answers. Then ask for Bridget. You don't have to mention me or say who you are.

Then give the phone to me. Do you mind? This favor?" He picked up the receiver from the phone on the front desk. "Can you keep this just between us?"

"Of course." I was curious, surprised.

He punched in the number, handed me the telephone.

"Hello." A deep masculine voice.

"Can I speak to Bridget?" I asked.

The doorman watched me.

"Sure," said the man on the phone. "Hold on a sec."

I heard him call out, "Hey, Bridget, honey, telephone. For you."

I handed the telephone receiver to the doorman. His face was flushed. He nodded in thanks, then whispered into the receiver. Endearments.

A sour, unpleasant feeling of kinship with Bridget rose in my chest, like a chronic dull ache, and I went outside to face the city.

Cars, taxis, the shrill call of sirens. Men with turbans or women with green hair or blue, teenagers wearing belts made of chains. Buses groaned, spewing their thick exhaust.

Men were sleeping on sidewalks or sitting there alone, talking to themselves.

Will I ever adjust?

I have been rereading your old letters. Late at night, after Lewis and the boys are asleep, I read by the dim light in the living room. Sometimes I have left the apartment and taken a walk alone, then returned to your words. *I have come to believe that a person is better off thinking of others who are worse off, instead of dwelling on the imperfections in one's own life.*

"Your husband is a very important man," the doorman said to me.

Look at the homeless person on the street. Say your prayers.

Uncle Sid and I will likely live in this house until one of us dies. Where would we move to?

February 1, 2003

This is what I left behind in Michigan: my work as an English teacher at a school where I had been for years. Dear friends. Holiday routines. The school where the boys were happy. The rough gray stone of our house. The comfort of understanding the patterns of seasons. Rhythms of daylight and dark. I knew by heart the gray world of January, February, and March, even April. The cold seemed to freeze all scent, except for the sharp odor of wood burning in fireplaces. The spring smells, sweet lilacs and yellow azaleas. In summer, the hot dry fresh-cut grass. Balmy air after the weather began to cool. Acres of apple orchards in the fall. The moist, tart taste of crisp red apples we'd picked ourselves. The view from our bedroom window. The tall old maple and green grape arbor in our yard.

These are not small things. They go to the heart of a person. To the soul. To the essence of memory and comfort.

I hoped the move to New York would be good for all of us. Lewis thought his new job here would be better than his work in Michigan. Now I realize we've left so much behind.

I have always wondered why in Michigan they say: *Weather is coming.* A storm, a freeze. When really weather of some sort always exists. I will have to look that up when I have fully adjusted.

You wrote to me once that most Jews used to live in apartments. Freestanding houses were for the wealthy. You would never say "goys"; you are too respectful for that.

New York is full of immigrants and Jews, rich people and celebrities, and those down on their luck.

I have much to look forward to. The boys growing up, a full life with Lewis, my teaching. When does that change? *You have so much to look forward to.* Now I have less. My mother has no memory. My father has a terminal illness. I am trying to adjust. You and Uncle Sid have even less. *I spend so much of my days looking backward,* you wrote.

Great gasps of pleasure. They help one look forward.

Since we've moved to New York, Aunt Z, I have stopped dreaming. Do you dream?

This is something I have wondered about—what it means when a person stops dreaming. The doctor I mentioned earlier in this letter was a therapist. Lewis told me, "You are not yourself. You say you can't talk to me. Find someone you can talk to."

She was a slim, serious woman with tight curly black hair and wide brown eyes, a steady gaze as if she could examine the soul of another by sight alone. I sat across from her in a small room in a tall building, both of us in armchairs.

I asked her about the dreaming.

She folded her slender hands on her lap and said, "Why do you ask?"

I wasn't sure how to answer. I wanted to ask her: If you stop remembering dreams, do you lose a part of yourself? I told her that I used to dream about my mother, about when she was well, before she had dementia. In my dreams, she was young and beautiful with golden brown hair. Not gray and forgetful as she is now. I told the woman about my father's illness, and that you are almost like a mother to me, in your letters. I explained that I had met Lewis twenty years ago, after a disastrous love affair. I told her I used to dream about having sex with him, doing it in the yard beneath our apple trees, but I don't have those dreams any longer. I talked about the boys. About Michigan. About my friend. I told her I was afraid I loved him. I asked if that was the answer she wanted.

"If that's the one you want to give," she said.

We spoke for a while. She said to me, "It's clear you're having adjustment problems."

Adjusting to *what*? I thought, but I was hesitant to interrupt.

She spoke with the harsh edge of a city person. "I have no doubt the apple fields were pleasant," she said.

I could tell she had never been to Michigan.

"You are going through a series of adjustments," she said.

"Series?"

"What does that mean to you?"

As I was thinking about how she used the psychiatric technique of throwing ideas back to me as if we were playing tennis, I saw her stare at the silver clock ticking loudly, like a bomb, on the table beside me. "I'm sorry," she said, "our time is up."

March 12

Is life a series of adjustments? You wrote me long ago, *Uncle Sid works day and night.* Who keeps you company? I wondered then. I looked at Lewis last night when he came home and thought: Without emotional connection, life is nothing, all *Sturm und Drang.*

You once told me, *Life is constant movement and change, and we have no time to cherish the day.* For a few hours with my friend, I cherish the day.

I have begun to think, Aunt Z, that in order to adjust, I must go away. I have always wanted to spend time in the West. I have, in fact, made plans for a trip. I will travel by train across the country. A slow, meandering journey away from home. I have made the arrangements and will hand-deliver this letter to you. Perhaps you can give me advice and help me adjust. Perhaps I can take care of you and Uncle Sid for a while. Thinking about this, I feel happy. I have become a street rat, want to put on my sneakers and walk away from this city. Perhaps this is foolish. One is always the same person inside. But I'm like the women who hovered near Rabbi Levinovich's grave. Afraid. I am frightened of life with Lewis and without him. Life with my friend and without. The boys are growing up. They have lives to look forward to.

Do you remember when you sent me the letter about Isadora Duncan? Last night I looked for that letter and found it. You told me that your mother took you to see the great ballerina when you were a girl. How the dancer wore a glittering blue scarf draped around her neck, like a ribbon of jewels. That she leapt across the stage as if she might leap like that forever. *Miracles seemed to happen as we watched. She danced in the Dance of Life.* You sent me the letter when I was young. I did not understand at the time how young I was. I knew nothing of burdens or secrets. I didn't know that I would meet Lewis, and then one day my friend. *My mother and I held hands as we sat in the audience,* you wrote. That's what I want to do, Aunt Z. Sit close to you, read your letters aloud, and hold your hand.

3.

Open House

I've been married once and divorced, and have always thought I'd never marry again. It's a conviction I've had, like being opposed to the death penalty, or voting Independent until you die. Through my work, I've gotten a glimpse of marriages. I'm a real estate agent in Nashville. I've lived here twenty-five years, have seen houses come on and off the market time and again, been a broker for clients and their ex-spouses, their new ones. You almost never hear a husband and wife exchanging pleasantries when they house-hunt. Hardly ever, "How do *you* like this, dear? or "We could be so happy here." It's often, "We're not paying that kind of money." Some spouses don't tour houses at the same time, as if they're leading separate lives.

I work with clients for as long as they need me. Like Nora Ruth. She's been searching for a larger house for two and a half years. Today, we're going to an open house at a beautiful contemporary built on a hill overlooking the city. I'm hoping this might be the one. Her husband owns a sporting goods store. I haven't been able to figure them out. How can they afford a more expensive house? Family money? But it's not my job to analyze where money comes from, just to be sure there's enough to get a loan.

Nora Ruth is a petite woman in her forties, with wavy light-brown hair and large black eyes, a quiet, intense manner. She wears color-coordinated pastel outfits. When we tour houses, she carries a green spiral stenographer's notebook and jots her impressions. Sometimes I feel as if we're girlfriends as we ooh and aah over a house. "This one is gorgeous," she said last month when we walked through a renovated Victorian. "I can see our sons here. There's a study for my husband. And the kitchen."

We stopped at the gleaming black granite counters. "The kitchen is to die for," I said.

Nora Ruth's husband rarely joins us. Still, I look forward to showing houses to her. We're becoming friends. She's told me about her children and many moves. "I want a house where we can live happily ever after," she said once. "I don't want to be a nomad anymore." I've mentioned my views on marriage, my brief affair with Sam, but I haven't spoken of Jim. Jim and I have a relationship. He's married. We've gone on like this for years.

Jim is solid, like the turn-of-the-century house Nora Ruth and I just saw, with its brick and plaster walls, a house that seems as if it could last forever. He's from the North like I am. He's a formal person, not knockout handsome. But I love to stare at his profile when we lie together in bed at a hotel. His wavy gray hair and the long, crooked nose. He has the broad shoulders and torso of an aging athlete, one who knows the value of exercise, manners, and the mind.

Nora Ruth doesn't talk much about her husband. I've met him just three or four times. "He doesn't want a Victorian, renovated or not," she told me last month. A few weeks ago, I showed them a 1950s ranch. It had unusual features, a swimming pool in the shape of a guitar, a red tile Jacuzzi in the master bath. While we toured, he talked about his business, the surplus goods, denim jeans, the camping items and hunting guns. Nora Ruth walked in silence, her dark eyes darting around the rooms, taking inventory. She jotted notes in her spiral notebook. After we'd walked through the house twice, her husband said to me, "This isn't us. We want something newer. Contemporary. And the pool will be a hassle. Nora Ruth doesn't want to live this far from town." He looked at her. "Am I right, dear? I can always tell what you're thinking."

Arrogant, I thought.

"I didn't say that," she replied in her soft drawl. "No. It has nice features. Interesting."

"It may look interesting now. But we're not going to buy this." His voice became louder, and the seller's agent eyed us as she walked by.

"Why don't the two of you take some time, discuss this at home,"

I said, though it occurred to me that Nora Ruth's husband might not be interested in buying any house.

"Don't waste Lacey's time, honey," he said to her. "You told me a pool was absolutely out. You don't want to redo bathrooms and neither do I."

"I never told you that." She stared at him and laid a hand gently on his, as if to cushion her words. "I said I'm giving it thought." Then she turned to me and said sweetly, "Lacey, I wouldn't rule this house out."

Sometimes I'm uncomfortable with what I do for a living. I love working with people, but I feel as if I'm selling *dreams.* Selling *hope.* I started in real estate after my divorce. I know the business well now. I never turn off my cell phone; I'm on call day and night. You have to be flexible, and have to take charge. I tell clients who want to sell exactly what to do to prepare. Selling is all about *illusion.* You clear the shelves of books to make them look like there's space for someone else's *stuff.* You remove photographs, personal things, even art. I don't want a buyer to get distracted. I often stage a seller's house, arrange furniture, bring accessories and flowers. Sometimes I go to a house early before a buyer arrives and bake cookies so the rooms smell like a happy home. I want a house to shine, want clients like Nora Ruth and her husband to concentrate on the *dream*, the renovated kitchen with stainless steel appliances or the landscaped yard. To fall in love with the whole picture. When they start nitpicking about details, I've lost them.

I often feel as if I'm trespassing through people's lives. I've seen husbands and wives argue about why a house hasn't sold. It's bad enough when people move for a good reason, to a larger house or new city. But divorce is the worst. No one is happy. A spouse may suddenly haul away furniture. I have to rearrange what's left. When a buyer and I peek in a closet and see no men's clothing hanging, see an empty space, like a gaping hole, there's usually a beat of uncomfortable silence, as if the tensions in the household might be contagious.

I worry this business has made me hard, that I've lost a softness I had when my children were young and I was married. I can fend for myself now. I'm proud of that. But there are days when I wish I were more helpless, so a man would want to take care of me. I know that's old-fashioned, even sexist. I would never tell Jim this. He does what he can, considering he's married to someone else.

He and I worked together before we became involved. Once, years ago, we were at a preview for an open house. The other realtors had already filed through. We were touring a sprawling ranch house on a wooded acre, the kind you often see in Nashville. This one had a master suite with windows that opened onto a garden. It was spring, the best time to sell. The leaves of the pear tree in the yard were a brilliant white, as if we were in an enchanted land.

Jim and I were still talking after the other agents left. We were in the bedroom. I suddenly looked at him, really *looked*, as if I wanted to see inside him. The way people assess houses when they want to buy. He seemed to gaze at me that way, too. He has ears that protrude, an endearing feature, and he was dressed in a navy sports jacket and khaki pants. He told me that he was saving money so he could go to law school or study social work, switch professions.

"At this stage of life," I said, impressed.

"I'm ready for change." His eyes were steady on mine. "If not now, then when?"

I looked away from him, at the garden. It seemed to me he was making a comment about the two of us. I thought: Why do I want a man who belongs to someone else? Then I gazed at him again, and we moved closer until we touched.

Jim has taught me about the real estate business. I'm sensitive to what buyers want. I advise clients to write out the pluses and minuses of a house. "You're never going to find the perfect house," I tell them. I think about this in relation to Jim. *Pluses and minuses.* I love him. Does he love me? Maybe. Can we talk to each other about meaningful *stuff*? Absolutely. Sex. I would follow him anywhere to have sex with him. *Minuses*: The relationship is going nowhere. Will it ever go somewhere? We may never live in any house together. That thought makes my heart catch.

Jim moved to Memphis two years ago. In a way, it's just as well. Nashville is a small town. I'm always bumping into people I know. When my ex-husband and I were in counseling, we saw more familiar faces in the waiting area of the therapist's office than I care to remember.

I miss Jim terribly, but what I like about his move is that I don't see him often enough, once a week if we're lucky. We talk on the phone when we can. That's the plus and minus of it. There's not much chance of bumping into each other as we navigate our real lives. I'm spared the embarrassment of encountering his wife, not a minor thing. Is she beautiful? I imagine them going to dinner, talking in intimate tones. Jim tells me they rarely make love anymore. Truth or dare? True or not? Nights when I'm lonely, I think about my ex-husband and Sam, the man I left my husband for. Things didn't work out with Sam. That first time I touched him I shocked myself. Then I realized I'd stumbled onto something I'd lost: desire. And now with Jim. Sometimes images of Jim's wife break into my thoughts. You never know where the mind will go.

Nora Ruth meets me at my house. I'm dressed in a black silk dress, high heels, and gold jewelry. I like to look professional, but feminine. We leave her car in the driveway and travel in my silver Lexus. It's a beautiful spring day. The air smells fresh; the trees are flowering. We drive west, away from the city, on tree-lined hilly streets.

"What did you and your husband end up deciding about the ranch house?" I ask.

"We never decided." She wears a white blouse and pale lime-green skirt, soft colors like sherbet. Her light hair is pulled back with a white headband. She looks like a young girl. "We just can't compromise. I told him that finding the perfect house is an illusion." Then she whispers, "Like finding the perfect marriage."

"You're right." I don't continue the conversation. I try to keep a businesslike distance from clients, even someone like Nora Ruth, who's become a friend.

We drive in silence. Both she and her husband have said they love contemporaries. I'm planning to remind her, hoping that if she likes this one, we can put theirs on the market. I could make two sales. But Nora Ruth's hands are folded tensely in her lap. She stares straight ahead. I decide to respect her mood.

As I drive, I admire the arch of magnolia and redbud trees, how they form a canopy of leaves and flowers above the street. Spring is the most beautiful time of year in the South. I'd always imagined I'd live in a big northern city, never expected to spend so much of my life here. I moved to Nashville with my ex-husband. We shared custody of the children, so I stayed. Then habit took over. I try to keep busy with work and friends, so I can forget I'm in a small town. I like to go to clubs to listen to bluegrass or country music. Thursdays, I volunteer at a homeless shelter. I love being there because I'm not selling anything. Regulars stop by, and you develop friendships. I often play cards with Charlie P. and Bo Smith. Charlie has small, beady eyes like a gangster. He wears a T-shirt with "Shit Happens" imprinted on front.

"Shit happens," Bo said last Thursday while we were playing hearts. "Today the goddamned sky opened up. Rain."

"Crap, it's all crap," Charlie said as he dealt. "I've lived in a house with all of it." Then he looked at me as if he had just realized I was there. "Excuse us. You're a lady."

"Thanks for noticing," I laughed. "All of *what*?"

"Look in any house. The crap's there."

Life has been hard for these men. They sleep on mats or cots. Men without women. I'm conscious of being female there. This never bothers me at work. I cut down on lipstick and perfume when I'm going to the shelter. Usually, I try to look as if I'm a woman who can take on the world, not a shrinking violet like my cousin. She and her family moved to Nashville a few years after my ex-husband and I did. Her husband is a lawyer and head of the legal department at a big record company here. They live in a house in the best part of town. But he says jump, and she jumps. If he says a dress is too expensive, then it *is*. If he says one of the kids is grounded, his wife doesn't argue. Is this what happens between Nora Ruth and her husband? I glance at her. She's still staring ahead, drumming her fingers on her lap.

That wasn't the problem with my ex-husband. He was devoted to his mother. At first, I loved this about him. He brought her presents, telephoned her every day. I was sure he would transfer that love from her to me. He never did. She lived with us for a while after she became a widow, and I began to feel like the maid, the secretary, the hooker. One day, I told him I wanted more from him. More emotion. He said he didn't know what I was talking about.

He's still living with his mother now. Is he really happy there? Then a thought breaks into my reverie that I don't want to acknowledge. *How happy am I*?

The contemporary is built of white stone and sits on the edge of a forest. A redwood deck encircles the back. The seller's realtor tells us about the house, and then Nora Ruth and I wander through the rooms on our own.

"A great location," I say to Nora Ruth. She's still pensive. I try to be upbeat. "And beautiful grounds." I don't remind her that maintaining this house and yard will cost time and money. I just point out how lovely it is. As I'm talking, I feel myself getting caught up in the *dream.* I imagine her here with her family, leading a picture-perfect life. In my mind, I tone down her husband, make him more like Jim.

She doesn't say much. How long will I have the patience to work with her? She must have seen fifty houses.

We wander to the large master bedroom, past the glass doors that lead to the deck. When Nora Ruth stops to look in the closet, my cell phone rings.

"Baby, can you talk?" Jim says.

"Nice to hear your voice. For a minute."

He tells me about a problem at work, asks about my day. Then he says, "I wish I could make love to you right now."

I smile and walk to the other side of the room. Nora Ruth is looking at her spiral notebook, as if she wants to ask a question. "I'm waiting for you," I whisper to Jim. "Wishing you were here." I can feel my breath speeding up, a tingling between my legs. "What's your day like?" I ask him huskily.

He tells me.

"I've got to go, baby," I say. "A client."

"I'll call later. You okay?"

"Fine. Except you're not here." I take a breath to steady myself. Sometimes talking to him is almost enough, gives me the jolt I need to get through the day.

"Look how sunlight pours into this room," I say to Nora Ruth. We're in the master bedroom again. The space is sparkling with afternoon light. "The house has a rec room, and an office for your husband. What do you think?"

She peers at the room, then at her spiral notebook. Finally, she looks at me as if my question is more complex than an inquiry about a house.

"I…" Her lower lip curls up, her eyes squint and fill with tears. "I had a talk with my husband. I don't know. I just don't know."

She starts to cry and turns away from me. Then I hear one loud sob. No one else is in the room. I don't know what to do. So I go to her, hug her.

"He doesn't want a house," she mumbles. "He doesn't want to be married to me."

"Oh, honey."

Nora Ruth feels frail and bony. Her shoulders quiver as she cries. I can tell she's embarrassed and so am I, but hugging her seems the right thing to do. We stand like this for a moment. Then I step away. So does she. Her eyes are red and blotchy. Mascara is smudged beneath them like swirls of finger paint. In the harsh afternoon light, she looks as if she's suddenly aged.

"I'm sorry." She wipes her eyes with the back of her hand. "I'm taking your time. I don't know what's gotten into me."

"Don't be sorry."

"He doesn't want a new house or an old one. With me. He's in love with someone else. He wants to marry her. I'm so alone with the boys." She takes a breath so sharp, it sounds like a whistle. "He doesn't care. He wants *her*, that *bitch,* that *whore*." She spits out the words.

"Oh, Nora Ruth," I say lamely. "Maybe he'll come to his senses. There's nothing wrong with looking at houses anyway." That's the wrong thing to say; I feel flustered and my palms are sweaty. I realize she could be talking about me. Is that who I am? "I mean, I've enjoyed showing you houses," I say. "We've become friends. One day you'll find a house you really like. Maybe he'll come through for you."

"No. He won't change." Tears fill her eyes again. She fumbles in her purse and pulls out a folded tissue. "And neither will I."

She stops in the master bathroom while I thank the seller's realtor. Then we drive to my house. Nora Ruth leans her head against the passenger seat, quiet. I push a CD of piano music into the slot, Edvard Grieg all the way home. When we reach my driveway, she says, "I'm sorry, Lacey. I've wasted your time. For so long. You've been wonderful to me. I knew things weren't right with him. I didn't want to admit it. I misrepresented myself to you."

I switch off the ignition. "With these things you don't know. Circumstances change," I say. "Don't feel any obligation to me."

She's silent.

I bite my lower lip, feel lipstick smear on my teeth. "Don't be hard on yourself. It will be okay." I'm not sure what "it" is. Our business relationship? Our tentative friendship? Her marriage? Her life? "It will work out," I say hopefully. "Would you like to come in for coffee, a drink? I'll make dinner. It's been a long day."

"You try to fill your life with other things," Nora Ruth says, as if she's talking to herself. "Then you don't have to think so much." She pulls off her headband and drops it in her lap. Her hair falls limply around her face. "Everybody has secrets. Now you know mine." She tells me about her marriage. Inattention. Neglect. Lies. Her husband's affair.

Which of these is worse? "Are you sure you don't want to come inside and sit down?"

"I appreciate all you've done. Another time I'd like to." She shakes her head with what seems like resignation. "One way or another, you have to make peace with your life." She gets in her car and slams the door.

After she drives off, I sit in the blue armchair in my living room and gaze through the French doors that open onto the yard. The azaleas are in bloom. The leaves of the pear tree are a pale white. They look fragile. I pull off my high heels, drink a glass of wine, pour another, then slip a CD, *Mozart Naturally*, into the Bose Wave player. I like this recording because the sounds mimic the natural world. You can hear the sweet tones of the piano, water rushing like a waterfall, and birds chirping as if it were morning in a forest. I listen to the graceful notes, the birds, and the whoosh of water. I know the sound effects are fake, but I like them anyhow, like to pretend I'm in the wilderness with nature around me.

Drinking my wine, I think about Nora Ruth. Damn. You just can't tell about people from the outside. Shit happens. My own tears when I understood my marriage was dead. The thought of this makes me feel weak. Maybe my relationship with Jim is just fine. Better than a marriage. Maybe I'm not cut out to be with a man all the time. I like my privacy and solitude. To be alone with my thoughts. I don't expect him to look at houses or to buy me one, don't expect much, except to hear his voice, listen to his words, be certain he'll listen to mine. From time to time, make love to him.

I feel woozy from the wine, the music and the birds. The sun is setting, and the sky is growing dim. I think of Jim, his wife and kids. Nora Ruth's tears. Suddenly, I feel my face getting hot, as if I'm ashamed of whom I've become. I'm sickened by the thought. I struggle to push Jim's wife out of my mental picture and imagine living happily ever after with him. Not in Nashville or Memphis. On one of the coasts. I'm tending a garden in the house we share, and he's doing something noble, not real estate anymore. "I want a house where we can live happily ever after," Nora Ruth once said. "I don't want to be a nomad." I don't want to be a nomad either. "You try to fill your life with other things," she said. "Then you don't have to think so much."

But what can you do? Life is threaded with losses. Of how you *imagined* your life would be. What kind of house you would live in, whom you would marry. How you would spend the rest of your life. I never thought I'd be alone. I realize I'm tired of fending for myself. Worn out. My secret.

So I turn up the music's volume and envision the house we toured this afternoon. I can see myself there with Jim. He'd love the bedroom and the round windows like portholes on a ship. He'd love the way the afternoon sun pours in. We could lie in bed together and count the stars. I can feel him next to me now, smell the sweet scent of his skin. This comforts me. But on the other side of my fantasy is another woman like Nora Ruth. I try not to think about this.

Instead, I think about houses, how we live inside them, and they contain us. Maybe that was the problem in my marriage. The house was wrong. We were in a traditional, but my ex-husband loved contemporary. I didn't listen to him. He didn't listen to me. If we'd lived in a different house, maybe I would have been a different kind of wife. I wouldn't have betrayed him. He might have been a different husband. He might have been more relaxed and loving. I would have been more at ease then, too. If he had *noticed* me, wanted to notice me. *What if, what if, what if?* Would any of it have mattered?

I wipe moisture from my eyes and walk to the French doors. Then I press my face against the glass. In the darkness, I can almost see us now, even though I fight it. Can't I just let go? It's like a *dream* that's stuck in my head. My daring is just *illusion.* I've never gotten over the end of my marriage, no matter how hard I've tried. The failure of that dream. I can see the two of us when we first married, moving into the white brick house on that tree-lined street with uneven sidewalks, the flowering magnolias. We chose the house together, a container for us and all our hopes and dreams. I can see the two of us…

But no, it's Jim and me I see, the wedding rings on our fingers and the smiles on our faces as we open the front door and hurry inside to see what awaits us.

Excavation

My writing teacher told me if I wasn't able to hand in a completed story, I should keep a journal and send him that instead. The most important thing is to keep writing. To move forward, whatever happens. Which can be difficult. I used to lead an ordered life, but now I'm reeling. From my mother's illness and death. My pending divorce. And there are decisions to be made about cleaning out and selling my childhood home. My trip there—to Chicago—is tomorrow.

In the past, I've sent stories to the teacher and thought: Where are you? He lives in another city. I began this arrangement when my husband and I lived in the South, in a town so small there were no classes for someone like me, a grown woman with children. I've discovered that writing is a way to excavate. Excavate parts of oneself. That's what appeals to me. Though I'm a high school librarian, when I was young, I dreamed of becoming a great writer. Now I just want to improve my skills.

This arrangement with the teacher resembles the one I have with my lover, who also lives far away—very far away, on the other coast. He and I knew each other in high school. When my marriage was floundering, I found him on Google and called. He came to New York on business. We spent the day together, and he finally said, "Sylvie, do you like to live dangerously?"

"What do you have in mind?" I asked.

"Well, here we are." We sat side by side on the bed in his hotel room. "I've always wanted to sleep with you."

"If I lived dangerously with anyone," I whispered, "I'd do it with you."

In the middle of the night, if I wake up, I lie in the dark and think about him. I consider myself lucky to have a lover, even an occasional one, at my age, fifty-four, though I'm not yet formally divorced and he's still married. This is not ideal, I know. If my daughter were involved with a man in this way and told me, I would say: "Life is complicated. It's easy to love a man you don't see often. There's no use making judgments about what people do, though; they try all sorts of things these days." Still, I would tell her that being involved with a married man is wrong in so many ways. But I can't help myself.

I began the arrangement right before Philip and I separated. Philip had become difficult. Prickly and controlling. We had moved from the small southern town to Manhattan. If I said, "Let's go to a movie," he'd frown and say, "I'd rather see a play." If I said, "Let's stay home, just the two of us," he'd say, "Don't you ever like to socialize, Sylvie? We live in the greatest city in the world." One day I looked at him and remembered couples I saw in restaurants, men and women sitting across from each other with nothing to say. I will die if I have to live like that for the rest of my life, I thought.

Philip's family was from Switzerland. My grandparents were from Russia. He liked to arrive at places early. I took my time—Russian time. If I'm there, fine; if not, most people wait. I've never had a problem waiting.

There are lots of things I don't understand about life and writing. For example, I wrote a story about my mother's death, about death in general. I wanted to correct the facts of what had actually happened.

In the story, I mentioned the doctors who treated the patient. The teacher said, "This is too clinical. Who cares about all the doctors?" I tried to understand and absorb the criticism. That's part of being a writer, being a person—learning to take in useful criticism. But I thought: Doesn't anyone want to know the truth?

The truth was: Being in a hospital was like this. There were doctors whose names you couldn't remember, their expressions grim, white coats draped over their bodies. They danced around the patient, whose name they didn't know. Every doctor made decisions and counter decisions, offered suggestions and counter suggestions, as we, the family, stood trapped in a cloud of confusion, with no one to comfort us.

My mother lay in bed in intensive care, her dyed blond hair coarse and unruly against the pillow, her mouth open wide, plastic accordion tubes from the ventilator jammed down her throat. She was frail and weak. She couldn't breathe on her own. She couldn't speak.

"You have to decide when to remove the breathing tube," a doctor said to my father, my sister, and me. "This needs to reflect the patient's wishes. It should be done soon to avoid complications."

"Do you want us to take the tube out?" my father asked my mother, bending toward her, grasping her hand, trying to comfort her.

She nodded vigorously.

"I can't predict what will happen," the doctor said. "Sometimes the patient is stronger, sometimes not."

No one was brave enough to say: When we take out the tube, you won't be able to breathe on your own. You'll die.

No one in that room with its bright lights and whirring machines and the tubes that snaked into my mother—not one person, not my father or sister or me, not the doctors who trudged in or the nurses—would tell the truth and say the word: die.

"If they take out the tube, it will make you more comfortable," my father explained. He stroked my mother's swollen hand.

She blinked and inhaled a raspy breath.

"Do you want to be more comfortable?" I said, standing next to my father.

She nodded again.

I imagined that when the doctors removed the breathing tube, she would talk. I would hear her beautiful, deep voice. But she never spoke. She shut her eyes and fell into a coma. Then she died.

In the story, I let the mother talk. I heard her voice again. She got well. This was a comfort to me.

When I was young and met my husband, all I wanted was sex. I loved Philip and sex. Now I long for comfort, a hand in mine, a body beside mine at night, a person who understands me.

On the airplane to Chicago, I sit in the window seat, my iPod plugged into my ears. I listen to Vivaldi. I'm not eager to visit my childhood home and clear it out, even with my sister's help. I haven't been back in four months, since my mother's funeral in September. I wish the recent events in my life would disappear. I wish that I were living with Philip, and that we loved each other like we used to. I wish my mother hadn't died. I wish I were married to my lover.

It's not easy to have a husband, I remind myself. I married on a whim, a considered whim. Philip and I lived a good enough life for a good enough amount of time, I suppose. We raised two children. Holly is in graduate school; Adam has just started his first job after college. Now I sit alone in my small rented apartment in Murray Hill, with the heat that doesn't always work, the sounds of mice scratching in the walls, and I wonder: Did I expect too much from Philip? From marriage? From life? Who did I think I was—Greta Garbo? Marilyn Monroe? Someone special? Since we've separated, I've dated, but the truth is, I'm not interested in dates. I'm interested in intimacy. That's why I'm working with the writing teacher. There is an intimacy in putting words on paper. An intimacy with oneself.

The writing teacher knows what he's talking about. Once you decide you're going to write, something happens. Words appear. It's like anything else. Once you decide you're unhappy, you are. Or that you'll get divorced; then you do. It's the same with my lover. I imagine that I'll have sex with him and find comfort, and then when we meet, I do. We touch each other as if we've always been together; we know the map of the other's body like our own. If you can imagine something, it often happens.

The teacher told me not to write a story about a fifty-four-year-old woman. "There's no audience," he said. "Who wants to read about a middle-aged woman with middle-aged problems?"

"Don't people want to know the truth?" I said.

"Not kids," he replied. "They haven't got a clue about middle age. They think they'll be young forever."

What can you put in a story? I consider this at work. I consider this when I wake up in the night. I try not to think about my divorce. Instead I think about stories or about my lover, all the ways he and I make love. We're working our way through the *Kama Sutra*. This was his idea. First we read *The Joy of Sex*. He has a great sense of humor and adventure. I used to read the *Kama Sutra* on my own, to prepare, but this made me long for him. Now we read it together.

When I can't sleep, I think about my mother. Her image always intrudes. I imagine conversations she and I didn't have. If I'd known she was going to die, I would have asked: Were you happy in your life? What was sex like for you? Disappointment? And love? Did you love me as I have always loved you?

I would have asked for guidance: What does a person do if she realizes she's living the wrong life?

Philip works in finance. I never understood what he did. There was no inventory. I had trouble reading the stock indices and understanding the symbols and mutual funds.

I like the quiet of the library, the companionship of books. I like things in place. Sometimes, when classes come to the library, I assign students to write in a journal during their library time. They complain they don't have ideas. "The blank page," I tell them, "is like the future. Unknown. You have to plunge in." I give them suggestions that my writing teacher has given me.

Philip loved to socialize with colleagues and clients. I went with him to gatherings, but I hated them. I preferred to be home with our kids when they were younger or to curl up with a book. My favorites are classics: *A Wrinkle in Time, Little Women, A Tree Grows in Brooklyn.*

The tried and true.

"The tired and true," Philip said with a frown.

But a preference is a preference, a feeling is a feeling, a passion is a passion.

In the taxi to my parents' house, my cell phone rings. It's my childhood friend Carla. She lives in New Mexico. We've known each other since grammar school.

I tell her I'm on my way to the house.

"You know how sorry I am about your mother's death," Carla says. "She was such a grand woman."

"I never thought of her that way," I say.

"My mother was so bookish," Carla says. "And your mother was an actress. Not a real one, of course. She was dramatic. With her grand presence and personality. That blond hair, her bangle bracelets, and the big pearls she wore. I envied you." Carla pauses. "You know, Sylvie, I had my serious mom and my grandfather living with us, and my father was never home. And you had a beautiful mother who was full of enthusiasm. She danced through life."

"Serious, bookish," I say. "I never thought of your mother that way. I admired her. She was refined. Smart. She was lovely."

"My mother was mousy. And then she died."

"You were young."

"Twenty-one," she says wistfully. "She wasn't even fifty. I didn't understand then how young she was. I'm too hard on her. She wasn't mousy—I'm wrong. I miss her. I would have appreciated her now."

"You should appreciate her. Well, my mother was the school counselor, and she knew everyone's business. But she never talked about sex. Your mother did. What does it matter? All those years, I wished my mother were different. Like you felt about your mother. Now I think: What was that about? They're both gone."

"Yeah," Carla says. "I'm still trying to figure out my relationship with her."

In the wintry January air I stare at the house from the sidewalk. Paint peels off the trim; the windows need washing. The house seems to exist on its own, abandoned. My father lives in a retirement community now. He didn't want to live in the house alone.

I'm determined to rescue the valuable stuff from the things that have been crammed in this house for fifty years. The definition of value is different for everyone. I learned this last week when my sister began cleaning the house. Ivy told me on the phone that she'd saved the pile of *Newsweek* magazines, to see if there was a reason our mother kept them. But she threw out a box that sat in the basement.

"What was in the box?" I asked.

"Just junk," Ivy said.

"What kind of junk?"

"Old things. Your letters from Cincinnati, notes I wrote from Denver. Photos."

"You threw those out?"

"Who needs them?"

"You threw those out!" I yelled. Letters I'd sent to my parents twenty years ago. Ivy had thrown out part of my history, her own.

"There's so much crap in this house, you can't keep everything," Ivy was explaining.

"Why the hell would you do that?" I interrupted.

"They didn't mean anything to me. Not my letters or yours. I saved the pictures. I wouldn't throw those out."

"But they meant something to me, the letters."

"I didn't know. How would I know? Next time, I won't do it."

"Can you get them from the trash?" I heard the desperation in my voice and felt foolish.

"I'm not looking in the trash. Besides, it was picked up yesterday. When you come here, save everything you want."

In my mother's house—I think of it as hers—I set my suitcase in the bedroom I shared with Ivy. She'll be here later to help. Despite the cold, the house is warm; the furnace still works well. I eye the mahogany dresser, oak desk, and the bookshelves crammed with childhood books. Then I change into sweatpants and a T-shirt and begin to excavate. I go from room to room and open drawers and closets. My mother saved everything, it seems. I am digging to find nuggets of value. I understand now why Ivy threw out the box.

My mother never wanted us to touch anything here. The closets are jammed with clothing and boxes. "Don't go in there," she used to say.

"Why not?" I asked a few years ago. "Let's take a look in that closet. We can clean. It will be cathartic, Mom."

"No. Absolutely not."

In my parents' closet, on my mother's side, on a high shelf, I see large pieces of cardboard tied together by string. I pull these down and find posters and a drawing I did in middle school, perfectly preserved: the black ink, washes of green, orange, brown, a city scene. Stories I wrote in middle school: "The Unruly Rag." "A Life of Shame." I see the grade of A+! written on the pages. I put them back on the shelf, planning to return to them later.

I move on to her dresser, struck by the items deemed essential to a life: panties, hosiery, socks, brassieres—padded and lacy—camisoles. Another drawer overflows with gloves—opera length, fur-lined brown leather for the cold, white cotton gloves that my mother wore long ago for special occasions, as if one day these would come back into fashion. A drawer full of scarves—oblong, kerchiefs, rectangular silks with bright patterns, geometric cottons, and soft paisley wools.

Greeting cards are tucked among the clothing in yellow paper bags marked "Hallmark." There are cards for all occasions. "To My Darling Husband…Happy Father's Day!" "To a Wonderful Couple!" "For a Special Daughter!" "Another Happy New Year!"

Cards that will never be sent.

In the bottom of the scarf drawer lies a worn, dog-eared copy of *Lady Chatterley's Lover*. I'm a little shocked. Was this my mother's *Kama Sutra*?

Folded among the clothing are pieces of lined white paper with her handwriting. They are drafts of letters. She always wrote a draft in her careful cursive, with the ebullient greetings: "My Dear Dr. ___, We were thrilled and we write to you with the greatest of gratitude…" "Dearest Rabbi Schlomovitz, Thank you for your kindest counsel and…"

Did my mother complete these?

A scavenger, I sit on the floor and rummage through the night table, where I find a typed letter addressed to my mother, written right after her father died.

> Dear Harriet,
>
> I want to tell you how much I feel your loss. To lose a friend, a good friend, is difficult enough at any time. To lose one when you need him as much as you need your father is indeed too bad.
>
> You told me how much you loved your father. The loss must therefore be doubly great. It is as if your entire emotional life were changed. I know it is hard.
>
> And yet we must learn to meet life as it comes. This is one of the signs of adequate living. Some of us must leave first. All of us leave at some time. New friends replace old ones; new attachments are made ultimately.

> I hope that you will meet the situation as painlessly as possible, and that you will soon resume your college work.
>
> Very sincerely,
>
> Professor Sterling James

My mother did resume her college work. She must have met life as it came. She loved her father, I realize with melancholy, as I loved her.

More letters are secured by rubber bands. My acceptance to the University of Michigan. Letters I sent:

> Dear Mom and Dad,
>
> I'm sorry I haven't written for 3 weeks! I hope you haven't forgotten me. College is just great, and…

Beneath this, I discover something my mother must have written when I was in high school.

> Dearest Sylvie,
>
> There are points in life when it is hard to have a real conversation. Then, letters will have to suffice. I am concerned that you don't talk to your father or me anymore. Please tell us what is on your mind. I want to understand you. I'm your mother. I love you. You brood in your room, you go off with your friends, you

It's unfinished. She never gave me this. I remember how I brooded, devastated, having just broken up with my boyfriend, who is my lover now, never mentioning the breakup to my mother. I lay her letter on Ivy's old bed.

On a shelf in another closet, old Marshall Field's boxes contain more correspondence.

> My darling Harriet:
> How fortunate you are to be at the University of Illinois! We are all so proud!! Uncle Seymour is sending you five dollars, and he…

There are lists, too, of what my mother wanted to accomplish. She didn't date these. The house is strewn with what was meant to be.

Each time she put pen to paper, she was having a conversation with herself, I realize.

Though I don't remember seeing her sit at a desk or table, recording her words, she clearly did. The evidence is here. The chronicles of her life.

I cannot stop. I empty the orange-and-gray tin that sits on her dresser. Papers tumble. I discover a small rectangular photograph of my father, my mother, and me, one I have never seen. I must be about a year old. My parents are smiling and young. They hold me between them, in their arms. My head, covered with sandy curls, tilts to the right, finger in my mouth; the full weight of my body rests safely on my mother's shoulder.

My mother is everywhere in this house, in the landscape paintings on the wall, the yellow cotton quilt that covers my parents' bed, in the cracked white linoleum kitchen floor. She is sitting on my bed, and I am ten and transfixed; she is telling me about Mozart, her favorite composer, about oceans and rainforests. "You can write about these things, Sylvie," she says, "in one of your wonderful stories."

I remember the rush of happiness I felt running up these stairs when the man who is my lover first kissed me in high school. And my mother tearing down the stairs in anger after me when, as a teenager,

I brooded and refused to help in the house and called her names: ugly witch, bitter old woman—anything to alienate her.

"It's just a stage you're going through," she yelled. "You'll see. Don't speak to me like that. God help us live through your stages, Sylvie."

In the afternoon, Ivy telephones and says she'll be late coming to the house. "I'm sorry," she says.

"It's okay," I say. "I'll be here." I'm not going anywhere, I think.

When the doorbell rings later, I wonder why she hasn't used her key.

Through the peephole, I see the rabbi. I open the door, surprised.

"Hello, hello." His breath curls in the cold air. "I came to see how you were."

He is dressed in a gray wool coat. He removes his black fedora and thrusts a veiny hand to shake mine. "We've met many times. I remember when you were a young girl. I'm Rabbi Victor Schlomovitz. Your mother was a student in my Torah class. She was the star student."

"Yes, please, come in." What Torah class? She never mentioned this.

"Your mother, may she rest in peace, was a princess among women." His white hair glows in the afternoon light.

"Thank you." I'm embarrassed. I'm wearing gray sweatpants and an old T-shirt that reads "Still Pure After All These Years." I feel dust in my hair, on my clothes. We stand in the front hall on the blue stone floor. How many times have I stood here? Entered the space, left, come back?

"Please sit down." I gesture to the living room. "And please forgive my appearance." My mother would offer the man tea. "Would you like tea or coffee? Something to eat?"

"No, no. I have only a moment. Although your mother is gone, she remains alive in your memories. You are doing the right thing by cleaning this house."

"Yes, Rabbi." He doesn't have to tell me about memories.

"You still have a relationship with her." His large, hooded eyes become misty. "We all must cope with death. We learn things about our loved ones, even after they pass away." He raises a hand to the ceiling, to the heavens. "We continue our relationship with the dead."

"Are you sure I can't give you tea? My mother respected you so."

"Oh, she was a wise and beautiful woman. You take after her and look just like her. But I must go." He hands me a brown paper bag and smiles. "For you."

Inside, I find a plastic jar shaped like a bear, filled with honey.

"May you know sweeter things in the days to come," he says.

"Thank you," I say, touched by his thoughfulness.

"Treasure your memories." He marches to the door. "You will keep her alive that way."

The man sets his fedora on his head, walks out, and climbs into an old blue Volvo station wagon with a dent on the right front. He disappears down the street, like a messenger from another world.

I know I must make progress here. I set the jar of honey on the kitchen table. Though I don't need it, I'll save it, to remember the man's kindness. I collect garbage bags from beneath the sink and climb the stairs. In my old bedroom, I stare at the dresser, but instead of opening the drawers, I toss the garbage bags on the floor, kick off my sneakers and sprawl on my bed. Ivy's bed is littered with papers I've put there. I shouldn't lie on the quilted pink bedspread—my mother would be displeased. But I lie there anyway.

All I can think of is my mother. I don't think of my divorce or my stories or my lover. My image of her is so strong, it's as if she is sitting next to me, her sweet jasmine perfume spilling into the room.

Then the image of her in the hospital intrudes. I am still standing next to her. They have removed the ventilator and stopped all medicines, except for morphine to make her more comfortable. Morphine, the doctors' definition of comfort. My mother's mouth hangs open, as if she is struggling to breathe. The face is hers, yet there is such an unnatural stillness about it. I can't believe she's gone. I try to close her mouth, but I can't—her lips are frozen open. The woman from hospice can't close them either. I am unable to leave that room, even in memory. I'm certain my mother will sit up and speak in her deep, mellifluous voice: This is a second-rate hospital. Why did you bring me here? Who are these doctors? Sylvie, I want to go home.

Home. I want to go home.

I remember when Philip and I moved to the southern town where there were no writing teachers for a woman my age. "This will be my new home," I explained to my mother as brightly as I could, although I worried about living in so small a place.

"You don't know anyone there, Sylvie," she said. "You'll be with strangers. I'll try to help you, my sweetheart."

After the doctor removed the breathing tube, she fell into a coma and survived for four days. My father, sister, and I sat at her bedside, but we went home to sleep. She died at night, alone, in that hospital, tended by strangers.

"Do you think she was lonely?" I asked the nurse when I arrived, breathless, to see my mother for the last time.

"A lot of people die alone," the woman replied. "The research shows that."

"I wonder why," I said lamely.

"No one knows for sure." She shrugged, ready to go to the next patient. Then she reconsidered. "Because death is so private," she said. "People wait to die alone. Because they want to spare the people they love. Spare them pain."

I want to stay in that hospital room, but the woman from hospice—with her gray hair and weak smile of concern, a gold cross dangling around her neck, the woman who should be our champion and lead us through grief—is saying, "I'm sorry, but you'll have to go now. The hospital needs this bed."

I stare at her. I don't understand. "The hospital needs this bed," I repeat.

"Yes. There are other patients who need a bed."

I've walked past so many empty rooms here. "How can they need this bed?" I say. "What can five more minutes mean to them?"

The woman doesn't answer.

This is why I wrote the story for the writing teacher, I realize—because I still can't leave that hospital room.

Dark descends early in January. Ivy has not arrived yet, and I am lying in my old bed, thinking. At the moment this seems to be what I do best. I am continuing my relationship with my mother.

I think of my daughter in graduate school in another state, moving into her own life. My son is busy with his job at a financial firm. Philip is gone. And my lover. "Where are you?" I whisper. I turn on my side and hug a pillow.

Spirals of moonlight seep into the room. There's no noise from traffic. This silence was my companion when I was a child. I remember all the nights I slept in this bed, and the quiet. The comfort.

A whole world seemed to take place in this room: all the joys, disappointments, and longings of life.

School was another world; I traversed the two with ease. There was no lover then, no failed marriage, no writing teacher, no job, no grown-up children. I used to lie here and map my future: I would go to college and fall in love, marry and have children. I would become a great author. Or maybe not. My dreams stopped there. I couldn't see beyond the early rush of love and motherhood.

I was certain that at the right time I would know what to dream next. I was smart, an excellent student, but naïve. I believed in happily ever after.

And if I didn't know what to dream next, I would discuss this with my mother. She would give me guidance.

But she is gone, and this house will soon be gone.

We must learn to meet life as it comes.

"Where are you?" I call out. Who am I talking to? My sister? My absent husband? My children? My teacher? My mother?

I realize I am asking this of myself.

It's time. I switch on the light and go to my old dresser to begin. At first, I want to keep everything. I force myself to throw items away: high school report cards, playbills from theaters, a few of my mother's lists. I find a letter Carla wrote to me in college. I set this aside. Then I find a piece of lined paper with my mother's handwriting:

> My teeth hurt. My eyes hurt. My neck is aching. I think I am dying. Can anyone help me?

I discover another:

> Tell the doctor my stomach hurts. I can hardly see. My neck does not stop aching. I need someone to help me.

She is continuing her relationship with us.

There are pages of these notes in the drawers. My mother's handwriting is faint and wobbly. There are no dates. This is the chronicle of her decline.

Perhaps she wrote these when conversation was no longer possible.

I imagine cataloguing the notes and letters as I would in an old-fashioned library, making order, creating folders, lining them neatly on shelves, organized according to topic: youth, college, marriage, birth of children, travel, old age, the terrible decline. I imagine telling Ivy this grand idea, and then I imagine her sisterly disdain.

What use would this be to anyone?

I hesitate, then pull the trash bag closer and throw in papers. I can't bear to think of my mother like this. I won't.

I keep a few stray sheets to show Ivy.

I will take life as it comes.

I am tossing out papers at a manic pace. Then I stop. I tie the handles of the bulging bag and open another. The whole span of my childhood fills my mind. My mind is a dresser drawer crammed with memories I must excavate.

I dive in and settle on this:

My parents were so proud when I looked at colleges. We visited the University of Michigan. I had an interview there. The admissions officer asked me a few questions. Then my mother, who loved to compliment people, who could be lavish in her praise, began to tell the man about my abilities and accolades. Her face became rosy, her voice fervent with excitement.

The admissions officer, a dour middle-aged man in a gray suit, with gray eyes, stopped her. "There are a lot of Sylvies," he said.

"I didn't know that was such a common name," my mother replied earnestly.

My father nodded.

"No, no." The man shook his balding head. "There are lots of kids like her—with great scores on the tests, honors, terrific prospects for the future. Talented writers or artists or gifted in math. They have great promise. We can't admit them all. We have limited spots for students from out of state. This may not be the Ivy League, but we're close. We have to choose."

I didn't know much about the Ivy League then. I'd never been to the East.

"I don't understand," my mother said. She clutched her pocketbook to her chest. She wore white cotton gloves and a blue-and-white polka dot dress, her pearls shimmering around her neck. She looked radiant, dressed to perfection. She looked grand, just like Carla said. It was a comfort to have her beside me. Even so, I was mortified by the turn of this conversation. They would never let me into this university. I was suddenly furious. My mother had ruined my future; I couldn't wait to leave home. I would tell her after the interview. Why couldn't she listen? Why couldn't she look more intellectual, more serious? Why couldn't she be silent like my father? He sat stupefied by the cost of college, I was sure, though we had been informed about loans and scholarships.

The admissions officer frowned, as if he didn't have time for such trivialities, and maybe he didn't. It occurred to me then he might be drunk. I was shocked by this.

"Michigan is a great university," he went on, slurring his words a bit. "It's in the Big Ten, after all. Those from out of state are the cream of the students. Think of it like this—the University of Michigan is a microcosm of the world."

My parents nodded. I shifted uneasily in my seat.

"And in the world, no matter how special you think you are," the man pronounced, "you learn that no one is special." He shook his head, as if he were talking about himself. He looked worn suddenly, used up by life. "The world is the grim reaper," he said. "Life doesn't care about anyone."

My parents blinked, shocked at his candor. I blinked too.

"I don't agree with that," my mother said briskly, defending me, protecting me. "I don't believe this is the policy of the University of Michigan. I want to talk to a supervisor."

"Oh, you'll see. But our time is up. I have another appointment." He shook my hand, gripping it firmly.

Then he eyed my mother. "I'm sorry to say, there's no one else to talk to here. If the director of admissions were in town, you could speak to him, but he's not. Anyone on our staff will tell you the same thing: Maybe your Sylvie will be a student here. That I can't say. We'll look at her application. We'll weigh her against the other applicants. She's on the cusp of her future. Whatever happens, if you're all lucky, she'll grow up and live her life. Doesn't matter if she's a student at this great university or at a school like it, she'll see as life goes on. No one is special at all."

Sitting on my childhood bed, surrounded by garbage bags and papers, I decide to write a story for my writing teacher. I don't need to reimagine the story, I realize. I can write the memory exactly as it happened, except I will change the end.

After we spoke to the admissions man, my parents and I walked out of the office, past a fidgety teenage boy and his father, and then along the tree-lined paths through the campus. My mother looked pale. I could see the man's words had shaken her. "Not special!" she muttered under her breath.

My father frowned and said, "Surely there was a supervisor."

"I'm going to look into it," my mother said.

I walked between them in sullen silence. I didn't care about a supervisor. All I cared about was being accepted at the school and going on to live a life of my own.

My mother thought I was upset and she tried to reassure me when she was really reassuring herself. "You *are* special, Sylvie, no matter what that man says." She put her arm around me.

My father nodded.

"But the most important thing is that, whatever happens, we'll always love you," she said.

This embarrassed me. My temper flared and I wiggled from my mother's grasp. She was cloying and overprotective; if she hadn't pushed me forward in the interview, the man wouldn't have felt the need to push back. It was she who had caused his gruffness, his absurd assertions. It was she who would get me rejected by Michigan.

I stormed away from my parents and flung words at them over my shoulder. I didn't know where I was going, but in my imagination I was striding into my future. "You asked too many questions,"

I yelled. "I hate you. You've ruined everything." I was a teenager, riddled with anxiety, brooding; I was trying to break away.

And yet I knew it wasn't a matter of greatness or ability, after all. Some people *were* exceptional, but I wasn't one of them. I wasn't a world-class figure skater or a musical genius or a math savant. I realized the truth of what my mother had said. She really didn't care if I was extraordinary. She just loved me for who I was.

I was my parents' daughter and to them, I was special. And my mother was special, too—at least to me. Not because she was grand, like Carla had said (and she was), but because she loved me whether I was happy or sad, a success or failure.

I let my parents down badly that day, but in the story, I can redeem the past, correct it, or at least try. Instead of running from her and yelling, I'll end the story like this:

My mother thought I was upset and she tried to reassure me when she was really reassuring herself. "You *are* special, Sylvie, no matter what that man says." She put her arm around me.

My father nodded.

"Whatever happens, we'll always love you," she said. "It doesn't matter what the admissions officer says."

Walking between my parents, my anger dissolved. I felt calmer, almost prescient. It finally didn't matter whether Michigan accepted me or rejected me. I'd go to college somewhere. Perhaps my mother and father were just another set of doting parents, but they were *my* parents. She was my mother, the only one I would ever have. I suddenly understood what her absence someday might mean to me.

"You'll always be special to us," she said. "What's important is who you are and how you live." She kissed my forehead. "Don't ever forget that, Sylvie."

I stopped walking. There would be other admissions officers and other problems, I knew, but my mother and father would be a bulwark against adversity for as long as they were able.

The three of us stood beneath a leafy tree on the campus. The sun was shining low in the sky. I was on the cusp of my future. I could feel it. I would go to college somewhere and I would live my life as I chose. A quiet voice inside me told me to take my time. The future was long and I would never again have companions quite like my parents.

I grasped my mother's white-gloved hand and squeezed it tight.

Bare Essentials

The room had just the bare essentials: a king-sized bed, desk, armchair, a dresser and coffeemaker, and, of course, a bathroom. It was in a functional hotel, but the space had everything a traveler needed. Todd and I met there three or four times a year, some years more, some years less, in a city where I once lived. I've lived in so many places: Chicago, Boston, Detroit, LA, even London. The exact location of the hotel doesn't matter. It could be anywhere. We had all we needed there. The place was without frills or pretension, without art or sentimental personal objects. It was bare enough to make room for passion.

Of course, it's difficult to try to quantify passion or the quality of feeling between two people. How can you be sure the same feeling is shared by the two who are together in the hotel room, in bed, in each other's arms?

I know that people can experience an act, an event, or a shared life differently. I'm aware of this from my own experience, from the end of my marriage. Perceptions can be so at odds that it's sometimes difficult to believe two people have shared time or even conversation. In the case of my ex-husband, this was true. My ex-husband, my former husband, my husband no longer, the man I once adored who fell out of love as easily as falling in love, a man I detest but sometimes miss.

In the hotel room, I don't think about my ex-husband. He is a vague, unpleasant memory, part of a past life, though we have been divorced only two years. I have forgotten the sound of his voice. I don't remember the characteristics of his body or the curve of his smile.

I know the length of time Todd and I have been meeting in the hotel, the exact number of years and number of times we've fucked or argued. I would never tell him this. I told my ex-husband too many things, and with Todd I am circumspect. What happens in real life seems beside the point.

Todd is married, and that's no surprise, I suppose, except to me, who was raised to believe that marriage was sacred.

The demise of a marriage doesn't happen in a vacuum, and I've come to believe intimacy may be an unattainable fantasy. Our first marriage counselor told Lou and me this. "He robbed the bank, and you're driving the getaway car," the counselor said. He was middle-aged, wore a wedding ring, and spoke in a warm but ironic voice.

Lou and I laughed uncomfortably.

"Maybe I should be driving the getaway car," Lou said.

"You'd leave me with the dirty work," I countered. "Rob a bank. Typical."

"I'd be better off robbing the bank and driving away myself," he said.

Lou was an angry, dissatisfied man, an economist who wanted everything to run perfectly. I had fallen for his quick charm and knowledge of the world when we met. He said he loved my sense of adventure, but in later years he accused me of being flighty, indecisive, indefinite. This was true, but I behaved this way only with him.

I edit medical research papers for a journal, studies about bacteria, *Campylobacter* or *C. difficile*. In my work, I am precise. I know that a hundred trillion good bacteria call the human body home. Even the mouth has several species of bacteria, and each tooth has its own ecosystem. The body is like space or the ocean, a vast unknown, like the mind. Like a relationship.

My work is painstaking, but in my life with Lou, I was anything but precise. I became carefree while he was dour. I rushed out at a moment's notice, leaving dishes in the sink and clothing on the floor, while he was meticulous about putting things in the correct place. I was flexible in reaction to his inflexibility, willing to give into his ideas about where to live, how to raise our two sons. He balanced the checkbook, and I didn't subtract my spending. He balanced our budget. I lost receipts and bills.

The demise of a marriage is a failure. Lou may have fallen out of love with me, but in my own way, I fell out of love with him. I did nothing to repair our fissures or leave them behind. I brought the fissures with me to the hotel, and only there, left them in the hallway before I entered the room to see Todd.

I've met Todd's two grown children. I know what his mother and sisters are doing with their lives. I know that Todd's sister is ill with lupus and lives near him. He takes care of her. His father died when Todd was young; his stepfather was a parent to him. Todd knows about my parents who are no longer alive, my brother and sister who live in different cities—the successful one, and the other who struggles—and about my sons, one of whom wants to live in a Zen monastery. The divorce has been hard for them. Todd doesn't know that in anger I slapped one son's face and feel great remorse, or about checks I've bounced, or my fear of being unable to support myself, or how I really feel about my divorce—fissures or not, I've failed.

I know he likes cream in his coffee, and apple pie, and he knows I am mostly punctual. Todd is unerringly on time. He's worried that the years ahead of him are fewer than those behind him, and there is not a thing he can do about this. He's growing older. I am, too. This is an intractable fact.

"Sometimes I think we have a love that's not usable," I say to Todd today. "I read that phrase in a book."

We are in bed, beneath the sheet, in the bare hotel room.

"We see each other." His arm is around me.

"I mean, I want to find a companion," I say to him dreamily. I'm the most candid after we've fucked. "I'm divorced now, after all." Of course, I don't need to qualify this.

"I hope you do find someone," he says. "But you don't have to be married to him."

My heart sinks a little, and I lay my head on Todd's bare shoulder. He has a lovely long, angular face, dark curly hair spotted with gray, and a solid, muscular body. I have found someone—him. "There are the leavers and those who stay," Lou always said. Lou was the kind of man who leaves, he told me. Todd is the kind who stays. I admire this about him. I hate this about him.

"No, I don't think I'll get married again," I say. "But I want that intimacy. Of being married." I think of the nights at home alone. I remind myself I have that intimacy at this very moment, in this hotel room.

"Some people have that in their lives," he says quietly. "Really, they're lucky. Others don't have a close connection, even if they're married."

I know this. The couple married thirty years who have lived like brother and sister for a decade—he's like my brother, my friend says. No sex. She's not interested. Another friend's husband hasn't wanted sex for years. She misses the passion, she says, but she doesn't want to leave or break up the family.

"There are all kinds of arrangements," I say to Todd. I love the blue of his eyes, like the color of the sea, and the shape of his lips and how they bore into mine.

"That's what relationships are." He kisses my shoulder. "Arrangements. People are always arranging and rearranging their lives. I want to see you more."

"We'll arrange it," I say. I want to see him more often, too. But then it will be difficult to part. I need just enough closeness so I can bear to leave, be a chameleon and slip back into my life without too many wounds.

Too much yearning is like a wound.

When we fuck, there are no wounds, no past and no future.

The truth is: I don't know how much longer I can do this with Todd. But I don't tell him. The leaving makes our arrangement difficult, the moment we part and after. The months of absence. I don't consider myself dependent, but I have become dependent on our passion, the ritual of it, the fact of its existence.

I know from my work that bacteria can only survive in a conducive environment, in a friendly host. When the conditions change, the bacteria die or leave. The conditions of my life have changed. I'm not sure that's a correct analogy, and I make a mental note to ask the author of an article I'm editing if my assumption about bacteria is true and my analogy to people correct. Even if a bacterium is eradicated, I think, there are millions more, and an organism can wander from host to host until the bacteria finds a safe and welcoming home.

People are, in the microscopic regions of the heart, not so different from bacteria.

I've read that bacteria have sex and reproduce. Some live a faster lifestyle and, in a sense, drive a convertible and take risks. Some are resilient. Others disappear in the struggle to survive.

My ex-husband bought a convertible before we divorced, and he started to live a fast lifestyle. He went to bars and acquired a girlfriend. The marriage fell away, and I didn't fight.

Since the end of my marriage, I've realized there aren't many things I need or want—material possessions, that is. This is a liberating feeling. A few days with Todd, dinner with friends or with my children is enough for me. I've had the house, albeit a small one, the wedding ring and vacations, the trappings of marriage. However, the bare essentials fell away. I didn't know how to say this to the marriage counselor: What was important between my husband and me was gone. The correct sequence of the genes of our relationship became scrambled. Something was wrong. This was my failing—not articulating my hunch. I don't know if telling the counselor or Lou would have made a difference.

What is the cost of desire? I think as I lie in bed next to Todd in the hotel room. Today is the last afternoon of our visit.

Is it worth it to be alone and then have a few hours or days of pleasure? Our relationship is a delicate balance. No, a relationship is like the body—full of things we cannot see and that we don't realize exist. A microscope doesn't help. If you look too closely, the mystery is gone. That happened with my marriage. You can label the stuff of a relationship, trace emotions, and conquer the science of it, but then you can lose the beauty of the whole. I didn't tell the counselor this, but I believe it's true: You can talk a relationship to death.

I've seen this phenomenon in scientific papers: the obsessive quality of research, the attention to the minute details of an organism. Scientists deconstruct an organism with such specificity that often nothing is left to the imagination. After the thrill of discovery, the researcher loses sight of the grace of the creation.

Is this merely passion between Todd and me, or is this an emotional connection? Or are the two intertwined?

Is there such a thing as "mere" passion? Maybe that's lust.

Perhaps if he and I continue to meet when we're very old, I'll ask. Not now, when I'm still greedy for him.

I've come to believe that some thoughts are better left unsaid. My grandmother used to quote an old Yiddish expression. My mother did too, during her last illness. A new side of my mother appeared as she was failing and about to leave life. When I told her about my marital problems, she shook her head. "Oh, honey," she said. "I'm sorry. You never know what's around the next corner. You have to be prepared for anything in life." Then she slipped into Yiddish, and translated: "The kiss is superficial, but the bite comes from the heart."

Sometimes I'm angry at Todd. I hate to admit this, even to

myself. It's not in my nature to be angry with him, but there are times when I think he isn't enough for me; there's too much absence. When we're apart, I wonder about us. Mostly, I believe he is enough, like now as we lie together, holding hands, his body cupped around mine.

I have a mantra for our relationship when I begin to have doubts. A story I tell myself: You don't own anything in life. Don't own a house or apartment, no matter what the recorded deed says. You're the guardian of the property for a while. A bacterium doesn't own its host. Bacteria are transient, like everything else. You don't take ownership of a person. You're the guardian of the relationship for a period of time. Then you let it go. Even with a marriage. Marriage is a contract. I had that contract with Lou. But how can you bind a person's soul?

The older I get—and I'm middle-aged—the more I understand the fluidity of the world. We travel through each other's lives, as if we all have a purpose, a place and time to be part of another's existence. People turn out not to be who they seem. "There are the givers and the users," my ex-husband used to say.

I told Lou in anger while we were at the counselor's: "You're like opportunistic bacteria that take advantage of their host."

Sometimes I pretend Todd is my husband. We are, after all, in a hotel room together now, a room that feels like our home. I know his habits: the way he undresses and lays his clothing on the chair, with easy care. I know his erection is a way of saying he's happy to see me. At first I felt awkward with him and undressed slowly. I felt guilty about Lou and about Todd's wife. Todd once said to me, "You used to be so inhibited, and now you're not." I said yes, and didn't tell him that I'm shy. Inhibition is a function of shyness. Now I undress easily when we meet in the hotel room and wrap my arms around him, happy to see him. I don't explain that my father said he didn't like to talk much about himself and worried he created a wall between other people and himself. I don't tell Todd that, in my own way, I do the same.

I don't go into psychological treatises about my parents and how they paid more attention to my brother than to me. Todd doesn't enumerate the stresses in his life. He doesn't tell me what lies he's told his wife. Or what he says when she asks about his day after he's spent the day with me. He doesn't tell me what feelings may or may not fester inside him, doubts or uneasiness or guilt. Or the way he keeps feelings at bay. I don't know the stories he tells himself. Like: I will see her one more time, we will fuck, and then I will go back to being faithful to my wife. Or, I'm a loyal husband in all ways except this, a good husband. Isn't that what matters?

We are careful about the data we share.

I know Todd is capable of keeping secrets from his wife, and from me. I am both grateful for this and disappointed.

"I wish you were free," I say to him in the hotel room. As soon as I say this, I regret the words. I don't want him to know all of my wishes, just as I don't know his.

"Free. I don't want you to think I'm a prisoner in my marriage. I'm not."

"I don't even know if you have health problems," I say.

"You know almost everything about me. Just my back. My damned tennis elbow."

In the bare room, we talk about our life together, our shared truncated history.

"How many years have we been doing this?" he says. "How many times do you think we've made love?"

"Oh, I don't know. Hundreds maybe." I pause to count.

"How many ways do you think we've done it?" he asks.

I smile and shrug. I know the year and the month and the day and the moment when we started. I was living in the city where I lived, and he was living in the city where he lived. I was visiting a friend in that city. Todd came over to drop off a package, and we had a lot in common. He and I had gone to the same college. We had some overlapping friends. He was a nephrologist and believed in humanistic medicine and the need to teach students about emotions and empathy. He used these concepts at the university and in his work at an inner-city clinic. I had edited a paper by his colleague. Todd was interested in ideas and art, like I was. Once he and I started talking, it seemed we would never stop.

The self-help books say distance sustains an affair. I wonder if this is true for Todd and me. Or if maybe we sustain our connection because of who we are and the mystery of what happens when we're together.

I will probably never find out.

There are no innocent bystanders in an affair. Nothing is innocent about it. The only innocence is preserved in the bare hotel room, in that bed, at the moment when time stands still.

It was easier to do this in another city when we began, when I knew my husband was occupied. I tried to smash my guilt then.

Maybe this isn't an affair anymore. An affair is fleeting. This seems like something else. A relationship. With borders.

Todd and I are Buddhists in the hotel room. We give up all worldly attachments, except for desire.

"What?" Todd says to me. "Something is on your mind."

"Nothing is." I lean my head on his bare shoulder.

"No, I know when something is bothering you." He looks at me closely.

I'm quiet. I can ask him anything. There are things I don't want to know.

"Don't ask me how I can do this," he says, as if he can read my mind. "I can compartmentalize. It's how I'm made."

"I've been willing to see you in compartments." The room is so bare;

there is nowhere to look except at him, at his lovely blue eyes.

"Are you having doubts?" he says.

"About what?"

"You and me. Doubts about us."

"No, I was..." I stop. "I was thinking this room is our compartment."

"Like a compartment on a train." He kisses me.

I don't ask: Where is our train going? What are your intentions? The questions my father or mother would have asked. What are my intentions?

"I think secrets are essential to your character," I say, and I suddenly know this is true.

"If I can't be honest with you, who can I be honest with?" he says quietly. He pauses. "Doesn't everyone have secrets?"

"I suppose." I have my own.

"Everyone has secrets of the heart."

I trace my fingers along the outlines of his face. What does our relationship say about him, I wonder, his character, about who he is? I don't ask: If I were your wife, would you be a loyal husband? Would the same level of comfort exist between us as exists now?

These are hypothetical questions. The only way to determine the answers is to do an experiment with controls, like the scientists do. That's not in the cards.

The things I did not say to my ex-husband:

- I am not 100 percent happy with our marriage.
- Does anyone deserve 100 percent happiness in life?
- I've read that every person behaves like a different person with each friend or lover or relative.
- I'm one person, a better person, with Todd, and another, more flighty, less happy woman, with you.
- When you asked me to marry you, I adored you. I thought you adored me. Still, I wasn't absolutely sure, but I said yes because I

wondered: Can I be 100 percent sure of anything in life?

- This is why I enjoy science writing: because there is no absolute certainty; there is always a variation, a new discovery, a refinement, another place to explore. And I like editing because of the precision.
- You admitted to the marriage counselor that you told me half-truths. "No," the counselor said. "Those are lies." Perhaps that's why I started with Todd. I loved you. You'd had an affair all those years ago. I wanted to get back at you. I didn't know my own affair would lead to real feeling with someone else. I learned about lies from you.
- I know that you sleep with your mouth open and snore. You keep the house at sixty degrees in the winter. These are very human habits. You have a temper. Everyone has minor quirks. I have habits that annoy you. Even so, you were a buffer against loneliness.
- I believed marriage was sacred. I would have stayed with you forever. Our marriage gave me comfort. I could solve problems that faced us because comfort surrounded me, an intimacy of presence with you, even if, after a time, there wasn't an intimacy of souls.

The things I do not say to Todd:

- The consequences of sex are different for a woman than for a man.
- We are equal partners in passion. My marriage did not have this equality.
- Someone said in ancient Greece that true friends have two bodies with one soul.
- I read that the sculptor Henry Moore said: "The secret of life is to have a task, something you devote your entire life to, something you bring everything to, every minute of the day for your whole life. And the most important thing is—it must be something you

cannot possibly do."

- The secret of my life is that I am in love with you.
- Since I've been divorced, I spend time after work checking Match.com, or going on a date, or talking to my kids or friends, or wandering around the city where I live, or reading. I reread a novel, *The Old Capital.* You and I read aloud from it once in the hotel room. Do you remember what a character said? "Good fortune is short while loneliness is long."
- You are my good fortune and my loneliness.
- Sometimes I think our relationship will not continue. Sometimes I think it must continue. That's called conflict.
- I am capable of telling half-truths, even to you. I wonder if I tell them to myself.

Todd explains the concept of "mattering" to me now.

"My daughter is making progress on her dissertation," he says. She's in graduate school, sociology. "She's decided to do research on 'mattering.' How this affects students and teachers. Does a student perform better in school because she feels she matters to the teachers? I think about that in my practice. Does a patient work harder to get well because he feels he matters to the doctor? Maybe so. People want to feel they matter and that taps the best in them." He smiles. "It's really what people perceive that counts."

"In all parts of life," I say, intrigued.

I can't extrapolate this to bacteria, except that the host matters for the bacteria's very survival, even a weak or compromised host.

"Would you miss this if we stopped seeing each other?" I ask.

He presses his head into the pillow, looks at the ceiling, then at me. "You can stop this any time you want," he whispers.

"But would you miss it?"

I think I see tenderness flicker across his face, a hint of pain. "Yes," he says evenly. "I would miss this, you. Very much." He puts his arm around me and pulls me closer. "And you?"

"Of course, yes." I have no answers, just questions. "I'm just surprised at the shape life has taken."

"The shape we give our lives. For me, too. It's one surprise after another."

I wrap my arms around him. In a small box of time, we matter to each other in a fundamental sense. Isn't this what everyone wants?

After we've fucked again, Todd drifts to sleep, and I lie awake next to him, thinking. There is no scientific method for measuring the cause of passion or if passion will last. Is our relationship love or need or both? Does loneliness intensify desire?

I've accepted that there are no explanations for what happens in our lives. No matter what the scientists say. Things occur or don't. So much is chance or luck combined with what feels like free will.

My mother always said there was no perfection. "We don't have to make the world perfect, honey," she told me. "God creates only so much. The world is cracked and incomplete. You do what you're able to and try to repair the world as much as you can. You won't be able to fix everything."

If the world is cracked and incomplete, relationships are as well.

Whenever it's time to leave, like now, Todd and I reluctantly shower and dress. I don't tell him about the feeling of absence. I say, "It was nice to see you. I'll talk to you."

He says the same, hugs me, and then slips out the door.

When he walks out, I wonder now, as I always do, if I'll see him again. There are so many uncertainties in life, and we're getting older. There is the clutch of terror when we part. Is this it? Is this all? Is this the end?

I can't bear more fissures or failures. I remind myself: In life there are no guarantees.

Over time, I know, during the absence, I will hear his voice on the phone, but I will forget the exact shade of blue of his eyes, the way he smiles—with his whole face—and how he tilts his head to kiss me, forget even the quality of emotion when we're together.

But I will remember our compartment of comfort.

If he leaves the room first, like today, I wait until he's gone, until his footsteps have disappeared. I have my rituals after we part. I stay in the hotel room and sprawl on the bed. I inhale the scent of him, and try to recapture the quality of feeling in my mind. This is silly and sentimental, but essential. I breathe in the remnants of passion. Then I rise and check the room twice to be sure I am leaving nothing behind. I slip the flat plastic hotel key into my purse, to put in the back of my drawer where I keep all the keys from all the rooms where we have met.

I eye the room again and brace myself for real life, as if bracing for a storm. I tell myself what I read once: There is no bad weather; only weather you're not dressed for. Then I leave the room, shutting the door behind me, and push my way outside, into the elements, whatever the season, and then drive or take a bus or plane or train toward home.

A Celebration of the Life of the Reverend Canon Edward Henry Jamison

1

When I was a child, my mother told me that no one dies in his or her own time. A person's lot may be seventy years, she said, but the veil of death appears before anyone is ready. So it happened with my cousin, Edward Henry Jamison. At his death, he was not quite sixty-seven.

My mother's family fled from Russia. She was the third child of four, the first born in America. She spoke with the nasal imprecision of a Chicagoan, and she was loud and tough like a city kid, with a brash way of stating opinions as if she were pushing onto a crowded El. But she was stocky and freckled like a Russian peasant, superstitious, and she often spoke Yiddish. I learned her phrases by heart. *Dos ponim fun an alt'n, iz a landkarte tzum keyver:* An old man's face is a roadmap to the grave. *Gey shray chay vekayom:* Go scream: Living and Eternal God, nothing further can be done. *Ainem dacht zich az bei yenem lacht zich:* One always thinks that others are happy.

My parents kept kosher and my mother, like most of her family, felt uneasy about gentiles, if not outright afraid of them. The family didn't adopt the tough, detached veneer I'd noticed in Jewish survivors of the Holocaust. But she and her family yearned to *belong* to something; the relatives cleaved to each other.

My father, a born Chicagoan, seemed to accept my mother's idiosyncrasies, that with her Russian parents and siblings she was more half-and-half than anything, part old world, part new. I hated this about her. She always seemed like a mix-up to me. I realized this when I talked with my friends' parents, who spoke no Yiddish and didn't mind whether you were gentile or Jew.

I recognized this, too, when Edward joined our family. He married my oldest cousin. He was nine years older than Eva, and an Episcopalian minister.

He and Eva made their bargain. She learned to sit in church, and he learned to attend seders and *Shabbat* dinners. I was shocked, yet admired that she could be so disloyal to the family and marry a man of a different faith.

Edward grew up in Scotland and spoke with a lilt. He had the bearing of a gentleman, cultured and genteel, like an ancient lord.

"He's even met the Queen of England, Pammie," Eva once told me dreamily.

Our family never saw Edward in his white collar or went to church to hear him preach. He never spoke with us about religion or God. He was just Edward to us, older cousin Edward to me, with his wavy brown hair, handsome chiseled nose, and bright brown eyes. He had long, strong fingers like those that could play a harp.

"Good afternoon, Pamela," he used to say. "What kind of day will it be for you?"

I blushed. I always did when he spoke to me. I was fourteen when they married, and secretly in love with him. We were all a bit in love with him. Except for Eva's mother, Aunt Fay, who was a widow herself. When Eva told her she planned to marry Edward, Aunt Fay wept.

Nights then, I lay awake and beseeched God—*Adonai Eloheinu,* hear me please—to allow me to marry a man like Edward, so I could walk down an aisle in a billowy white dress, circle my husband seven times, and kiss him. So I might live happily forever after, as I was certain Eva would. I would live near her, I imagined.

After they married, I spent summer weekends at the Belmont Beach with them. The crowded, littered shoreline stretched in the shadow of downtown Chicago. We basted ourselves with coconut butter, lay close on a blanket like sardines. The burning sunlight toasted our bodies. Edward read aloud to us, "Leda and the Swan," excerpts from Shakespeare, or even *A Child's Christmas in Wales.*

Often, he recited from memory. His clear voice rose above the thumping waves of Lake Michigan. I hated for him to stop. When he did, the three of us discussed the meaning of life.

One winter, as a surprise to Eva, he arranged ballroom dancing lessons for the two of them. On cold Sundays when I visited them, they switched on the record player and demonstrated a tango or waltz. I watched, transfixed. The way each anticipated the sway of the other seemed the physical manifestation of love. Then Edward danced with me with great patience.

But I went away to college and never lived in Chicago again. Eva and I kept in touch by telephone. She gave birth to a daughter. I visited them all on occasion and married a kind man whom I loved for his intellect and compassion. Lennie was a sociology professor. We settled in New Jersey and had two children. I taught art at a high school there.

Lennie was Jewish, but barely. He was *milkhik*. He was tall and wiry, with sandy hair and kind, pale-blue eyes. He didn't understand the dietary laws, the difference between *milkhik* and *fleyshik*—the biblical injunction against eating foods made from milk with meat. He didn't know Yiddish words or prayers. He preferred to read a sociology book instead of going to synagogue on the holiest days. I loved this about him. He and his family were completely American. I felt *fleyshik,* steeped in the muddy, meaty, heavy gravy of Yiddish words and ritual, drowning. I couldn't wait to break away.

When we met, he lived in Brooklyn. I was in graduate school in the city and often stayed overnight at his apartment. It was a mixed neighborhood. Lennie liked the diversity. "Only two percent of the population of the United States is Jewish. Why limit yourself?" he said.

Across the street, in a walk-up, lived a group of Hare Krishnas. They strolled on the sidewalk in bright, flowing orange robes and had pinched expressions.

One night in May, at 3:00 a.m., they started to chant. It was impossible to sleep. Lennie and other neighbors asked the chanters to shut the windows. They refused. A neighbor called the police. "Hare Krishnas have a right to religious freedom," the policeman said when he arrived. "If you don't like it, change the Constitution. I can't change them or you either. It's human nature."

A few weeks later, the Hare Krishnas began to chant in the night again. Lennie had a job interview the next day. He was a patient man, but he bolted from bed, grabbed a hose from a shelf, hooked it to the faucet, opened the window, and sprayed.

"Don't," I said.

I saw the Krishnas bowed in prayer; I watched the water spiral against their shaved heads until they slammed shut the windows.

That July Fourth, neighborhood kids threw firecrackers under the robes of some Krishnas. The firecrackers exploded. A flurry of orange disappeared into the building, then the members emerged carrying baseball bats. A fight broke out. Again, the police arrived. The officer said religious freedom was protected, but violence was not. He herded the kids and a few of the Krishnas into a patrol car.

Just before Lennie and I moved away, a fire erupted in the neighborhood and the Krishnas' building burned down.

After Eva married, she announced to the family many times that religion made no difference to her. "Edward could be a Buddhist. Hare Krishna. Or Christ himself. I'll love him until I die."

He wore a *yarmulke* at our apartment, as if not being Jewish was a mere oversight. He played pinochle with the men, but he never drank *schnapps.* He was quieter than the family, more polite. He waited for people to finish their sentences rather than shouting out his opinion. He often quoted poetry. My father made a point to sit next to Edward and talk to him.

One night before *Shabbat* dinner, Edward pulled a chair next to mine and said kindly, "Pamela, have you given thought to what you want to do with your life?"

I shrugged, pleased. No one else in my family seemed to have noticed me. I didn't have an answer for him.

"You're smart," he said. "You have many gifts. Set your dreams high. There's a big world out there. Don't close your eyes to it."

At dinner, he lifted the silver goblet and gulped sweet red wine. And another cupful. Another. That night, he laughed loudly and wobbled when he left.

"Drunk," my mother said to Aunt Fay after Edward and Eva had gone home. "You let your daughter marry an English drunkard. Gentiles drink. Thank God, our mother isn't alive to see it."

"He's from Scotland, Edith. You'll see when Pammie and Janet grow up." Fay blinked hard. "Small children, small problems. Big children, big problems."

My mother's frown deepened. She turned to me. "Pamela," she said, "stop staring and making useless marks on that paper."

I was at the dining room table and set down my pencil. "They're not useless," I muttered. "They're art." I had been drawing Aunt Fay's nose. It was long and ugly and sat off-center, like the beak of a hawk.

As a child, I was pudgy with coarse, stringy brown hair. Unathletic. Buck teeth. Loud. I felt great enthusiasm for life, though also a fear I would not measure up. I hugged my old grandmother with too much vigor. Dashing to answer the telephone, I tripped on a wire and watched helplessly as a lamp crashed to the floor.

Eva was the opposite. She was eight years older than me. She had a willowy, feminine charm with her small waist and her height (almost five feet, ten inches), her shining green eyes, slender nose, and a perfectly shaped oval mole above her lips, like Marilyn Monroe had. She taught me to file my nails, round the tips, how to apply pink lipstick within the contours of my thin lips.

"Remember the importance of brushing your hair," she told me. She flicked the Fuller brush in the same downward stroke a hundred times against her gleaming brown hair.

She read Shakespeare and Tolstoy. I read *Archie* comics, locked myself in my room, and drew pictures with crayons and ink. She wore rose-scented perfume, dressed in stylish clothing she sewed on an old Singer, and copied the designs from *Vogue*.

She used to read aloud to me from Edith Hamilton's *Mythology*. "To be an educated person, to greet the world head-on, you have to know these things, Pam," she said.

And she had boyfriends before Edward. After she married him, she explained to my sister and me the best technique for kissing (encourage the boy to insert his tongue in your mouth and press your tongue against his, suck on his hard, don't be afraid). She instructed me to walk with a book balanced on my head. "Stand straighter, Pammie," she said one afternoon, and set a second dictionary on top.

"Like this?" I asked.

"Push out your breasts. Perfect." She smiled. "This will teach you confidence. Help you discover your passion."

I discovered passion with my boyfriend, Christopher. And later, with Lennie. Then after we married, I found passion in a studio in our garage. At night, when our children had gone to sleep, I built life-sized wooden sculptures. I sawed, painted, soldered, and glued. I felt like Geppetto or God.

I constructed a couple; the woman stood naked, as tall as me. Eyes of black buttons, hands made of forks, legs from an old table, hair I twisted from wire. The man was a chair painted to be a man. *Adam and Eve in the Garden of Eden*. I thought of Eva and Edward and sent them photographs. "Beautiful," Edward wrote in a letter. "You have found your voice."

I made a woman with arms outstretched, as if she were flying. *Persephone Arising in Triumph*. And a man whose heart you could open; his heart was a box. In my sketchbook, I scribbled ideas. I had never done anything that felt so right to me, as natural as the Yiddish that rolled off my mother's lips.

Often I locked myself in the garage studio to think. It was the one place I could be alone, away from Lennie and the children, my students at school. I retreated there happily. Cut off from the world, surrounded by my wooden figures, I felt as if this was my secret life. Or as if, like my sculptures, I, too, was immune to illness, age, and loss.

Sometimes I wrote letters there to Edward and Eva. Or I leafed through old correspondence I kept in the studio.

> Your letter was quite beautifully printed—a true joy to read. Well, my lover, for now my thoughts are washed away like a rippling river. Don't forget how much I love you. I never want to be away from you again. Let's get married ASAP.

Christopher was Catholic and a believer, a painter. I had been in love with him before I met Lennie. In my studio, I imagined what life might have been like had I married him. I once shyly asked Edward's advice. "Follow your heart, Pamela," he told me. "Don't be afraid to meet life head-on." But I hadn't been able to bring myself to introduce Christopher to my family.

This was the story Eva told me: Edward had been feeling oddly for a few months. Nothing alarming. But he had lost weight and felt lethargic. He couldn't remember appointment times for the bulimics and families of recovering alcoholics he counseled at his office in a rundown area of Chicago. He thought a vacation would help. She insisted he see a doctor and made the appointment. The doctor examined Edward, said he needed tests, and admitted him to the hospital. He noticed that Edward's skin looked yellow.

Eva had telephoned me. Lennie came to the studio to get me so I could take the call. I didn't have a telephone there. I hadn't talked to her for a few months.

She told me Edward was in the hospital. They had just received the diagnosis, two days after the doctor's appointment.

"I didn't know he was ill," I said, wiping glue off my hands.

"Cancer, Pammie," she said. "It's spread. They don't know from where. What kind." Her voice had a terrible pitch, like a broken instrument.

"That's awful." I wound the phone cord around my sticky fingers and remembered our idyllic summers long ago at Belmont Beach. "You'll get another opinion."

"There's nothing they can do." Her voice was a screech. "He's not eating. Oh, Pammie, why don't they feed him?"

She and I had spoken only sporadically in recent years. Not because of lack of affection. Work and family had kept us both busy. Their daughter Lynn was grown now. My children were in high school. My exchange with Eva fell into a familiar rhythm; the old intimacy between us resurfaced.

"They'll feed him," I said. "Do you like the doctor?" Though I wasn't sure what difference that would make.

She sighed. "I never see her."

I imagined beautiful Eva in the hospital room, sitting next to Edward. I wanted to talk to him, but I envisioned him sleeping. In my mind, they held hands.

"The doctor at the hospital is an oncologist," she said. "By the time I arrive, she's gone."

I felt like the older cousin, felt the limits of distance, being a thousand miles away. "Go early then, talk to her," I said, determined to calm Eva. "I can get you the name of another doctor if you'd like." A friend of Lennie's was a physician in Chicago. He could recommend someone. I shivered. I tried to avoid the details of illness. My father once had a mild prostate cancer. Lennie's mother had developed colon cancer years ago, but she had recovered. Illness seemed ready to pounce at will.

"I don't need another name yet," Eva said.

When we hung up, I said to Lennie, "I wish I could help them."

"Go there," he said. "Or call her. That's all you can do. Listen to her."

I nodded. Certain things in life were *bashert*, preordained, my mother had always said, as if a correct order existed for the events of one's life. When I stopped dating Christopher, she told me the relationship wasn't meant to be. Eva and I had once been close; now, the threads of our lives seemed intertwined again. There must be a reason. Perhaps I could help her. I promised myself I would call her often.

The next night, I telephoned her instead of going to my studio.

"He's still in the hospital," she said. "I stayed at my mother's apartment the last few nights. It's my first night home alone." Her voice vibrated with terror.

I envisioned Eva's and Edward's townhouse. The elegant oak floors that snaked through the rooms. He and Eva both loved beautiful things. Shelves of leather-bound poetry and art books in Edward's study. The delicate flower bouquets on the William Morris wallpaper design. The photograph in the silver filigree frame of Edward bowing to the Queen of England.

Lennie sat at the kitchen table. The newspaper crinkled as he turned a page. I felt guilty he was healthy.

Though when I talked to Eva, I often felt clumsy, not beautiful or smart enough, I said with confidence, "Go back to the hospital. You don't have to stay home alone."

"Oh, Pammie. I'm trapped in the underworld. Edward and I are. I'm like Persephone, but I can't get out."

The myth flashed back to me with the promise of the bright

summer afternoons when Eva had read aloud to me. "You don't have to stay home alone," I repeated.

"But I'm here. I'm tired, Pammie," she said. "And my mother. She comes to the hospital and sits. She's not well herself. I can't talk to her about this. She never liked Edward, but she's beside herself about his illness. And Beverly has more in her life than she can handle." Beverly was Eva's younger sister, twice divorced, in debt.

"It will be better when Lynn is home." Lynn lived in Chicago and had gone on vacation before her father became ill.

"Yes," said Eva faintly. "It will be better then."

No one answered Eva's telephone the next evening, so I tried her cell phone. Static spotted the connection. "You're not supposed to use this in the hospital room," she whispered. "Hold on."

After a minute, she said, "He's still not eating. They feed him through a tube." Her voice was small. "He'll waste away."

"You have to get another opinion."

"I don't know if I have the energy for that. The doctor said nothing would help."

"You can do it," I said fiercely. "Some doctors are good, some bad." For a moment I wondered if she wanted Edward to die. I bit my lip and reminded myself not to get carried away. When I talked to Eva, I felt like a girl, at the mercy of my imagination. We both sounded like girls when we talked to each other, I realized.

Then she whispered, "The doctor told me he has months. Maybe three. Maybe six."

"Oh, Eva. How can I help? I can come to Chicago if you want." There were three weeks of school left until summer break. The annual school art fair began in a week and a half; I was in charge. It would be hard to leave. But I would go.

"I wish you were here, Pammie." She choked back tears. "I can't imagine how this feels for Edward. I wish you lived here."

"I do, too." I wedged the telephone receiver against my ear, as if

I could burrow into it, emerge from the other end. "Tell me when you want me there."

"Not yet," she said, regaining her composure. "But I'm so glad to talk to you. I haven't even asked how you are. I'm sorry. Maybe something good will happen."

"Hospice?" I said with alarm the fourth night after Eva had told me the diagnosis. I called her as I sliced cucumbers for a salad for dinner. "Are you sure you want that? There must be something they can do." I thought of Lennie's mother, of my father and his illness. He still swam a mile every day.

"That's what the doctor advised." An odd calm filled Eva's voice.

"But with hospice, the doctors can't help. I mean, give him medicine. Right? It doesn't seem like he was sick a few weeks ago. He was still working."

"They don't know what medicine to use. Edward says it's God's will."

"He's wrong. God wouldn't will this. Where is he?"

"Still in the hospital. He'll come home tomorrow. We've made arrangements. The hospice people will visit us. Edward will be happier at home. They even gave us a hospital bed."

Gloom settled over me. I had a terrible time concentrating. The next day, I forgot about a meeting with our daughter's teacher. I spilled paint on a student. My sketches looked forlorn. I realized I'd miscalculated—there wasn't enough room to hang all the artwork I'd chosen for the school fair.

I couldn't explain to myself why Edward's illness had this effect on me. Eva was like a dear sister; he was like my older brother. Perhaps he had been my first romance, I realized, unrequited, the image of what I thought a man should be. He had the aura of "other," wonderfully different from my family. Worldly. Educated. An aura I envied. It was irrelevant to my emotions that years had passed since I spent weekends at the beach with him and Eva or since he taught me to waltz. I had visited them during trips to Chicago. On occasion, I still sought his advice, sometimes in the letters I wrote to him and Eva. Whenever I thought of Edward, youthful longing flickered in me.

I stopped going to my studio. Instead, each night when Lennie went to his desk, and our daughter and son to their rooms to do homework, I telephoned Eva.

"The hospital bed is in the living room," she said two nights later. "Our poor little room. It's torn apart. I sleep on a mattress on the floor there. I can't leave him. If he wants me, I have to be there."

A groan echoed in the background.

"Hold on," she said. "Can you?"

"Of course." I stretched out on my bed and pressed my head into the pillow, waiting.

Then I heard Eva's voice. "Edward, honey, do you need something? To go to the bathroom? Talk to me. I'm speaking with Pam. Do you want to say hello?"

I couldn't hear the response.

"Would you like to speak to Edward?" she said to me. "He's having trouble talking, but I know he would love to hear your voice."

"Yes," I said, ashamed I hadn't thought to ask.

After a moment, the sound of breathing came through the phone, like the scratching of sandpaper.

I said, "Edward, hello, it's me, Pam."

I heard only his breathing, so I went on quickly. "I think of you every day," I said. "I'm sorry you're sick. No, I hate that you're sick. I hope you're comfortable."

He grunted. Then another grunt, as if someone had clasped hands against his mouth. Now there were moans, repeated moans. I knew Edward was responding to my words, but I could not bear to hear the sounds, that I would not hear his lilting voice.

I interrupted. "I love you." I realized I was shouting; I lowered my voice. "You're wonderful. You've always been wonderful to me."

Silence hung between us.

"I'm so happy to talk to you," I said, desperate to fill the silence. "Good-bye." What on earth was I saying? "Not good-bye," I corrected. Moisture filled my eyes. "I meant I'll talk to you when you're feeling better. In a few days."

I heard a grunt like the longest last note of the *shofar* that sounds on the holiest days, when we beseech God to write us in the Book of Life for another year. A low, steady moan like *tekiah gedolah.*

Then Eva's voice, cheerful, hopeful. "He liked talking to you, Pammie. I can tell."

"You're so loyal to him," I said to Eva the next night. I sat in the living room, talking on the telephone. "I admire that. You're taking such good care of him."

"He's been my husband for thirty-five years. I'm more hopeful. I called another doctor. He has medicine that might help. I'll take Edward to the doctor's office. I don't know how I'll do it, lift him. But I guess I'm making up for being mean to him."

"Mean?"

"Oh, I don't know." She laughed softly. "You marry someone. You think they'll change. They never do."

I considered what she meant, what form her meanness took. But I didn't ask. I thought of my meanness. Lennie's. We hadn't been ill-tempered when we first married, but impatience and anger had crept in.

"The house is always sloppy," he yelled yesterday. "Piles of junk all over. Table legs, paint, glue. You're always on the telephone. I'm sick of it."

"Because we don't have enough space," I said, although I knew I could straighten up and pay more attention to him.

"That's because you're sloppy. You live in your own world."

"I like it that way. That's me."

Eva interrupted my thoughts. "When we were in marital

counseling," she said, "the counselor said Edward was a workaholic. Edward walked out. But he was. Left the house at seven every morning and didn't come back until nine. He drank too much. We never went far on vacations. He didn't want to leave his counseling patients—the alcoholics, their families, the bulimics." She spoke with aching regret, as if she were already a widow. "That's Edward. A relationship has to be reciprocal."

"Lennie is like that," I said. "He works every night at home."

"Not like Edward. I almost left him."

"You did?" I said, surprised.

"But what does it matter now?"

"Why would you want to leave him?"

She didn't answer.

I didn't know what to say. "Does Edward have a will?" I blurted out. Of course he does, I thought. Lennie had advised me to be direct in this situation. He had dealt with this issue when his father was ill.

"A will?" Panic threaded through her voice. "No."

"You have to have one," I said.

"I do?"

"You should get a will right away. Not necessarily for now." That was a lie. I paced as I spoke to her. Lennie's father hadn't written a will. I remembered the problems his mother had had because of this. I wanted to spare Eva. "You write a will so you have it when you need one," I said. "If not, it can be difficult to get money. Even to pay bills."

"I haven't looked at the bills since we went to the doctor."

"Call cousin Ben." He was a lawyer. "Tell him Edward needs a will right now."

"If you think I need to."

Three nights later, she said, "I'm more hopeful. It's better at home."

"Is Edward comfortable?"

"Yes; he talks to visitors. Your parents were here. He loves your father. Your father was the only one who welcomed him into the family. He has medicine for pain."

"Did he sign the will?"

"It never came."

"Came?"

"They sent it."

"In the mail? You'd better ask Ben to bring the will to you. Or my father. He'll help."

"He could barely write," Eva said in our next conversation. "Your father brought the will."

"Did Edward sign it?"

"Just his initials. Do you think that's okay? Do you think I really need it? I felt so badly asking."

"You did the right thing." I hunched over the kitchen table, the telephone receiver at my ear. Why didn't he write his will sooner? Why did I delay making a sculpture or telling Lennie or the children I loved them? Though I locked myself in the studio or became impatient, I loved them.

"Pammie, you wouldn't believe the things I have to do." She sighed. "I haven't been to work since he got sick. It will cost thousands of dollars to buy a plot for him. He wants to be cremated. Buried in the church. He loves the church."

"He does?" I had almost forgotten that Edward was a minister. I imagined him with his *yarmulke* at my parents' table. "He never talked about church. I didn't know he still went. I thought he'd given that up."

"No. He went to church all the time. But when we got married he decided not to work as a minister so much anymore. He wanted to do his counseling, too, and help people in a lasting way." She paused. "Maybe in deference to me. But if he's buried there, then I can't be next to him. I wouldn't want to be buried in a *church*. I don't know where I'll go." Her voice trailed to a whisper.

"You have plenty of time for that," I said, but anxiety skittered inside me. I didn't know where I would go either.

Then she said quickly, "I did something."

I waited, worried. Eva had spoken in such a hushed manner, as if she had done something illegal. "What?"

"I went to Edward's desk. It was a mess. Things everywhere. I opened the drawers. I threw out everything. Notes. Old letters. Papers. Newspaper articles he had clipped. He had saved them for years. They're all in the trash."

"Oh." My body tensed. A sudden longing filled me. I pressed one arm against my side, as if I needed conscious effort to prevent my hand from reaching into the telephone wires, to the piles of Edward's papers, to scoop them up and save them.

"I didn't feel guilty," she said. "Not a bit. He had saved them for what? They're no good to anyone now."

"But maybe you'd want to see them, or Lynn would. Or Edward would want to look at the papers again." I imagined letters I'd written to him about my art, and old letters I kept in my studio, the sketches in my notebook, how they nourished me. And the documents Lennie meticulously filed in his metal cabinets, tidbits about sociological studies that had no meaning to anyone else.

I made arrangements to see Edward. I would leave for Chicago on the weekend and stay as long as Eva needed me. I would miss the opening of the art fair and would have to work hard to finish the preparations.

I realized I didn't know the core of Edward, just who I imagined he was. Still, I couldn't wait to hold his hand, to tell him what he'd meant to me, that I had measured all men against him.

But on Friday morning, Eva telephoned me at school. I spoke to her from the office. My eyes rested on the large calendar on the wall. It was two weeks and two days since Edward had first consulted the doctor.

"It's over, Pammie," she said simply. "He's gone."

2

Faded brown wallpaper peeled off the corners in my parents' front hallway. I hadn't been home for three years, though my parents had visited us in New Jersey. Still, I felt like a stranger. The musty, dark Russian tapestry of a castle that had belonged to my *bubbe* still hung here. I set my suitcase on the green stone floor. I knew the smells by heart. Sticky scents of cooking oil. Onions, garlic. Chicken livers. The heavy odor of fried *schmaltz*.

The windows and curtains in the small living room were shut. The apartment felt sealed in.

"Tea, let's have tea, Pammie," my mother said wearily.

It was late, after ten; the flight had been delayed. My mother trudged into the kitchen, her back more bent than I remembered. She wore gold house slippers and a blue silk robe. I could see the wide slope of her drooping bosom through the thin fabric. A wave of brown hair streaked with blond curled against her forehead. Bunches of wrinkles swallowed up her face and freckles. I hugged her. She was so small. Much smaller than me now.

"Tea would be nice," I said.

"Eva asked me to read a selection," my father said.

"A selection?" I said.

We walked into the kitchen.

"At the funeral tomorrow." He rummaged through a pile of papers on the green Formica counter.

"It's in the bedroom," my mother said.

"Oh, yes." My father disappeared into the hall.

"He's fine for his *age*, Pammie." She glanced toward the hallway. "He swims every day. But he doesn't remember so well." She sighed. "That's the way life will be from now on."

My father reappeared, clutching a piece of paper. "I am to read Izeeya," he said.

"What?" I sat at the table.

He handed me the paper. It was titled "Isaiah, Section 55:10-13."

"You're going to read this?"

"Yes." He smiled proudly. "It's an honor to be asked. I will go to the *bimah* and read aloud at the funeral tomorrow."

"You'll be in a church," my mother said. "There is no *bimah*. You'll go to the stage. What do they call it? I wish Edward were here. I could ask him."

"He's not here," said my father. He sat next to me. "You'd better get used to it."

"You should read a blessing," she said. She set the teakettle on the old white Roper and switched on the gas burner. Grease splatters dotted the wall behind it. She stared at the small blue flame that danced beneath the kettle.

"You need to practice, Dad," I said. "Before you read in front of all those people."

"What people?" asked my mother.

"At the funeral," I said.

"I hate funerals." She turned to face me. "I wonder who will be there."

"They have friends," I said. "Family."

"Some of them will be *ongeshtopt*." She frowned and handed my father and me each a mug of tea. "Stuffed with money. And Edward was an only child. His parents are dead. Who from his family will be there?"

"Who cares?" I said. "We're his family. The point is, Dad doesn't want to stumble over words."

"I'm alive and here." My father slapped his hand against the table. "No reason to talk about me in the third person. I'll go practice."

He left again. A few minutes later, he walked in and stood in the center of the kitchen. His face was round, eyebrows white like snow. His belly pressed against his blue cotton shirt, the buttons almost bursting open from the pressure of his body. His shoulders sagged; the crown of his balding head glistened. He was an old man, I thought. I hated to see it.

"Izziya," he said. "Section 55:10-13."

I corrected him. "Say it like this. I-zay-a."

He repeated it, and then said, "Eva chose this passage. It's about hope, I think. Life. Death." He read the first stanza aloud.

When he stopped, he looked at my mother, then at me, as if he were a boy, pleased with his performance. Wanting praise.

"That was wonderful, Dad."

"You read too fast," my mother said. "No one can understand you."

"It was a little fast," I said. "But I can work with you."

"Please do," my mother said. "I don't have patience tonight."

"You never have patience," my father shouted. He turned to me. "You're a teacher, Pamela," he said quietly. "A great teacher."

"Thank you. That's sweet."

"You know how to speak aloud," he said.

"She's an *art* teacher," my mother said. "Pam, move your mug away from the edge. It will fall. I don't want a broken mug. We have enough to worry about."

I folded my hands on the table. "It won't fall."

My mother slid the mug to the center of the table and left the room.

I pulled the mug closer to me, lifted the paper from my father's hands, and wrote on the paper. "Emphasize this," I said to him. "Emphasize words. Like 'joy' and 'peace.' 'Lord.'" I demonstrated. "Remember how beautifully Edward spoke. And breathe, Dad. I'm your audience."

"Okay." He squared his shoulders and recited in a strong, clear voice:

For you shall go out in joy and be led back in peace;
the mountains and the hills before you
shall burst into song,
and the trees of the field shall clap their hands.

Instead of the thorn shall come up the cypress;
instead of the brier shall come up the myrtle;
and it shall be to the LORD for a memorial,
an everlasting sign that shall not be cut off.

That night, in the narrow bed where I slept as a child, layers of me seemed to peel away. I felt thirteen again. I had always blamed this on my parents, this feeling, when with them, of being small, the vulnerability that rushed inside me now. But perhaps it was no one's fault. I was made this way. I suddenly felt as if I had never left home, never left my parents' world. For an instant, I wished I hadn't.

Restless, I thought about the psalm, and my mother's words: "That's the way life will be from now on." The room felt stuffy. I switched on the lamp on the night table and opened a window. Then I sat on the floor and fished through drawers in the old oak bureau. My mother had left papers and possessions here for years—like Edward must have done, like I did in my studio—as if she could preserve the illusion of my youth. Or hers. In part, she didn't care to bother with housekeeping. Better to get an education and hire others for housework, she used to say. She had taught English to Russian immigrants.

She had always told people that my father held an important position in the textile business. But he had, in fact, been a salesman for Ship & Shore. Nothing more. He lugged his heavy suitcase crammed with samples from customer to customer. Growing up, I owned only clothing I needed, that we could afford, except for blouses. My father had given me hundreds for free. White cotton blouses. Polka dot. Seersucker. Long-sleeved, short-sleeved. Irregulars. Damaged goods.

Some still hung in the closet here. My mother inflated the truth; she spun a *meise* about people. My father in the textile business. Lennie was a famous professor (he was a professor, but not famous). Cousin Eva had reached the top of her profession; she taught reading to children *and* taught the teachers (she supervised student teachers in her classroom). Cousin Edward *used* to be active in the church but he wasn't anymore, and now with his counseling degree he made an important contribution to the world. Just last year, she told me she wouldn't be surprised if he finally converted and became a Jew.

In a moment of childish self-pity, I wished I had proclaimed my feelings to him long ago. But he was Eva's husband. Even now, I felt disloyal. I didn't know how he felt about me. I would never know.

The bureau drawers were stuffed; some I could barely pry open. In one, I found old catalogues, and beneath those, papers with clumsy doodles of flowers and horses, and a torn ticket stub for *The Sound of Music* at the Michael Todd Theater. In the bottom drawer, beneath manila folders, sat a small white faux-leather book zipped on three sides. "AUTOGRAPHS—8th GRADE."

On the second page, I saw Eva's graceful handwriting: "LOVING CONGRATULATIONS!" And following that, Edward's neat script: "Pamela, on to the next! You'll always be my favorite. Follow your dreams. You are the one person in the family who can do anything she sets her mind to. My love to my swell new cousin."

"There are rituals, Pam," my mother said the next morning. "Eva wants to sit *shiva.*" She looked at me. "The rituals of mourning are for the mourner, not the dead." Her voice rose, as if someone had contradicted her. "Eva is Jewish, no matter who Edward was."

My father nodded. He wore a neat, dark suit, as if he were an undertaker. We were drinking coffee at the kitchen table. "She talked to the rabbi," he explained.

"He said she can do what she wants. She wants four days of *shiva.* Not seven." My mother smoothed the wrinkles in the bodice of her black linen dress. "After the *shiva*, after they bear their grief, the next day Eva and Lynn will walk once around the block. They cannot look back. They say good-bye to the past. Greet the future." My mother sounded hopeful. "You have to do that in life. I've explained this to her. I did it when my parents died." Then her tone became mournful. "Edward died so fast. No one should know by this kind of loss their whole life."

We didn't speak. I imagined Lynn and Eva strolling around the block, arms outstretched to greet the uncertain future.

My mother broke the silence. "Then the first Friday night after the *shiva* ends, Eva, Aunt Fay, and Lynn will come to synagogue with us."

"Custom," my father said matter-of-factly. "When you're our age, Pam, you'll know these customs by heart."

I suddenly envied how these rituals comforted my parents. "That's nice," I said.

"It's more than nice." My mother tapped her hand against the beige plastic tablecloth. "It is what *must* be done."

My father nodded.

"When they sing *Lecha Dodi*—do you remember, Pammie?" She began to hum.

"Of course," I said defensively. "I go to synagogue sometimes."

"The song greets the Sabbath Bride." Her eyes were bright and moist. "We sing, the congregation does. Then Eva will walk into the sanctuary, in her new status in the community, and we turn and greet her."

I imagined the congregation, which was mostly elderly, singing, bowing to the new widow. My throat ached.

St. John's Cathedral sprawled over an entire block downtown. The day was hot and humid. No cool breeze wafted here from nearby Lake Michigan.

In the white stone building, many relatives whom I hadn't seen for years mingled, as well as people I didn't know. My sister, Janet, was dressed in black, like a widow herself, though she was divorced. She stood with her arm around Lynn, who had a bewildered expression and Edward's long, slender fingers and bright brown eyes.

My cousin Mo had grown fat and bald. He had planned to become a doctor when he was a boy, but went into sales. Cousin Beverly, pale and teary-eyed, walked into the chapel with Aunt Fay. Aunt Fay, ninety now, was thin and bent like a bow, her expression sad and pinched. A six-cornered star dangled from a gold chain around her neck. As she gazed at the stained glass windows that glistened in the sunlight, at their representations of saints, her mouth opened into a surprised "O." Cousin Ben sat in a pew. He had left his first wife years ago. His children had stopped talking to him then; he had a perpetually wistful smile. He sat with his new wife now. Her makeup was layered heavily, as if she were a geisha, her expression hard. She must have fought for him, I thought.

Finally, I caught sight of Eva. From a distance, she looked beautiful to me, like a princess, in her flowing black chiffon dress. When I hurried to her, I saw layers of wrinkles on her face. Her dress hugged her stomach; her skin sagged with sadness. Even her mole seemed shriveled. She was old. We all were old now. I blinked away the thought. Then her eyes met mine, and I threw my arms around her.

She wrapped hers around me, her long wrists thin and bony like the necks of swans.

"Oh, Pammie," she whispered. "I love you. Thank you."

Lennie had arrived on an early flight. He could stay just for the morning service. I slid into the pew next to him and held his hand. I had been afraid he would be too busy with work to join me. You marry someone, you think they'll change, and if you are lucky, on occasion they do.

My parents flanked us like bookends. An usher handed each of us a program: "A Celebration of the Life of the Reverend Canon

Edward Henry Jamison." This seemed a long and strange title for Edward. I had never thought of him as a reverend or father. The Reverend Canon Edward Henry Jamison was a mystery to me. Perhaps all people were a mystery.

The priests filed into the chapel wearing beautiful robes of gold and orange, like Hare Krishna garments. A figure of Christ hung suspended over the altar. He wasn't nailed to a cross and he seemed as if he were floating in air. All of a sudden, I feared him, like I had as a child. I imagined blood spurting wildly from his veins. When I squinted, the figure of Christ returned to being inanimate, unreal, like a sculpture. I studied the smooth shape of his hands, his face with its beatific expression. For a moment, I wished I could believe in him, too. Then organ music resounded, and the priests gathered at their places.

"A man's life is like a breath," a priest began.

Edward had worn robes such as these, I realized; he had climbed to this altar. He had preached, eaten wafers, and been devoted to Christ. He was a Christian, a gentile, a man of God, and he had not spoken a word of this to us.

Soon people began to sing. The hymns surrounded me and lifted me up.

I noticed my mother's cheeks become rosy, with shock, I surmised. Shock that this was how Edward had lived, in the halls of this great cathedral, like a Scottish fortress, protected from the world. Our world.

"This is what comes from marrying out of the faith," she whispered to me.

"I like it." I breathed in sweet incense. "It's what Edward believed. It's beautiful."

"Beautiful to those who believe." She frowned and sniffled. "Pleasant but strange to those who do not."

"He was a person. That's what matters." I imagined the Hare Krishna building swallowed by flames long ago.

During the service, my mother and Aunt Fay wept. My father studied his portion until a priest gestured to him. At the pulpit, he began to read, stuttering at first, but then as we had practiced. His luminous words flooded the room. My father shouted the word "joy" with perfect elocution and fervor, as if determined to seize that joy for as long as he could.

After he read, the service continued, and finally the priest began the Liturgy of the Eucharist. The mourners walked to the front for the communion. My family and I sat alone in the pews, like outcasts. Then the congregation rose and sang one last hymn. Their voices surrounded us again and swelled with faith and hope.

Later, we huddled outside in the church garden beneath the hot glare of the sun. Lynn and Eva stood next to a priest. The man lifted the green metal urn filled with Edward's ashes, a vessel so small it seemed impossible that it contained the remains of a human being. The priest knelt and placed the urn in the earth. Then my cousin Mo chanted the *Kaddish* off-key. Eva bent and scattered handfuls of dirt on top. The other mourners waited their turn to do the same. Jew and gentile. White bougainvilleas, like teardrops, draped the ground near Edward's spot. I wondered if each petal contained a soul.

Lennie stood at my right, my father at my left, then my mother next to him. She leaned to me and murmured, "He lived a double life. A secret life. He preached at a church and sang at our seders."

I frowned. "It's not our business. It never was."

"This is how Edward lived," my father said before I could finish my reply. "And how he died. Dust to dust." He shrugged and spoke with uncharacteristic authority, his voice hoarse. "Everyone has some kind of secret life."

I wondered what his secrets were. And my mother's. I might never know.

"And loyalty runs deep, Pammie," he said. "Don't forget that.

Tell the children." He kissed my cheek and stared at the gravesite, as if ready to meet life head-on.

I forced myself to look in the same direction. I was more half-and-half than anything, I realized, a mix-up too.

"You have to give your children a legacy," my father said. He pointed to my mother, then himself. "Leave something to the world. We're Jews. When you're young, you don't think that's important. You'll see. You grow old, and what's important changes."

I swallowed my grief and stepped closer to him.

"Loyalty runs to the grave," he whispered.

My father breathed deeply. His chest heaved. He was eighty-six years old. In his lifetime, he had seen many people born and many people die. He wasn't ready to die himself. But standing by the gravesite now, I knew he would go soon. They would all die soon. *Gey shray chay vekayom.* I mouthed the Yiddish words fiercely, as if they were a plea. My eyes swept over the mourners. Five years. Ten years. Fifteen. My mother would go, my father, Aunt Fay. And later my sister, Eva, other relatives, Lennie and me, the children. We would die and be replaced on this earth. I had been fooling myself. Cut off from the world, in my studio, I had tried to fool myself.

I slipped my arm through my father's. He wobbled from the weight of me. Then he caught his balance. We leaned against each other, as if each one held the other up.

Thanks

Thank you to those who have encouraged my work. The Ragdale Foundation gave me the gift of uninterrupted time during the writing of this book. My gratitude as well to the Bread Loaf Writers' Conference and especially to the New York Foundation for the Arts for awarding me a fellowship in fiction.

I couldn't have become a writer without the help of my wonderful colleagues and friends. I'm deeply grateful to David Milofsky for his unwavering support and insights about my work.

Thank you to Louise Farmer Smith, Anne Korkeakivi, Eva Mekler, Susan Malus, and Mina Samuels for advice and camaraderie. My appreciaton to Donna Baier Stein, Lois Winston, Jules Hucke, Dallas Hudgens, Lauren Cerand, Margot Livesey, and to the Two Bridges Writers' Group. Great thanks to Betsy Werthan, Bart Schwartz, Melissa Bloch, Monica Glickman, Lois Nixon, S. K. Levin, Danielle Ofri, Robert Roth, David Richman, Jeanette Mall, Stuart Fischer, Diane Pincus, Madeleine Austin, and the Uslans for friendship and encouragement.

An immense thank-you to my loving, sprawling family. They have wrapped me in comfort and warmth. My gratitude especially to Nancy Levine, Gloria Henllan-Jones, Connie Rubin, Lisa Rubin, Doris Schechter, Belle Lippman, Julius and Bernice Wineberg, and my cousins.

I'm grateful to the editors of the literary journals who have provided a home for my work, to my teachers, New Rivers Press, Relegation Books, and to *Moment Magazine* for honoring the final story in this collection.

Thank you to Steven Bauer, a gifted editor, for his suggestions.

I am indebted to Walter Cummins and Serving House Books for their belief in my work, their kindness, and for helping shape the individual stories into a book.

Above all, my greatest debt of gratitude is expressed in the dedication.